Where Love Grows

Laurel Ridge Series, Book #13

Tara Baisden

Sterling Ridge Press LLC

Copyright

Zondervan. All rights reserved worldwide. The "NIV" and "New International Version" are trademarks registered in the United States Patent and Trademark Office by Biblica, Inc.™

Cover designed by Sterling Ridge Press LLC

Published by: Sterling Ridge Press, LLC www.sterlingridgepress.com

ISBN: 978-1-966093-30-5 Printed in the United States of America

First Edition: August 2025

For permissions, contact: tara@tarabaisden.com or visit www.tarabaisden.com

Also by Tara Baisden

<u>Riverbend Valley Series</u>

#1 A Cowboy's Second Chance

#2 Wanderlust & Wild Horses

#3 Heartstrings on the Horizon

#4 Runaway in Riverbend Valley

#5 Mended Hearts

#6 Healing Hearts

<u>Laurel Ridge Series</u>

#1. Season of Hope

#2. Finding Grace

#3. His Perfect Plan

#4. Love Redeemed

#5 Snowbound Blessings

#6 Sheltered Hearts

#7 Restoring Faith

#8 Love Rekindled

#9 Where She Belongs

TARA BAISDEN

#10 Shelter in His Arms
#11 Where Love Stands
#12 The Pieces We Mend
#13 Where Love Grows

About The Author

Tara Baisden is a Contemporary Christian Inspirational Romance author who proudly calls the beautiful state of West Virginia her home. Nestled on a sprawling mountainous property, she is surrounded by the peace and serenity of nature. Her days are happily spent in the quiet of country life, writing heartwarming stories of love, faith, and second chances. Tara also enjoys quilting, working in her garden, tending to her beloved pets, and soaking in the beauty of her surroundings.

With deep roots in West Virginia, family is everything to Tara. One of her favorite pastimes is gathering on the front porch with loved ones, sharing stories, laughter, and enjoying the simple, meaningful moments that life offers. When she's not crafting her novels, Tara can often be found exploring the rich history of her home state, visiting local historical sites, and, of course, stopping by every bookstore she passes! Her passion for reading and discovery always fuels her next adventure.

Tara is the author of the Laurel Ridges series of novels, as well as the Riverbend Valley series of novels, of which have been beloved by fans of inspirational romance. Her novels reflect her love for faith, family, and the timeless beauty of the world we live in.

Known for her sweet and clean romances, she creates characters that feel like family and settings that make readers want to visit again and again.

You can find out more about Tara and her latest releases at www.tarabaisden.com or follow her on social media for updates and behind-the-scenes glimpses of her writing process. Stay connected—you won't want to miss the heartfelt stories of love and family she has in store!

About Laurel Ridge

Welcome to the fictional town of Laurel Ridge, West Virginia!

Nestled deep in the heart of the Appalachian Mountains, Laurel Ridge is a place where time slows down, allowing visitors and residents alike to enjoy life's simple pleasures. With its quaint, brick-paved streets, historic storefronts, and the ever-present backdrop of rolling hills and dense forests, Laurel Ridge is a hidden gem that attracts tourists looking for both serenity and adventure.

A Rich History

The town was founded in the early 1800s by pioneering settlers who were drawn to the fertile land and abundant natural resources of the region. Laurel Ridge began as a small logging community, relying on the towering forests that covered the surrounding mountains. The New River, one of the oldest rivers in the world, provided an essential transportation route for lumber, as well as a lifeline for the early settlers.

As the years passed, the town evolved from a logging outpost into a thriving hub for craftspeople and artisans. By the late 19th century, it had developed a reputation for its hand-crafted furniture, textiles, and pottery, all made by skilled locals. The town's proximity to the New River also made it a destination for adventurous souls seeking to kayak, fish, or hike along the riverbanks.

A Place of Renewal

Though the logging industry faded by the early 20th century, Laurel Ridge adapted to the changing times. Its natural beauty and deep connection to West Virginia's mountain heritage drew travelers from near and far, transforming it into a beloved tourist destination. Local shops, run by generations of the same families, line the town square, offering handmade goods, locally sourced foods, and, most of all, warm hospitality.

The town's signature event, the Harvest Festival, began in the 1930s, celebrating the craftsmanship, music, and traditions passed down through the generations. Each year, visitors flock to enjoy live Appalachian music, taste locally grown produce, and witness demonstrations of old-world techniques like blacksmithing and weaving.

A Town of Faith and Community

At the heart of the town stands Laurel Ridge Community Church, a small, white clapboard building with a steeple that reaches toward the sky. Built in 1876, the church has been a pillar of faith and strength for the community for over a century. Its bell, crafted by the town's original blacksmith, has been ringing on Sunday mornings ever since, calling townsfolk to worship and reminding everyone of the enduring values of faith, hope, and love.

The church's history is intertwined with the town's, serving as a refuge in difficult times and a gathering place in moments of joy. Over the years, the church has grown to include an outreach center that supports local families and tourists in need, providing everything from free meals to spiritual counseling. The church's welcoming atmosphere reflects the town's deep sense of unity and service.

A Growing Tourist Haven

Today, Laurel Ridge has grown to a population of around five thousand people, yet it has managed to retain its small-town charm.

Dedication

For anyone who has ever felt caught between who they were and who they're becoming.

For those who tend their dreams like gardens—patiently, hopefully, with dirt under their fingernails and faith in what isn't yet visible.

And especially for you, dear reader, who understands that the most beautiful blooms often appear in the most unexpected places, at just the right time, when we've created enough space for them to grow.

May you always find the courage to plant new seeds, even when you're not sure what will come up.

Love, Tara

Contents

Chapter 1   1

Chapter 2   8

Chapter 3   18

Chapter 4   26

Chapter 5   35

Chapter 6   41

Chapter 7   51

Chapter 8   59

Chapter 9   68

Chapter 10   77

Chapter 11   87

Chapter 12   98

Chapter 13   107

Chapter 14   117

Chapter 15   127

Chapter 16   138

Chapter 17   149

Chapter 18   158

Chapter 19   168

Chapter 20   176

Chapter 21   184

Chapter 22   193

Chapter 23   202

Chapter 24   212

Chapter 25   221

Chapter 26   232

Chapter 27   244

Chapter 28   253

Chapter 29   261

Chapter 30   270

Chapter 31   278

Chapter 32   285

Chapter 33   292

Chapter 34   299

EPILOGUE   308

Leave A Review   317

Chapter 1

Anna Mitchell twisted the stubborn weed from between two brilliant orange blossoms, her hands deep in the rich mountain soil. "Come on, you little monster," she muttered, feeling the satisfying snap as the taproot finally surrendered.

"And that," she informed her golden retriever sprawled in the shade of a nearby flower cart, "is why we pull them when they're small."

Daisy thumped her tail against the warm earth but made no move to leave her shady sanctuary. The July sun beat down on Anna's shoulders, turning her auburn ponytail into a fiery beacon among the rainbow rows of zinnias. She straightened, arching her back and wiping a forearm across her damp forehead.

From this vantage point, Blooms Farm unfurled like a patchwork quilt of vibrant color against the backdrop of the Appalachian Mountains. Acres of carefully tended flower fields cascaded down the gentle slope—broad sunflower faces tracking the morning light, marigolds creating rivers of gold and orange, and lavender lending its soothing purple hue to the landscape.

The white farmhouse where she'd lived her entire life stood sentinel, its wraparound porch visible even from here. Home. The word settled in her chest with the same warmth as the summer sun on her skin.

"Anna June Mitchell!" Her mother's voice floated down from the direction of the house. "Lunch is waiting!"

Anna smiled. "C'mon, girl, lunchtime," she called to Daisy.

The dog perked up immediately at the prospect of food, trotting ahead on the path that wound between the flower beds. Anna followed more slowly, savoring the symphony of summer—buzzing bees drunk on nectar and the distant trickle of the creek that bordered one edge of the property.

By the time she reached the farmhouse, Daisy was already inside and sprawled on the kitchen floor, hopefully eyeing the plates of sandwiches and glasses of sweet tea glistening with condensation.

"Hands," June Mitchell reminded her, not looking up from the cucumber she was slicing.

Anna smiled and detoured to the sink.

"I finished weeding the front half of the zinnia beds," Anna reported, scrubbing soil from under her fingernails. "Should have the rest done and several potted for an order by dinnertime if the heat doesn't kill me first."

"Not worth heatstroke," June replied, setting the plate of cucumber slices on the wooden table. "Those blooms can wait till evening when it cools down."

Anna dried her hands and slid into her usual chair. "Tell that to Mrs. Henderson. She wants thirty potted plants for her grandson's wedding by this evening, and you know she'll inspect every pot for weeds poking up through the soil."

June's eyes, the same cornflower blue as Anna's, crinkled with amusement. "Martha says Mrs. Henderson's been driving her crazy. She's added to the wedding menu four times this past week alone. And poor Shirley at the bakery has had to redo the decorations for the cake twice already."

Anna laughed and shook her head before biting into her sandwich.

The old kitchen ceiling fan stirred the warm air while they ate in companionable silence. Through the open window, Anna could see the greenhouse complex where Jake would be watering the potted mums they had growing for the fall season. Beyond that, the farm stand where Katie would be arranging the day's cut flowers in mason jars for the afternoon customers. The rhythm of the farm—of her life—flowing exactly as it should.

"I've been thinking," June said casually.

"Mmm?" Anna reached to scratch behind Daisy's ears as the dog pressed hopefully against her leg.

"About slowing down a bit."

Anna looked up, sandwich halfway to her mouth. Something in her mother's tone made her stomach tighten.

"What kind of slowing down?" she asked carefully.

June shrugged, eyes on her plate. "Semi-retirement, I suppose you'd call it. Not all at once, of course. But I'm thinking by next spring…"

The kitchen suddenly felt too warm.

"But you love the farm," Anna said, setting her sandwich down.

"I do," June agreed, meeting her daughter's gaze. "But I'm fifty-six, Anna. There are places I'd like to see. Things I'd like to do while my knees still work properly." Her smile was gentle but determined. "I've spent over half my life building this place up. Maybe it's time to enjoy some of the fruits of that labor."

Anna nodded mechanically, trying to process the implications. Her mother had always been the backbone of Blooms Farm—not just in the fields, where Anna excelled, but in the office where the actual business happened. The contracts, the invoices, the spreadsheets that made Anna's palms sweat just thinking about them.

"You've been learning more and more of the business side," June continued, oblivious to Anna's internal panic. "We could shift things around, maybe hire another full-time worker or two."

"Sure," Anna managed, reaching for her tea to wet her suddenly dry throat. "That sounds... reasonable."

"We can afford it, especially with those new wholesale contracts we gained. I've run dozens of reports and projections... we're sound, and I don't think my stepping down and adding more employees will hurt us that much," June said with a smile. "It's all just getting to be a bit much for me lately, and I'm finding more and more I just don't want to work full time anymore. I want to get out and do things. I want to be a normal middle-aged woman, enjoying life... going out with friends in the afternoon for coffee and gossip... maybe attending Bible study more regularly. Geez... I haven't traveled outside this state in over ten years."

The mention of reports and projections made Anna's chest tighten. Numbers had never been her friend. Spreadsheets were like a foreign language, incomprehensible despite her repeated attempts to understand them. The creative side, the growing side—that was where she shined. But the business aspects and marketing? That was June's domain.

"I've been putting some ideas together," her mother was saying. "Nothing urgent. We can talk about it when you're ready."

Anna forced a smile. "Of course. Whenever you want."

June patted her hand and stood, gathering their empty plates. "No rush. I'm not going anywhere just yet." She paused at the sink, gazing out the window toward the greenhouse. "But I have to say, the idea of visiting the Pacific Northwest in spring... all those gardens they talk about in Seattle..."

As her mother continued, Anna's mind raced. The business side of the farm had always intimidated her. Despite June's patient tutoring, Anna found herself freezing up whenever confronted with balance sheets or profit margins. What if she couldn't handle it? What if she made mistakes that cost them everything they'd built?

The farm was her world—the only place she'd ever wanted to be. While her high school friends had scattered to colleges across the country, Anna had stayed, certain that her future lay in the soil beneath her feet rather than in textbooks or dormitories. She'd never regretted that choice. Not once.

But now, the prospect of shouldering the full weight of the farm—including the parts that made her stomach churn—loomed like a storm cloud on the horizon.

"—anyway, like I said, no rush," June finished, turning back to her daughter. Her expression softened. "Anna? Everything okay?"

Anna blinked, realizing she'd been staring at nothing. "Fine," she said quickly. "Just thinking about all those zinnias waiting for me." She stood, forcing a brightness into her voice she didn't feel. "Better get back out there before the afternoon heat really kicks in."

June's eyes—the same ones that had watched Anna grow from toddler to woman—studied her face. "Alright then," she said finally. "Just remember to take extra breaks and keep hydrated."

Outside, Anna breathed deeply, trying to recapture the peace she'd felt earlier. She should be happy for her mother. June deserved to travel, to experience life beyond the borders of Laurel Ridge. To want more than endless days of soil and seeds and office work.

Anna made her way back down to the zinnia area of the farm, Daisy trotting faithfully beside her.

She had just knelt down to resume weeding when Daisy's ears perked up, her head swiveling toward the western edge of the property. A low, curious whine escaped the dog's throat.

"What is it, girl?" Anna asked, following her gaze.

Beyond the creek that marked the property line, movement caught her eye. The neighboring hundred acres had been vacant for as long as Anna could remember—the old farmhouse there slowly crumbling back into the earth, the fields growing wild. But now, she could make out the distinctive white trucks of the electric company, their cherry-picker arms extended toward power poles.

For a few weeks now, there had been signs of activity—surveyors with their tripods, a crew clearing the old access road, and the sound of heavy machinery echoing across the valley. After years of the property sitting abandoned, the sudden sale had been the talk in town for days.

"Looks like we're finally getting neighbors," Anna murmured to Daisy, who was still watching intently, tail wagging uncertainly.

A strange uneasiness settled in her stomach. First her mother's talk of retirement, and now this. Changes were coming from all directions at once.

As if sensing her unease, Daisy pressed against Anna's leg, looking up with concerned brown eyes.

"It's okay, girl," Anna said, rubbing the dog's soft ears. "I'm sure whoever it is likes peace and quiet as much as we do."

But even as she said it, doubt crept in. What if they didn't? What if they had plans that would disrupt the careful balance of her world?

What if they were developers looking to carve up the pristine acreage into vacation homes or a resort?

Anna turned back to her flowers, trying to focus on the task at hand. But her eyes kept drifting toward the neighboring property, where more trucks had appeared.

"Don't borrow trouble," she muttered to herself, echoing one of her mom's favorite sayings.

Yet she couldn't shake the feeling that something fundamental was shifting, like the ground trembling before a landslide. Her mother's words echoed in her mind: I'm thinking by next spring...

Less than a year. Less than a year to become someone she wasn't sure she could be—someone who understood profit margins and quarterly reports, someone who could sustain every aspect of the farm business her mom had worked tirelessly to build up.

"Wasn't part of the plan, was it, Daisy?" she whispered.

Chapter 2

"Well, I heard he's from Colorado of all places," Mrs. Whitaker announced, her voice carrying across the farmers market.

Anna nearly dropped the bucket of pink peonies she was arranging at the Blooms Farm booth. She straightened, tucking a strand of hair behind her ear, pretending she hadn't been listening to every word of the conversation happening just a few feet away.

"Colorado?" Martha Kincaid echoed, leaning forward over her table of homemade jams, pies, cookies, and other sweets. The morning sun glinted off her silver hair, neatly pinned in her signature bun. "What in heaven's name would bring someone from Colorado to Laurel Ridge?"

Anna busied herself with the flowers, fingers working deftly to arrange the peonies in their water-filled vases. The Saturday farmers market buzzed with its usual energy—vendors calling to customers, children laughing as they chased each other around the town square's white gazebo, and the scent of fresh bread from Shirley's bakery stand mingling with the sweetness of Anna's flowers.

"The mountains, maybe?" offered Pastor Andrew as he examined a jar of blackberry preserves at Martha's booth. "Though I've heard theirs make ours look like hills." He smiled, his kind eyes crinkling at the corners.

"Hmph," Mrs. Whitaker sniffed, adjusting her straw hat against the July sun. "Well, I just hope whoever it is isn't planning some fancy development that'll ruin this place. You know how those Western types are—always wanting to build something bigger and shinier than what was there before."

Anna pressed her lips together, resisting the urge to join the conversation. The mysterious new owner of the property neighboring Blooms Farm—the same property where she'd watched utility trucks installing power lines yesterday—seemed to have the town all abuzz today.

"Need help with those?" Katie Reynolds appeared at Anna's side, clipboard in hand and a knowing smile on her face. Her blonde ponytail was pulled through the back of a cap with the Blooms Farm logo, and despite the growing heat, she looked as crisp and organized as she had at dawn when they'd loaded the trucks.

"I've got it," Anna replied, glancing toward the gossiping neighbors. "They're talking about our new neighbor again."

Katie's eyebrows shot up. "Any actual information this time, or just the usual speculation?"

"Apparently, whoever it is... they're from Colorado." Anna kept her voice low. "Beyond that..." She shrugged.

"Colorado," Katie repeated thoughtfully. "That's new. Yesterday at the diner, I heard it was an older man, a retired banker from Charlotte." She chuckled, checking something off her clipboard. "The day before that, it was a famous female novelist seeking seclusion coming from Vermont."

From under the booth table, Daisy whined softly. Anna reached down to stroke the golden retriever's head. "It's okay, girl. Just town gossip."

"We've sold four flats of marigolds already," Katie said, shifting to business. "And the arrangements you made this morning? Gone in the first hour." Her blue eyes sparkled with satisfaction. "I've already taken three more orders for similar ones."

Katie's natural ease in working for June and Anna had been clear from her first day working at Blooms Farm two years ago. While Anna thrived with her hands in the soil, Katie was efficient and could do it all; juggling many hats at one time came easy to her.

"Mrs. Henderson stopped by and paid for her wedding flowers," Katie continued, flipping a page on her clipboard. "And I've set aside the miniature sunflower bouquets for the mayor's luncheon this afternoon—Jake will deliver them in a little bit."

June approached, carrying two paper cups of lemonade from the stand across the square. "Thought you girls could use these," she said, handing them over. "It's getting warm."

"Thanks, Mom." Anna took the cool cup gratefully. The ice clinked against the sides as she lifted it to her lips, the tart sweetness cutting through the summer heat.

"Our new neighbor is a hot topic this morning," June said, nodding toward where Martha and Mrs. Whitaker were still deep in animated discussion.

"I'm starting to think this person is a figment of the town's imagination," Anna said. "A different story every day."

"Well, whoever it is, they'll have to show their face eventually," June replied pragmatically.

Martha bustled over to their booth. "June Mitchell, please tell me you know something about this mystery man who bought the Harmon place next to your farm."

June laughed, shaking her head. "I know exactly as much as you do, Martha."

"Which is practically nothing!" Martha exclaimed, clearly frustrated. Her hands landed on her ample hips. "Do you know, I've been asking everyone—everyone—and not a soul can tell me much about this person. Even Mitch, who was the real estate agent that sold the property, is being tight-lipped, and that man couldn't keep a secret if his life depended on it."

"Maybe the new owner values privacy," Anna suggested.

Martha waved this off. "Privacy is all well and good, but I need to know the dirt. How are we supposed to welcome someone properly if we don't even know their name?"

Katie grinned. "I'm sure you'll have a welcome pie ready the moment they arrive, Martha."

"Two pies," Martha corrected with a sniff. "Blueberry and apple. I intend to cover my bases." She leaned in conspiratorially. "But I did hear one interesting thing this morning. From Becky at the post office."

Anna found herself leaning forward despite her determination to appear only casually interested.

"She said their mail is already being delivered—addressed to a 'B. Knight.' That's all she'd say." Martha's eyes gleamed with the thrill of new information.

"B. Knight," Katie repeated.

"I also heard a man hired Roy's construction crew to demolish that old farmhouse on the property next week," Martha added.

This caught Anna's attention. "They're tearing the house down?" The abandoned farmhouse had been a fixture on the neighboring property for as long as she could remember—a weathered sentinel slowly deteriorating over time. The thought of it being demolished stirred an unexpected sadness in her.

"Can't say I'm surprised," June commented. "That place has been falling in on itself for years. I heard someone inspected the house last month, and not a bit of it's salvageable."

A customer approached, examining the potted plants at the edge of their booth, and Katie smoothly stepped in to help. Anna watched her friend's easy rapport with the woman, the way she suggested companion plants and offered care tips without hesitation.

"Anyway," Martha continued, lowering her voice, "I was told a man flew out here a little over a month ago, walked the property, looked around town, and bought those hundred acres on the spot. Never said a word about his plans, just that he wants to enjoy a new, slower-paced life. And that came from the real estate agent's secretary, Wilma." She emphasized the phrase with finger quotes.

"Sounds reasonable to me," June said mildly. "That's why a lot of people move."

"But from Colorado!" Martha persisted. "What's wrong with the pace there? They have mountains too, don't they? And why all the secrecy?"

Anna found herself staring across the town square, past the gazebo where two young mothers were sharing a bench while their toddlers played at their feet. Beyond them, the rolling mountains that cradled Laurel Ridge rose in gentle waves of green. What would bring someone across the country to this specific spot? And what did he plan to do with a hundred acres of prime land?

"He has his reasons, I'm sure," June replied diplomatically. "And we'll all find out soon enough."

Martha sighed dramatically. "Well, if you meet him before the rest of us, June Mitchell, you call me right away. The suspense is killing me."

"I promise," June assured her with a laugh.

As Martha bustled away, Anna turned to her mom. "Are you really not curious?"

June's eyes twinkled. "Of course I'm curious. But unlike Martha, I can wait to satisfy my curiosity." She nodded toward a family approaching their booth. "Looks like the Babcocks are here for their weekly flowers."

The rest of the morning flew by in a flurry of sales and conversations. The Blooms Farm booth was never without customers—locals who came every week for fresh flowers and tourists drawn in by the vibrant display. Anna worked on autopilot, wrapping bouquets and individual potted plants in brown paper, answering questions about different flower varieties, and letting children pet Daisy, who soaked up the attention with a constantly wagging tail.

But her thoughts kept drifting to the property next door to their farm and its mysterious new owner. B. Knight from Colorado. A man seeking a slower pace. What did that mean for the land? For her farm? For Laurel Ridge?

"Earth to Anna," Katie's voice broke through her thoughts. "Mrs. Clark wants to know if we'll have those purple dahlias next week."

Anna blinked, focusing on the elderly woman smiling patiently at her. "Yes, sorry, Mrs. Clark. They should be ready by Thursday at the latest. You're welcome to stop by the farm and pick some up, or just call Friday morning, and we'd be happy to bring them here to the farmer's market next Saturday for you to pick up."

"Wonderful, dear. They remind me of the ones my mother used to grow." Mrs. Clark patted Anna's hand affectionately. "Your farm is such a blessing to this town."

As Mrs. Clark moved on, Katie nudged Anna gently. "You okay? You've been somewhere else all morning."

Anna sighed, rearranging a display of potted marigolds. "Just thinking about Mom wanting to step back from the farm. And now this new neighbor... It feels like everything's changing at once."

Katie's expression softened. "Change isn't always bad, you know. Sometimes it's exactly what we need."

"Says the woman who rearranged her spice rack alphabetically and lines her canned goods up in the same manner," Anna teased.

"Hey now, I'm organized to a fault... what can I say," Katie said with a grin.

June joined them, counting cash from the morning's sales. "We've already exceeded last week's total," she reported. "Katie, your idea to add those dried flower wreaths was brilliant."

Katie beamed at the praise, tucking a strand of hair behind her ear. "I thought they'd appeal to the tourists. Something they could take home that wouldn't wilt."

"Speaking of brilliant ideas," June continued, "I was thinking we could take some potted flowers over to welcome our new neighbor when he arrives. Maybe a good variety of colors... I'll add that to my to-do list this week and set aside a few pretty ones in the greenhouse."

Anna raised an eyebrow. "Now who's curious?"

June laughed, the sound as warm as the July sunshine. "It's not curiosity; it's called being neighborly. Besides, he's going to need friends if he's starting over. And his property borders ours—we should establish a good friendly relationship from the beginning. I wonder how old he is... it sure would be nice to have someone my age living over there."

"Best to be neighborly from the start in case he has some type of crazy idea for the property, like a subdivision or a McMansion... a lodge..." Katie added thoughtfully. "Better to have a foot in the door right away, for sure; that way you know what's coming."

The thought sent a ripple of unease through Anna. Their new neighbor could be planning just about anything next door. Which could mean noise, traffic, and disruption to the peaceful setting that made Blooms Farm special. It could mean chemicals drifting across property lines or construction runoff affecting their creek water.

"Let's not borrow trouble," June said, echoing the phrase she'd repeated throughout Anna's childhood. "For all we know, he could be planning a bird sanctuary."

"Or another flower farm," Katie suggested with a teasing glance at Anna. "A little competition never hurt anyone."

Anna rolled her eyes but couldn't help smiling. "As long as he's not planning to build a resort or subdivision, I'll welcome him with open arms."

"Well, we'll find out soon enough, I imagine," June said.

Anna looked toward the road that led out of Laurel Ridge at the edge of town and wound up into the mountains—the same road that passed both their farm and the neighboring property. "I just hope this B. Knight understands what this place means to the people who live and vacation here."

"If he doesn't," Katie replied, squeezing her arm reassuringly, "we'll just have to show him."

The market began to wind down as noon approached. Vendors packed up unsold goods, counted their earnings, and called out farewells across the square. Anna helped Katie and June load the remaining flowers and booth equipment into the farm trucks, Daisy supervising from her spot in the shade.

As she closed one of the truck's tailgates, Anna caught sight of Martha and Pastor Andrew deep in conversation near the gazebo, their expressions animated. No doubt still discussing the mysterious newcomer. Anna shook her head, smiling. In Laurel Ridge, a new resident was bigger news than the presidential election.

"Ready to head back?" June asked, twirling a set of truck keys around her finger.

Anna nodded, but her gaze drifted toward the mountains again. "I think I'll take Daisy for a walk by the creek when we get home," she said. "Check on the wild blackberries near the property line."

June and Katie exchanged a knowing look.

"What?" Anna demanded.

"Nothing," Katie said innocently. "Just thinking those blackberries must be very interesting this time of year."

"They are," Anna insisted, feeling her cheeks warm. "And I need to see if the recent rain has affected the creek level."

"Of course," June agreed solemnly. "Very important farm business."

Anna climbed into the passenger seat, Daisy jumping in to settle between her and June. "It is farm business," she muttered. "Someone has to keep an eye on things."

As they drove out of town, the Saturday morning hustle in Laurel Ridge faded behind them, replaced by the peaceful rhythm of country roads winding through the mountains. Anna watched the familiar landscape roll by, wondering how it might look to someone seeing it for the first time.

Had B. Knight fallen in love with the misty mornings when the valleys filled with fog like a sea between mountain islands? Had he noticed how the light changed throughout the day, painting the hills in different shades of green and gold? Did he appreciate the night sky here, unpolluted by city lights, where the stars hung so close you could almost reach up and touch them?

Or did he see only the potential for profit, for transformation, for imposing his vision on a landscape that had existed long before any of them?

"Penny for your thoughts?" June asked, glancing sideways at her daughter.

Anna scratched behind Daisy's ears, the dog's warm weight reassuring against her side. "Just wondering what B. Knight saw when he visited here."

June was quiet for a moment, navigating the truck around a curve in the road. "People come to places like Laurel Ridge for a reason," she said finally. "Usually because they're looking for something they couldn't find where they were before."

"Or running from something," Anna added.

"Sometimes," June acknowledged. "But either way, they're searching. And there's something about these mountains that calls to certain souls." She smiled at Anna. "It called to your grandfather when he first came here. To your father, for a while at least. And it's called to countless others over the years."

The mention of her father—who had walked away from both the farm and his family when Anna was ten—sent a dull ache through her chest. She looked out the window, focusing on the blur of trees and fence posts.

"I just hope," she said, "that whatever this person is searching for, it doesn't end up changing everything we love about this place."

June reached over to squeeze her hand. "Some change can't be helped, sweetheart. But that doesn't mean it has to be feared."

Chapter 3

Brad Knight eased his foot off the accelerator as his black F-150 rounded the last bend in the long gravel driveway. The silver Airstream trailer gleamed behind him, catching the late afternoon sun that filtered through the canopy of oak and maple trees. His hands relaxed instinctively on the steering wheel as the property opened up before him—his property.

"Well, would you look at that," he murmured, a slow smile spreading across his face.

The hundred acres he'd purchased just over a month ago—after a whirlwind forty-eight-hour visit to walk the land and sign the papers—unfolded before him like a painting come to life. The newly mowed rolling green lawn stretched across the property, embracing the old homesite and weathered barn. Along the edges of the lawn, wildflowers nodded lazily in the breeze, their colors brushing against the dense woodland that ringed the land like a secret kept close. And beyond it all, the mountains rose in quiet splendor, their summer greens deep and unbroken beneath the July sky.

Ahead on his left, the dilapidated farmhouse with its sagging roof and broken windows was a stark contrast to the vibrant landscape surrounding it. Brad carefully backed the truck and Airstream toward the newly installed electrical hookup where he'd arranged for his temporary home to be situated.

As he turned off the engine, the sudden silence enveloped him. No phone ringing. No notifications pinging. No assistants rushing in with urgent messages. No concrete buildings or people rushing around as if their lives depended on speed and constant motion. Just the whisper of wind through trees and the distant calls of birds he couldn't yet identify.

He stepped out of the truck, his boots landing on soft earth with a solid thud. The July air wrapped around him—thick with humidity but softened by a breeze that carried the scent of freshly mown grass and something sweeter. Wildflowers, maybe. Or the variety of flowers from the neighboring farm. He stretched slowly, working the stiffness from his shoulders after the long haul. He'd left Lexington, Kentucky, early that morning after spending the Fourth of July with his parents.

The cross-country trip from Colorado had stretched across three unhurried weeks. No deadlines. No pressure. Just a long string of highway at times, several quiet side roads to enjoy the views, and multiple spontaneous detours. He'd stopped wherever curiosity led—small towns, scenic overlooks, national parks he'd always meant to see. It wasn't just a drive. It was the beginning of his new goal in life... learning to really live and appreciate every moment.

Brad moved to the back of his truck and dropped the tailgate with a solid thud. He reached into the bed and pulled out a stack of leveling blocks. One by one, he knelt beside each stabilizer on the Airstream, sliding the blocks into place, checking the bubble level with a calm familiarity, the result of a few weeks' worth of trial, error, and quiet determination.

There was no timeline breathing down his neck, no one waiting on him to hurry and get the job done. Just the quiet rhythm of settling in, of claiming this stretch of earth as his own.

He adjusted each stabilizer, cranking them down slowly until the trailer eased into position with a soft groan of shifting weight. When he stepped back to assess his work, the Airstream sat solid and true—silver skin catching the late afternoon sun, wheels braced, balanced, and ready to be lived in.

A few yards away, the large propane tank a local company had installed the day before sat in the shade, right where it was supposed to be. The hookups were ready. Everything was exactly as he'd arranged through a month's worth of calls, emails, and polite but persistent follow-ups.

Brad checked his watch—just past four. Plenty of daylight left in the day. He pulled his phone from his pocket, reflexively checking for messages before remembering he'd silenced all but emergency notifications. The screen showed only the time and the signal strength—surprisingly good for such a rural area.

"Old habits," he muttered, shaking his head.

He opened his mapping app instead, orienting himself on the property. The hundred acres stretched primarily to the west and north, with the eastern border defined by the creek that separated his land from the flower farm he'd noticed on his initial visit. That visit had been brief but decisive—one look at the homesite, the gently rolling landscape on most of the property, the pristine forest, the babbling creek, and the surrounding mountains, and he'd known this was where he wanted to be.

As the app loaded, Brad's eyes were drawn across the creek to the neighboring farm. From this vantage point, he could see neat rows of multicolored flowers for what he guessed to be several acres. Three greenhouses gleamed in the afternoon sun, and beyond them, a white farmhouse sat atop a small rise, its wraparound porch facing his direction.

Movement caught his eye—a figure moving among the flower rows. A woman with auburn hair pulled back in a ponytail bent to tend the plants. Even from this distance, there was something graceful about her movements.

Brad found himself watching longer than he'd intended, struck by the tableau—the woman, the flowers, the farmhouse on the hill. It was like something from another time, a snapshot of a life so different from the one he'd been living that it might as well have been on another planet.

His former life in Denver felt increasingly distant with each passing day—the sleek modern condo he'd owned with its floor-to-ceiling windows and minimalist furniture chosen by an interior designer he'd barely spoken to. The endless meetings of his former business life, the constant pressure, the perpetual feeling that he needed to be three steps ahead of everyone else.

That life had nearly killed him. Literally.

The official term was stress-induced cardiomyopathy, though the nurse had quietly called it "broken heart syndrome." That label had unsettled him more than he cared to admit—because the truth was, it hadn't just been his body breaking down. His life was breaking, too. And it had been a wake-up call for him.

Brad's hand unconsciously moved to his chest, where beneath his gray t-shirt lay a small scar—a reminder of the heart episode that had changed everything. At thirty-two, he'd been the founder and CEO of LocalLens, a travel app that had revolutionized how people experienced new destinations. Twelve years of long workdays, of sacrificing everything for success, culminating in a company valuation of well over $150 million.

And a heart that had nearly given out under the strain.

The memory of that hospital room—stark white walls, the steady beep of monitors, the look on his doctor's face—still had the power to make his breath catch. That was when he'd known something had to change.

Then came Michelle's exit when he had told her he had sold the company, bought land in West Virginia, and was moving.

"I didn't sign up for some middle-of-nowhere mountain man fantasy. And I certainly didn't sign up for a long-distance relationship," she'd said, her perfectly manicured nails gesturing dismissively. "Call me when you're done with this... whatever phase this is you're going through."

But it wasn't a phase or a fantasy. It was survival.

Brad turned his attention back to his land, to the present moment. The old farmhouse would be demolished next week—too far gone to salvage, according to the inspector. Some things couldn't be saved; they needed to be cleared away to make room for something new.

He wasn't sure yet what that "something new" would be. For the first time in his adult life, Brad Knight didn't have a five-year plan, a strategy deck, or measurable goals. He just had land, time, and the freedom to breathe and live.

Well, that wasn't entirely true. Ideas had kept bubbling up in his brain—old habits of an entrepreneurial mind that never fully quieted. Walking the western ridge when he first viewed the property, he'd immediately spotted the perfect location for a small lodge with panoramic views. Or the natural clearing near the creek that would make an ideal location for a few upscale glamping sites. He'd spotted another area on his property that would be ideal for several tiny homes, and he envisioned an upscale camping resort.

Brad shook his head, smiling ruefully at himself. "One day at a time," he reminded himself aloud.

He turned his attention back to setting up his temporary home, finishing unhitching the Airstream and removing the stabilizing bars and chains. The gleaming silver trailer wasn't a top-of-the-line model, but it had certain comforts he wanted—a far cry from roughing it, despite what Michelle had implied. But it was modest intentionally so. A physical reminder of his commitment to simplify.

As he worked, he found his gaze repeatedly drawn back to the flower farm. The woman had moved to another section, now accompanied by a golden retriever that bounded between the rows. Something about the scene tugged at him—the obvious care being taken with the land, the steady rhythm of work timed to the seasons rather than quarterly reports.

It was what he'd come here seeking, wasn't it? A life measured in sunrises and sunsets instead of four office walls and multiple computer screens constantly running. A place where success meant a day well-lived, not another buck in the bank.

He wondered about his new neighbors. Were they friendly? Or did they prefer to keep to themselves? In Denver, he'd lived in his condo for several years and couldn't have named a single person on his floor. Here, with only a creek separating his property from his neighbors, he'd likely run into them at some point. The thought was both appealing and slightly daunting. It had been a long time since Brad had introduced himself to anyone without his company or reputation preceding him.

For twelve years, he'd been "Brad Knight, the LocalLens guy"—a tech wunderkind who'd built a travel app empire from his college dorm room. His identity had been so wrapped up in his company that when he'd signed the papers selling it to Expedia, he'd felt a momentary panic: Who was he now?

That question still lingered as he stood on his land, watching the sun begin its descent toward the mountains. But the not-knowing felt like freedom rather than failure.

Brad turned his attention back to the Airstream, deciding to set up the rest of his camp before losing daylight. He unfurled the awning, positioned his chairs and outdoor table facing the best view, and strung the solar-powered café lights between nearby trees. By the time he finished, the clearing had transformed into a cozy outdoor living space.

As dusk approached, Brad lit the smokeless fire pit he'd positioned in front of the chairs, the dancing flames casting a warm glow across the clearing. He'd just settled into one of the chairs with a cup of coffee when a sound caught his attention—barking, growing closer.

He looked toward the flower farm just as a golden blur burst into view near the creek bank. The dog—the same one he'd seen earlier with the woman in the flower fields—paused at the water's edge, barking excitedly at something in the shallows.

"What have you found, buddy?" Brad called, standing up.

The dog's head whipped toward him, ears perked in surprise. For a moment, they regarded each other across the creek—man and dog, strangers sizing each other up.

Then the golden retriever's tail began to wag furiously.

Brad couldn't help laughing. "Well, at least someone's happy to see the new neighbor."

The sound of a voice calling from beyond the creek bank reached him—a woman's voice, melodic even in its urgency.

"Daisy! Daisy, come here!"

The dog—Daisy, apparently—gave one more look at Brad before bounding back toward the voice.

Brad smiled to himself as he settled back into his chair, stretching his legs toward the fire. Tomorrow maybe, he'd cross the creek and introduce himself to his new neighbors. What would it be like to simply be Brad, the new neighbor? Not Brad Knight, tech mogul. Just a man starting over, with nothing but time on his hands and a new outlook on life.

As full darkness settled over the mountains, the stars appeared one by one, then in clusters, until the night sky was awash with more stars than he'd seen in years. The city's light pollution had hidden this view from him for too long.

Brad leaned back in his chair, letting his eyes trace constellations he'd forgotten he knew. The fire crackled softly. In the distance, an owl called, the sound echoing across the valley.

For all his success, for all the luxury and status he'd achieved, Brad couldn't remember the last time he'd felt this content simply sitting still. No laptop open, no phone in hand, no deals to close or problems to solve. Just the night sky, the mountain air, and the quiet certainty that he was undoubtedly where he needed to be.

Chapter 4

Anna jerked upright at the sound of Daisy's excited bark as she ran toward the creek.

"Daisy! No! Come back here!"

The dog paused just long enough at the creek's edge to glance back, mischief gleaming in her brown eyes, before dashing through the water and disappearing on the other side of the creek bank

"Perfect. Just perfect," Anna muttered, breaking into a run. The heavy July air clung to her skin as she followed the well-worn path down the gentle slope. Her boots slipped on the damp earth near the bank, sending pebbles skittering into the water.

The creek that separated Blooms Farm from the neighboring property wasn't deep—barely knee-high in some spots. Anna hesitated at the edge, scanning for the shallowest point.

"Daisy!" she called again. The only response was more excited barking, now accompanied by unfamiliar laughter.

Great. Just great. Her dog was harassing the new neighbor.

Anna spotted the old footbridge about twenty yards downstream and headed for it. The weathered wooden planks creaked beneath her weight as she hurried across, mentally composing the apology she'd offer for her dog's behavior.

She eased around a tangle of wild raspberry bushes, their thorns catching at her t-shirt. She emerged into a clearing just in time to see Daisy leap up to plant her front paws on the chest of a tall man standing beside a gleaming silver Airstream trailer.

"Daisy! Down!" Anna commanded, mortification heating her cheeks.

The man laughed, a warm, rich sound that seemed to belong. He scratched behind Daisy's ears before encouraging the dog to settle on all fours.

"No harm done," he said, looking up at Anna with a smile that reached his eyes. "She was just being neighborly."

Anna found herself momentarily caught off guard, not just by his easy manner with Daisy but by the warmth in his brown eyes that crinkled at the corners when he smiled. She hadn't expected the neighbor to be so... approachable.

Anna crossed the clearing, apology ready on her lips, but the words stalled as she took in the scene. The man before her wasn't what she'd expected. Dressed in a simple white t-shirt, jeans, and hiking boots, he looked more like someone who'd stepped out of an outdoor gear catalog than the wealthy developer she'd conjured up in her mind. He was young too, not the older silver-headed man she'd envisioned.

"I'm so sorry," she managed, reaching for Daisy's collar. "She doesn't usually take off like that. There must have been a squirrel or—"

"Rabbit," he supplied, nodding toward the edge of the woods. "Big one. Can't blame her for the pursuit."

His eyes were warm brown, crinkled slightly at the corners as if he smiled often. His hair was the same rich shade and casually tousled, like he'd run his fingers through it recently. Something about his relaxed stance and direct gaze made Anna suddenly aware of her dirt-smudged jeans and the messy bun that had long since escaped its elastic.

"I'm Brad Knight," he said, extending his hand. "And you must be from the flower farm?"

His hand was warm and strong against hers. An unexpected flutter of awareness traveled up her arm at the contact, catching her by surprise.

"Anna Mitchell," she replied, withdrawing her hand quickly, suddenly conscious of the dirt under her fingernails and the smudges on her work clothes. "Blooms Farm is ours—mine and my mom's."

She glanced around the clearing, noting the perfect spot he'd chosen for his campsite. The Airstream was positioned to capture both the mountain view and a clear sightline to her farm. Two comfortable-looking chairs faced a modern fire pit, and strung between the trees, café lights waited for evening to transform the space into something from a magazine spread.

The unmistakable rumble of construction equipment drew her attention to the old farmhouse a few hundred yards away, where Roy's crew was beginning demolition work. A bulldozer stood poised near the sagging structure, its bright yellow paint a stark contrast to the weathered gray timber.

"So you're the Colorado transplant everyone's been talking about," Anna said, turning back to him.

"Word travels fast around here, I see."

"Small town," she said with a shrug. "We don't get many newcomers who buy a hundred acres outright."

"Fair enough." Brad gestured toward one of the chairs. "Would you like to sit? I was just about to make some coffee."

Anna hesitated, conscious of the work waiting for her back at the farm. But curiosity—about this man, his plans, what had brought him across the country to her corner of West Virginia—tugged at her. Something about his easy smile and the genuine interest in his eyes made declining harder than it should have been.

"I can't stay long," she said, perching on the edge of the offered chair. Daisy immediately flopped at her feet, seemingly content to remain in the presence of their new neighbor.

Brad disappeared into the Airstream, returning moments later with two steaming mugs. "I hope you like it strong," he said, handing her one.

The rich aroma rising from the mug wasn't the standard drip coffee she'd expected. "This smells amazing," she admitted, taking a careful sip. The flavor was complex and smooth—nothing like the utilitarian brew that fueled her mornings.

Brad watched her reaction with unexpected attentiveness, a small smile playing at the corners of his mouth as though her enjoyment genuinely pleased him.

"I have an addiction to coffee," Brad explained, settling into the chair beside her. "Some might say I'm a coffee snob." A self-deprecating smile crossed his face. "Though I'm sure that makes me sound like a pretentious city boy."

Anna couldn't help but return his smile. "Maybe a little. But I won't hold it against you since the coffee's good."

He watched the construction crew for a few moments; the sounds providing an odd backdrop of noise to the normally quiet world.

Anna studied him over the rim of her mug, trying to reconcile this man with the various personas Laurel Ridge had assigned him over the past few weeks.

"So what brings you here?" she finally asked. "It's a long way from Colorado."

Brad's gaze drifted toward the mountains, something thoughtful settling in his expression. "A change of pace," he said simply. "I needed somewhere with more... space. Room to breathe."

It wasn't the whole story—Anna could sense that much—but she nodded anyway. "You certainly found that here."

"That I did." His attention returned to her, curious and direct. "Have you lived here your whole life?"

"Born and raised," she confirmed. "Never wanted to be anywhere else."

"That's... remarkable," Brad said, and the genuine admiration in his voice caught her off guard. "To know exactly where you belong."

Anna shifted suddenly self-conscious. Most people from outside Laurel Ridge viewed her lifelong residency as provincial, a sign of limited horizons rather than a deliberate choice.

"The farm's been in my family for three generations," she explained. "My mother expanded it from a small vegetable plot to what it is today—over twenty acres, mostly flowers now. We supply florists throughout the state, plus our retail stand on the farm and our farmers market presence in town."

Brad leaned forward, elbows on his knees, his interest clear. "That's impressive. Family businesses with that kind of longevity are rare."

"What about you?" Anna asked, redirecting the conversation. "What did you do in Colorado?"

A shadow flickered across his face, so briefly she might have imagined it. "Tech industry," he said, and Anna noticed he didn't elaborate. "Nothing so tangible as what you do."

Before she could press further, Daisy's head lifted, ears perked toward the woods. A moment later, she was on her feet, racing toward something only she could detect.

"Daisy!" Anna called, rising from her chair. "Not again."

This time, the dog circled back after a few yards, tongue lolling as she pranced around them both before settling at Brad's feet.

"She likes you," Anna said.

Brad smiled, reaching down to ruffle the golden fur. "Dogs have good instincts about people."

"Better than mine sometimes," Anna admitted, then immediately wished she hadn't.

Brad's eyes met hers, warm with understanding and something else—a quiet intensity that made her pulse quicken. "I've found animals and children usually get it right. The rest of us overthink things."

The construction noise suddenly grew louder as the bulldozer lurched into motion, beginning to clear debris from around the old house.

"Any plans for after the demolition?" Anna asked, nodding toward the activity.

Brad shrugged, a casual gesture that didn't quite match the thoughtful look in his eyes. "Not rushing into anything. I want to get to know the land first, see what it wants to be."

It was such an unexpected answer—so different from the development schemes she'd had running through her mind—that Anna studied him again.

"That's... a nice way to think about it," she said slowly. "Most people would probably come in with blueprints and bulldozers, ready to impose their vision whether the land agrees or not."

"I've done enough imposing in my life," Brad replied, his voice quieter now. "This place deserves better than that."

The sincerity in his tone struck Anna, along with the realization that there were layers to this man she hadn't anticipated. Not just an outsider playing at country living until the novelty wore off.

"So," Brad continued, "any recommendations for a newcomer? Best places to eat in town? Best stores? Hidden spots worth exploring?"

Anna smiled. "Martha's Diner has the best food in the area, hands down. Talbot's General Store in town carries everything you could possibly need, though Earl might send you to his hardware store for specialized tools."

"What's your favorite hiking spot around here?" Brad asked, his gaze direct.

The question caught her off guard. "There's a spot up on Ridge Trail—Sunset Point. You can see the whole valley from up there." She hesitated, then added, "The wildflowers should be incredible this time of year."

"Sounds interesting." Brad's smile was infectious. "Any chance you'd be willing to show me sometime?"

Anna blinked as an unexpected flutter came to her chest.

"I... might be able to free up some time one day. The farm keeps me pretty busy this time of year, though."

"I understand busy," Brad said, and something in his tone suggested he truly did. "No pressure. Just thought it might be nice to explore with someone who knows the area."

The construction crew's voices carried across the clearing as they called to each other. Anna glanced at her watch, suddenly remembering the dozen tasks awaiting her.

"I should get back," she said, rising from the chair. "Thanks for the coffee, and welcome to Laurel Ridge."

Brad stood as well, taking her empty mug. "Thanks for crossing the creek," he said, his smile genuine. "Even if it was just to retrieve your dog."

"Speaking of which—Daisy, come," Anna called. The dog looked up from where she'd sprawled at Brad's feet, her expression almost apologetic before she reluctantly obeyed.

As Anna turned to leave, Brad's voice stopped her. "Hey—would you ever consider being my unofficial Laurel Ridge tour guide? I promise I'm a quick study." He hadn't planned to ask, but the words tumbled out before he could stop them, surprising himself with how much he wanted her to say yes.

Anna glanced back, taking in the hopeful expression on his face, the easy way he stood in this clearing that somehow already felt like it suited him. Something tugged at her—curiosity, perhaps, or the surprising realization that she might actually enjoy showing him around.

"I might," she said, a half-smile curving her lips. "Depends on whether you're planning to be a good neighbor or not."

"I intend to be the best," he replied, and the sincerity in his voice made her believe him.

Anna nodded, turning back toward the creek with Daisy at her heels. As she crossed the old footbridge, she couldn't help glancing over her shoulder. Brad still stood by his Airstream, watching her go.

The smile lingered on her face long after she'd crossed back onto Blooms Farm territory. There was something about Brad Knight—something genuine and unexpectedly thoughtful—that didn't fit neatly into any of the boxes she'd prepared for the new neighbor. His warm laugh and the way his eyes had held hers when they spoke kept replaying in her mind, a pleasant distraction she hadn't anticipated.

"Come on, Daisy," she murmured, scratching the dog's ears. "We've got work to do. And you, troublemaker, can stop looking so pleased with yourself for introducing us."

Chapter 5

Anna adjusted the mason jar of pink zinnias, turning it slightly so the fullest blooms faced forward. The morning air hummed with the familiar Saturday morning farmer's market energy—vendors calling greetings, children weaving between booths, and the distant notes of someone playing guitar near the gazebo. She brushed a stray auburn strand of hair from her forehead, surveying their display with critical eyes.

"Those look perfect already," Katie said, appearing at her side. "You've rearranged that same jar three times."

"Just want them to catch the light right," Anna murmured.

June approached, handing them each a cold bottle of water. "Stay hydrated, girls. It's going to be another scorcher."

"Thanks, Mom." Anna twisted the cap off, grateful for the coolness against her palms.

"Quite a crowd today," June observed, looking around the bustling square. The white gazebo at its center anchored the scene, surrounded by market booths arranged in neat rows. Local farmers displayed their summer vegetables, bakers offered crusty fresh loaves of bread and a wide array of sweets, and craftspeople spread handmade wares across colorful tablecloths.

"Martha says it's because the Greenbriar magazine had an article this month that mentioned our market," Katie reported. "Apparently we're 'a charming slice of authentic Appalachia that hasn't sacrificed its soul to tourism.'" She mimicked a pretentious accent, making Anna smile.

"Well, that explains the influx of cameras and fancy sunglasses," June said, nodding toward a couple examining honey jars at the booth across from theirs.

From her shady spot beneath their table, Daisy suddenly raised her head, ears perked forward. Her tail began a slow, tentative wag that quickly accelerated to full-speed enthusiasm.

"What is it, girl?" Anna asked, following the dog's gaze.

Her breath caught as she spotted him. Brad Knight, moving easily through the market crowd, then pausing to speak to Pastor Andrew near the fresh berry stand. Even from this distance, she could see the genuine smile that lit his features as he listened to whatever the pastor was saying.

He looked different here—his tall frame no longer set against mountains and trees but among the brick buildings and cobblestone paths of Laurel Ridge. More real somehow, in jeans and a casual blue button-down with sleeves rolled to his elbows. His dark hair caught the sunlight as he nodded at something Andrew said, then glanced around the market. The easy confidence in his movements drew her eye in a way she wasn't entirely comfortable acknowledging.

When his gaze landed on her, his smile widened, a flash of genuine pleasure in his expression that sent an unexpected warmth through her chest. Anna busied herself with the flowers again, pretending she hadn't been watching, her fingers suddenly clumsy among the familiar blooms.

"Looks like the best display in town," a warm voice said moments later.

Anna turned to find Brad standing before their booth, hands in his pockets, eyes bright with genuine appreciation as he surveyed their colorful array of blooms. Standing this close, she noticed the way the blue of his shirt brought out flecks of gold in his brown eyes.

"Thanks," she managed, oddly flustered. "We try."

Daisy scrambled out from beneath the table, tail wagging furiously as she greeted Brad like an old friend.

"Hey there, girl," he said, crouching to ruffle the goldens fur. "Glad to see you remember me."

"She clearly has terrible judgment," Anna quipped, finding her voice. "Abandoning her post for the first person who scratches her ears."

Brad laughed, the sound drawing Katie's attention from where she'd been helping a customer.

"You must be our mysterious new resident," Katie said, stepping forward with undisguised curiosity.

"And you must be the town welcome committee," Brad replied good-naturedly, extending his hand. "Brad Knight."

"Katie Reynolds," she said, shaking his hand. "Assistant flower angel at Blooms Farm and chief gossip collector, according to Anna."

"Don't give away all my secrets," Anna protested, shooting her friend a warning look.

June approached, wiping her hands on her apron. Up close, Anna could see the quiet assessment in her mother's eyes as she took in their new neighbor.

"Mom, this is Brad Knight," Anna said. "Brad, this is my mother, June Mitchell."

"It's a pleasure to meet you, Mrs. Mitchell," Brad said, his handshake firm and respectful. "Your farm is absolutely stunning. I've been admiring it from my side of the creek."

June's smile warmed. "Thank you. And please call me June. Mrs. Mitchell makes me sound like my ex-mother-in-law."

"June it is," Brad agreed easily.

A customer approached, examining their potted herbs, and Katie moved to help them. June gestured toward their booth.

"First time at our market?" she asked Brad.

He nodded, glancing around the square. "First time in town since I arrived. I've been busy enjoying doing absolutely nothing and dealing with the demolition crew at my place."

"And how are you finding Laurel Ridge so far?" June inquired, her tone casual but her eyes sharp.

"Honestly? It feels more like home than anywhere I've lived in years... probably not since I lived in Lexington with my parents," Brad replied, and something in his voice—a simple sincerity—made Anna look at him more closely.

"That's quite a statement for someone who's only been here a few days," June observed.

Brad's expression turned thoughtful. "Sometimes you just know when you're where you're supposed to be."

The words resonated with Anna. She'd always known where she belonged—had never questioned it. But hearing someone choose this place deliberately and with such certainty made her see her hometown through fresh eyes.

"Well, we're glad to have you," June said. "Have you met any of the locals yet?"

"Just Pastor Andrew so far; I just got here maybe twenty minutes ago," Brad said, nodding toward where the young minister was now chatting with Martha near her booth. "He stopped by my place yesterday to welcome me officially. Brought cookies his wife had baked."

"That sounds like Lily," June said. "Always baking for newcomers."

"And what brings you to our humble booth today?" Anna asked, trying to sound casual. "Looking for flowers for your Airstream?"

Brad's eyes met hers, warm with amusement. "Actually, I came looking for you."

The simple directness of his answer stilled her.

"For Anna specifically?" Katie asked, eyebrows raised in exaggerated interest. "How intriguing."

"Katie," Anna warned.

Brad laughed, not at all bothered by Katie's teasing. "I'm hoping for a tour of Laurel Ridge. Who better to show me around than someone who grew up here?"

"I'm working," Anna pointed out, gesturing to their busy booth.

"We can handle things here," June replied promptly. "It's slowing down, anyway."

"It absolutely is not," Anna protested, though a small part of her was already considering what route through town she might take him on. "We're still—"

"Go," Katie interrupted, giving her a gentle nudge. "Show the man around before Martha corners him for an interrogation."

Anna glanced over to see Martha indeed watching their booth with keen interest, clearly plotting her approach.

"You'd be doing me a favor," Brad added, his voice lowered conspiratorially. "I can already guess this Martha person is probably ready with a dozen questions, some of which I might not want to answer."

The hint of a genuine plea in his tone made Anna relent. "Fine," she said, untying her apron. "But only because I don't want Martha scaring you back to hibernating in your camper."

"My hero," Brad said, his eyes crinkling with a smile that seemed to be just for her.

"We'll watch Daisy," June offered, taking the apron Anna handed over. "You two enjoy yourselves."

"Just be back by closing," Katie added. "I've got a date tonight, and I want to break down the booth as quickly as possible and then get home."

Anna nodded, suddenly aware that she was about to spend the morning alone with a man she knew very little about. She smoothed her t-shirt self-consciously, wishing she'd worn something nicer than her oldest Blooms Farm logo shirt and cutoff jean shorts.

"Shall we?" Brad asked.

"Let me just grab my bag," Anna replied, reaching beneath the table for her small crossbody purse.

As she straightened, she caught Katie mouthing "He's cute!" behind Brad's back and shot her friend a warning glare.

"Ready," she announced, perhaps a bit too brightly.

As they set off across the square, weaving between market-goers and booths, Anna was acutely aware of the curious glances thrown their way. She was even more aware of Brad walking beside her.

Chapter 6

"This is Martha's Diner," Anna said, gesturing toward the red-and-white striped awning that stretched across the front of the brick building. "Best comfort food in three counties, according to just about everyone who's ever eaten here."

Brad studied the cheerful exterior with its gleaming windows and hand-painted sign. Through the glass, he could see red vinyl booths filled with Saturday morning regulars and plates piled high with pancakes and eggs. Anna watched his profile as he took it in, struck by how his expression of genuine interest made his features even more appealing.

"Martha's the silver-haired woman who was eyeing me at the market?" he asked, glancing at Anna with a smile.

"The very same. Town matriarch, unofficial therapist, and keeper of every secret worth knowing." Anna tucked a strand of hair behind her ear. "She'll feed you the best meal of your life while extracting your entire life story without you even realizing it's happening."

"Sounds dangerous," Brad replied, his voice warm with amusement.

"You have no idea." Anna shook her head, but her lips curved into a smile.

They continued down the sidewalk on Main Street, the sun bathing the storefronts in golden light, glinting off window displays and the hanging flower baskets that adorned every lamppost. Laurel Ridge's downtown stretched before them, multiple streets lined with well-preserved historic buildings, most dating back to the early 1900s.

Anna was acutely aware of Brad beside her, his tall frame and easy stride drawing glances from passersby. She'd lived in Laurel Ridge her entire life, knew every crack in the sidewalk, and knew every local face they passed. Being seen with the mysterious newcomer felt oddly exposing, as if she were suddenly visible in a way she hadn't been before.

As they passed Leslie's Blossoms, the local florist, Anna nodded toward the display window. "Leslie's been in business almost as long as Mom. We supply her with some specialty blooms she can't get from wholesalers."

"Competitors?" Brad asked, raising an eyebrow.

Anna shook her head. "More like colleagues. She focuses on formal arrangements—weddings, funerals, corporate events. We're more about field-grown blooms, farm experience, and bulk flowers. Different customers, different needs."

"That's Taste of Heaven Bakery," she continued, pointing to a cheerful yellow building with pink trim. "Shirley makes the best cakes that should probably be illegal. And next door is the Sugar Maple Sweet Shoppe—handmade chocolates and candies."

"You're hitting all my weaknesses," Brad said, his gaze lingering on the window displays. "I have a terrible sweet tooth."

"I'm guilty as well," Anna replied. "Even the most disciplined dieter caves, eventually."

They paused outside Talbot's General Store, its wide front windows displaying an eclectic assortment of goods. Wooden benches and several rocking chairs sat beneath the covered front porch. Currently, two elderly men engaged in what appeared to be a serious discussion over a checkerboard sat at one end.

"Now this," Brad said, his expression brightening, "looks like the real deal."

"It is," Anna confirmed. "Talbot's has been here since 1908. They've modernized the inventory, but the bones of the place are original. You can find penny candy jars next to smartphone chargers."

Brad's genuine interest made Anna smile. Unlike the tourists, who sometimes treated Laurel Ridge like a quaint museum exhibit, his curiosity seemed rooted in something deeper—as if he were trying to understand the town's rhythms, not just observe them.

"Mind if we go in?" he asked, already moving toward the door. There was an almost boyish eagerness in his expression that Anna found endearing.

"Sure," Anna replied, following him through the wooden doorway that announced their entrance with a jingling bell.

The interior of Talbot's embraced them with the mingled scents of coffee beans, beeswax candles, and the indefinable aroma of a store that had stood witness to over a century of community life. Original hardwood floors creaked beneath their feet as they navigated narrow aisles lined with practical necessities and local treasures.

Brad moved with unhurried interest, examining handcrafted wooden utensils, jars of local honey, and shelves of practical household goods. He paused at a display of locally roasted coffee beans, breathing in the rich aroma appreciatively.

"I'm in heaven," he said, selecting a bag of dark roast.

"Blue Ridge Roasters," Anna said, nodding toward the label. "Family operation just outside town. They do small batches, different roasts seasonally."

As Brad continued exploring, Anna found herself watching him with growing curiosity. There was something disarming about his genuine appreciation for each discovery—the way he turned a hand-thrown pottery mug in his palms, testing its weight and balance; how he read ingredient labels on jars of local preserves with actual interest rather than just performative browsing.

He selected blackberry preserves from a shelf of jewel-toned jars, adding it to his small basket. "My grandmother used to make these," he explained when he caught Anna watching. "Nothing from a grocery store ever tastes the same."

Near the register, a display of leather-bound journals caught Brad's attention. He picked up one with a simple but elegant mountain design embossed on the cover, running his thumb over the texture.

"Those are made by Leroy Withers," Anna said. "A distant cousin of mine. He does leatherwork as a hobby."

Brad looked up, surprise evident in his expression. "Your cousin made these? They're beautiful." He added the journal to his growing collection of items.

Emma Talbot herself rang up Brad's purchases. "You must be the new fellow at the old Harmon place," she said. "Welcome to Laurel Ridge."

"Thank you," Brad replied, extending his hand. "Brad Knight."

"Emma Talbot. Third generation to run this store. If you need anything you can't find here, you just ask. Odds are I can order it, unless it's something truly outlandish."

"I appreciate that," Brad said, accepting the paper bag of purchases. "Though I'm trying to keep things simple these days, so I can't imagine wanting anything too crazy."

"Simple's good," Emma said with a smile.

Outside on the sidewalk again, Brad seemed thoughtful as they continued their walk. "Everyone is so..."

"Nosy? Curious?" Anna supplied with a wry smile.

He laughed, the sound warm and genuine. "I was going to say welcoming. But yes, also very interested... I can kind of tell who's a local and who's a tourist. The locals have a way of looking curiously in my direction with a smile. Tourists just walk right on by without eyeing me."

"Ahh... the charms of a small town. You might as well understand right away that nothing is really private here. It might take some getting used to."

"I don't mind," Brad said after a moment. "It's actually refreshing, in a way. Where I lived before, I could go days without having a real conversation with anyone in my building."

Something in his tone—a hint of isolation behind the casual words—made Anna glance at him more closely. "That sounds lonely."

Brad's smile turned rueful. "I can see now that it was. Rather depressing if you ask me."

They passed the Mountain Chic Boutique, its display window featuring summer dresses and handcrafted jewelry. Next door, The Book Nook's open door released the comforting scent of paper and binding glue into the summer air.

"Coffee?" Anna suggested, nodding toward Lily's Café on the corner. "They have a nice patio out back."

"Lead the way," Brad agreed, seeming pleased by the suggestion.

The café's interior was cozy and bright, with checkered tablecloths covering sturdy wooden tables and local artwork adorning the walls. They ordered iced lattes at the counter—Anna's with an extra shot of espresso, Brad's with a splash of hazelnut—and made their way through the French doors to the small patio garden in the back.

The space was a green oasis, sheltered from the street by trellises covered in climbing roses. Only two other tables were occupied—an elderly couple sharing a scone and a young woman engrossed in a book. Anna chose a table beneath the shade of a maple tree, settling into a wrought-iron chair.

"This is kind of cool," Brad said, setting his bag of purchases by his feet. "Hidden in plain sight." As he took the seat across from her, dappled sunlight played across his features, highlighting the warmth in his brown eyes. Anna caught herself noticing how the setting somehow suited him—peaceful yet full of life.

"One of my favorite spots," Anna admitted, stirring her drink. The ice clinked against the glass, a cooling counterpoint to the humid July air. "In high school, I used to come here to study when the weather was nice and I didn't want to sit in my house."

Brad leaned back in his chair, surveying the little garden with appreciation. "I can see why. Nice little place to just enjoy being outside and let the world just roll on by."

For a moment, they sipped their drinks as the distant hum of Main Street traffic blended with birdsong and the gentle rustle of leaves overhead. Anna found herself relaxing despite her initial wariness. There was something surprisingly comfortable about sharing silence with him, as though they'd known each other much longer than a day.

"So," he said finally, setting his glass down. "If I wanted to explore beyond the town limits, where would you recommend? I want to do some hiking, maybe hit some local trails."

Anna's face brightened. "Ridge Trail System is the closest to your property—it connects right to the national park trails. There's everything from easy walks to pretty challenging climbs all around Laurel Ridge." She paused, considering. "Sunset Point is one of my favorites, though. About three miles round trip, moderate difficulty, but the view is worth every step."

"I remember you mentioning that the other day," Brad replied, his interest evident. "What about river activities?"

"Well, the New River is what runs through this area," Anna said. "It's actually one of the oldest rivers in the world, despite the name. Great fishing, if you're into that. Some spots in the river are smooth if you prefer calm boating, and then the rapids range from beginner to expert, depending on which section you're on. There's canoeing, white-water rafting, paddle boating..."

"I'd love to try the whitewater rafting here," Brad said, his eyes lighting up. "It's been years since I've had time for anything like that."

"What kept you so busy?"

"Work, mostly. The tech industry isn't exactly known for work-life balance."

"And that's why you left?" Anna ventured, watching him over the rim of her glass.

He nodded slowly. "Partly. Do you hike much?" Brad asked, redirecting the conversation.

Anna smiled ruefully. "Not as often as I'd like. The farm keeps me pretty tied down, especially during the growing season."

"But you enjoy it when you do?"

"I love it," she admitted. "There's something about being on a trail, away from everything, that just....resets things." She traced a pattern in the condensation on her glass. "Mom and I used to hike every Sunday after church when I was younger. It was our thing."

"And now?"

Anna shrugged. "Life got busy. We expanded the farm. There's always something that needs doing."

Brad studied her for a moment, his expression thoughtful. "Sounds like we both could use more trail time."

"Probably," she agreed with a small laugh. "Though for completely different reasons."

"I don't know about that," Brad said, his eyes meeting hers directly. "Sometimes I think people are more alike than different once you get past the surface stuff."

The simple observation carried a weight that made Anna pause. There was an earnestness to Brad that kept catching her off guard—moments of depth beneath his easygoing exterior.

"Maybe," she conceded, taking another sip of her latte.

"What about other water activities?" Brad asked. "Do you ever go rafting or canoeing?"

Anna nodded. "We have a canoe, though it doesn't get used as much as it should. The stretch of the New River near here is pretty calm—perfect for lazy summer days."

"Love the sound of that," Brad said, genuine enthusiasm warming his voice. "I haven't been canoeing since summer camp when I was fourteen."

"Fourteen?" Anna raised an eyebrow. "That's practically ancient history... what, you're probably around thirty?"

Brad laughed, the sound rich and unguarded. "Thirty-two, and thanks for that reminder of my advanced age."

Their conversation flowed easily after that, moving from other local attractions to childhood memories and favorite books to worst cooking disasters. With each exchange, Anna found herself relaxing further, her initial wariness giving way to genuine enjoyment of his company.

"So you've really never lived anywhere but Laurel Ridge?" Brad asked as they finished their drinks.

Anna shook her head. "Never wanted to."

"And you never got curious about what else was out there in the world?"

"Not everyone needs to leave home to find themselves," she said, more sharply than she'd intended.

Brad held up his hands in a conciliatory gesture. "I didn't mean it that way. I actually admire it—knowing where you belong and not second-guessing. That's rare."

The sincerity in his voice defused her irritation. "Sorry," she said. "I'm used to people assuming I stayed because I lacked ambition or something."

"That's not the impression I get at all," Brad said, leaning forward slightly. "Building a life where you have roots—where you're connected to the land and the community—that takes its own kind of courage and commitment."

Anna studied him, surprised by the insight. Most people who left places like Laurel Ridge viewed those who stayed behind with either condescension or nostalgia, rarely understanding the deliberate choice it could be.

"What about you? You came here from Colorado, but you mentioned Lexington," she asked.

"Born and raised in Lexington, Kentucky. But I left for college in Colorado and never really went back to Kentucky except to visit family."

"And now you're here," Anna said, a question in her tone.

"Now I'm here," Brad agreed. "Looking for something different. Something real."

Anna wanted to ask what he meant—what hadn't been real about his previous life—but something held her back. Perhaps the same instinct that made her step carefully around new seedlings, giving them space to establish themselves before disturbing the surrounding soil.

Instead, she glanced at her watch and was surprised to see how much time had passed. "I should probably head back," she said reluctantly. "The market's closing soon, and I have to help with the breakdown of our booth. Katie's all excited about her date tonight, and goodness knows she'll spend the whole afternoon fussing over clothes and makeup."

Brad nodded, gathering his purchases as they stood. "Thanks for the tour, Miss Mitchell," he said, his eyes warm with genuine appreciation. "You're better than any guidebook."

Anna rolled her eyes, but couldn't suppress the smile that tugged at her lips. "Hardly. I didn't even cover half the town."

"Then I guess we'll have to do this again sometime," Brad suggested, his tone casual but his gaze direct, lingering on her face as though committing her features to memory.

"I guess we will," she replied, surprised by the small thrill of anticipation that accompanied the thought.

Chapter 7

Anna adjusted the pleated skirt of her favorite navy-blue dress and slid into the familiar wooden pew beside her mother. Sunlight streamed through the stained-glass windows of Laurel Ridge Community Church, casting prismatic patterns across the worn hymnals and aging floorboards. The sanctuary hummed with quiet conversation as families filed in, greeting each other with warm smiles and gentle updates on summer gardens, grandbabies, and family activities.

She'd been attending this church her entire life—knew every crack in the ceiling, every squeak in the floor, and every face that would soon fill the remaining seats. The predictability brought comfort, like the steady rhythm of seasons on the farm.

"Looks like a full house today," June observed, smoothing her floral dress. "Pastor Andrew's sermon series on 'Finding Peace in Chaos' seems to be a winner."

Anna nodded, shifting the hymnal in her lap and glancing up—only to freeze when she saw him stepping through the church doors.

Brad paused in the entryway, taking in the scene with quiet attentiveness. Dressed in pressed khakis and a simple blue button-down, he blended in easily with the congregation—except for the fact that he was new, and in Laurel Ridge, new was always noticed. The sight of him standing there, respectful and somehow both confident and humble, stirred something in Anna's chest.

Her pulse quickened unexpectedly as Brad's gaze swept the sanctuary. When his eyes found hers, a small smile of recognition lifted the corners of his mouth. Without hesitation, he made his way up the aisle toward them.

"Morning," he said softly, gesturing to the space beside Anna. "Is this seat taken?"

"It's all yours," June replied before Anna could answer.

As Brad settled beside her, Anna caught the scent of his cologne—clean, musky, and understated. Their shoulders nearly touched in the close quarters of the pew, and Anna grew acutely conscious of the narrow space between them, the warmth of his presence somehow both comforting and slightly nerve-wracking.

"I didn't expect to see you here today," she whispered, aware of her mother's attentive ear just inches away.

Brad's smile was easy but genuine. "Pastor Andrew stopped by yesterday evening to visit again... this time with a welcome basket from the church. We got talking, and..." He shrugged. "It's been a while since I've attended regularly. Seemed like a good time to change that."

The piano began the opening notes of the first hymn. The congregation rose, and Anna handed Brad her hymnal, opened to the correct page. His fingers brushed hers in the exchange, warm and steady.

"Thanks," he murmured, his voice low enough that only she could hear.

As the congregation's voices rose in familiar harmony, Anna stole a glance at Brad. His eyes were on the hymnal, his voice joining the others—not particularly strong or practiced, but sincere. There was something unexpectedly moving about seeing him here, participating in this ritual that had shaped her life since childhood.

The service progressed with its familiar rhythm—announcements about the upcoming community potluck, prayers for Mrs. Wilson's hip surgery, and finally, Pastor Andrew's sermon. The young minister stood at the pulpit, his kind eyes scanning the congregation before landing briefly on their pew, a flicker of pleased recognition crossing his face when he spotted Brad.

"In our busy world," Pastor Andrew began, "we've forgotten the art of being still. Of surrendering control and trusting that not everything requires our constant management. I've been thinking a lot about that over the past few days."

"We fill our lives with noise—with tasks and goals and endless to-do lists," Pastor Andrew continued. "But what if our greatest growth happens in the quiet? In the moments when we stop striving and simply be?"

The sermon unfolded around the theme of surrender—not as weakness, but as wisdom. About recognizing the difference between what we can control and what we must release. About finding peace in letting go of the illusion that we can manage everything perfectly if we just work hard enough.

Halfway through, Anna realized she'd been holding tension in her shoulders and consciously relaxed them. The pastor's words touched something raw—her worry about taking over the business side of the farm, her fear of failing at something that mattered so deeply. Her instinct was to control what felt uncontrollable.

Beside her, Brad sat with quiet attention, his expression thoughtful. Once, when Pastor Andrew quoted a verse about finding rest for weary souls, his gaze dropped to his hands, clasped loosely in his lap. Something in his posture—a subtle vulnerability—made Anna wonder what burdens he carried beneath his easy smile.

When the service ended and the congregation rose for the final blessing, Anna was surprised by the sense of connection she felt with Brad. Not from conversation or shared activities, but from this quieter sharing—of worship, of reflection, of the simple act of sitting together in a space that invited truth.

As people began filing out of the pews, exchanging greetings and making lunch plans, Brad turned to her with a smile that seemed different somehow—more open.

"That was exactly what I needed to hear today," he said, his voice carrying a note of quiet revelation.

Martha Kincaid materialized beside them, her silver hair perfectly coiffed despite the July humidity.

"Well now, isn't this a pleasant surprise!" she exclaimed, eyes bright with undisguised interest as she focused on Brad. "Welcome to Laurel Ridge Community Church, Mr. Knight. I'm Martha Kincaid—we haven't formally met, but I believe you've heard of me."

Brad's smile was warm as he shook her offered hand. "The owner of the famous diner. Anna's given me the full rundown on your cinnamon rolls and information network."

Martha laughed, delight evident in her expression. "Both are extensive and reliable, I assure you. You simply must come by the diner this week. Tuesday mornings I make coffee cake that'll make you reconsider every life choice that kept you away from Laurel Ridge until now."

"That's quite a claim," Brad replied good-naturedly. "I'll have to test it for myself."

"See that you do," Martha said with firm approval before turning to June. "June Mitchell, your flowers on the altar are rather beautiful today. Those pink peonies with the Queen Anne's lace—just perfect! Reminds me of my mama's flowers growing up."

"Thanks, Martha," June replied. "Anna did the arranging this week. She has a better eye for it than I do these days."

Martha patted Anna's arm. "Talent runs in the family, clearly." Her gaze slid meaningfully between Anna and Brad. "As does good taste in company, it seems."

Anna fought the urge to roll her eyes at Martha's less-than-subtle implications. "We should probably head outside," she suggested. "We're creating a traffic jam."

Indeed, several church members were waiting patiently behind them to exit the pew, including the elderly Parker twins, whose synchronized nods of greeting always made Anna smile.

As they made their way down the aisle, Brad was stopped repeatedly by curious townspeople. Earl Smith clasped his hand firmly, welcoming him and letting him know that the hardware section had been expanded in his store recently. Shirley from the bakery pressed a business card into his palm, mentioning that she took special orders with twenty-four hours' notice. Even Leroy, Anna's cousin, gave Brad a measuring look before offering a gruff but genuine, "Nice to meet ya. Welcome to Laurel Ridge."

June moved ahead to speak with Pastor Andrew, leaving Anna and Brad to navigate the gauntlet of introductions together. Anna watched with growing appreciation as Brad responded to each person with genuine interest—remembering names, asking thoughtful questions, and never showing impatience despite the obvious curiosity driving many of the interactions.

"You're handling the Laurel Ridge welcome wagon like a pro," she commented as they finally reached the church steps.

Brad chuckled, glancing back in the sanctuary, where a small queue of people watched them go.

They stepped out into the bright sunshine, where clusters of congregants had gathered on the church lawn. Children darted between groups, their Sunday best already showing signs of grass stains and play. Beneath a massive oak tree, a table had been set up with lemonade and cookies—the church's summer tradition after service.

"Let me guess," Brad said, nodding toward the refreshments. "That lemonade is homemade, not from a mix."

Anna smiled. "Mrs. Hinley's closely guarded recipe."

"I love it," he said, his tone warm with appreciation rather than mockery. "The church I grew up in had donut holes every Sunday. I can still smell them if I think about it."

Anna found herself wondering about the boy Brad had been, sitting in a Kentucky church, looking forward to donut holes after the service.

June rejoined them, her expression brightening as she took in the two of them standing together. "Well," she said, checking her watch, "it's nearly noon. We should probably head home."

Brad nodded, taking a small step back. "Of course. Thank you both for sharing your pew. It made being the new guy a lot less awkward."

Something in his polite withdrawal—the assumption that their time together was ending—prompted June to add, "We're just having chicken salad sandwiches, nothing fancy; but if you're free, you're welcome to join us for lunch."

Anna held her breath, suddenly very invested in his answer.

Brad's expression opened with genuine pleasure. "That sounds like the perfect Sunday lunch to me." He hesitated, then added, "Are you sure I wouldn't be imposing?"

"Not at all," June assured him. "Sunday lunch is meant for company."

Anna nodded, a small smile playing at the corners of her mouth. "Mom's right. Besides, you haven't lived until you've tried her chicken salad."

The three of them walked toward the parking lot, exchanging greetings with other departing church members along the way. As they reached their vehicles, June suggested Brad follow them back to the farm.

"We're the driveway past yours," she explained. "Our driveway is in a curve, and if you're not watching for it, you'll pass it."

"Works for me," Brad agreed.

As Anna climbed into the passenger seat of the truck, she caught her mother's knowing glance.

"What?" she asked, buckling her seatbelt with more concentration than necessary.

"Nothing at all," June replied mildly, starting the engine. But the slight curve of her lips told a different story.

They pulled out of the church parking lot, Brad's truck following. Anna watched the familiar landscape roll by—the town slowly giving way to country roads, fence posts, and wildflowers blurring together in the summer heat. She glanced in the mirror more than once, catching glimpses of Brad's truck behind them.

"It was nice of you to invite Brad," she said.

June nodded, eyes on the road. "He seems like someone who could use a home-cooked meal and good company. Living in that Airstream, eating alone…"

"His choice," Anna pointed out.

"People choose all sorts of things for all sorts of reasons," June replied philosophically. "Doesn't mean they don't appreciate alternatives when offered."

As they slowed at the approaching tight curve and then turned onto the gravel drive leading to Blooms Farm, the flower fields came into view—a patchwork quilt of color stretching toward the mountains.

"He fits in well here," June said, glancing in the rearview mirror at Brad's truck. "Not at all what I expected."

Anna nodded thoughtfully. "He's different from what I expected too."

"In a good way?" June asked, her tone casual but her interest evident.

Anna considered the question as they pulled up to the farmhouse. Brad was indeed different—quieter, more grounded, more thoughtful, and more genuine than the stereotypical man she'd imagined. There was a depth to him that belied his easy manner, a thoughtfulness behind his warm smile.

"Yes," she admitted finally, watching in the side mirror as Brad parked behind them. "In a good way."

June smiled, reaching over to pat her daughter's hand before she opened her door and called out to Brad as he approached. "Hope you're hungry! Anna makes brownies that could start a church bake sale bidding war."

Chapter 8

"I hope you're not expecting anything fancy—this is Sunday lunch, not Sunday best," June called over her shoulder as she rummaged through the refrigerator.

Anna paused momentarily, stunned by the sight before her. Brad stood at the farmhouse sink, sleeves rolled up past his elbows, rinsing tomatoes from their garden. Sunlight streamed through the gingham curtains, painting golden patterns across the worn wooden countertop beside him. He handled each tomato with surprising care, turning them under the cool stream of water as if they were precious stones rather than everyday produce.

"Fancy is overrated," he replied, glancing up with that easy smile that somehow transformed his entire face. "Besides, I've been living off frozen dinners and canned soup for days. Anything homemade sounds like a luxury."

June emerged from the refrigerator with a container of chicken salad. "Well, we can certainly manage better than canned soup. And heaven forbid... frozen dinners! Those things should be declared a sin." She set the container on the counter and gave Anna a pointed look. "Honey, don't just stand there. Grab the bread from the pantry, would you?"

Anna blinked, shaking herself out of her momentary trance. "Right. Bread." She moved past Brad, catching the clean scent of his cologne.... again.

From beneath the kitchen table, Daisy watched the proceedings with bright, interested eyes before abandoning her post to pad over to Brad. The golden retriever sniffed his legs once, then flopped down contentedly at his feet as if she'd known him for years.

"Traitor," Anna murmured to the dog.

Brad laughed, the sound rich and warm in the kitchen's close quarters. "Dogs know good people when they meet them. It's a gift." His eyes met Anna's with a playful spark that made her pulse quicken.

"Is that right?" Anna raised an eyebrow, setting the bread beside the cutting board. "And what makes you think you qualify as 'good people'?"

His eyes met hers, warm and unexpectedly earnest. "I'm working on it every day."

She'd meant it as light teasing, but his response held a quiet depth that seemed to be a pattern with him—moments of genuine reflection beneath the effortless charm.

"Well," she recovered, reaching for a knife intending to cut the tomatoes, "Daisy's standards aren't particularly high. She once made friends with a skunk."

June laughed, pulling plates from the cabinet. "That was a disaster. Three baths with tomato juice, and she still smelled for a week."

"Let me help with that," Brad said, reaching for the cutting board and then the knife in Anna's hand. "I think I can handle slicing tomatoes."

"Anna, why don't you get some mint from the garden for the iced tea?"

Anna grabbed a pair of kitchen scissors before she slipped out the back door to the herb garden. She heard Brad asking her mom about the farm's history. His interest seemed genuine—not the polite small talk of a guest, but the curiosity of someone who truly wanted to understand the place and its people.

The herb garden welcomed her with a rush of scents—rosemary, thyme, and basil releasing their oils in the midday heat. Anna knelt to clip sprigs of mint. Through the open kitchen window, she could hear Brad and June laughing about something. The sound of male laughter in their kitchen was so unfamiliar and odd it made her pause, scissors hovering over the mint plant.

How long had it been since a man had stood in their kitchen? Her father had left when she was ten, and in the twenty years since, it had mostly been just her and her mom, occasionally joined by Katie or one of the other employees on the farm. Her boyfriend from a few years back had rarely joined them for a simple lunch or dinner. The last date she'd brought home had sat awkwardly at the table, clearly uncomfortable with the domesticity of their farm life.

But Brad moved through their kitchen with natural ease, as if he belonged there.

By the time Anna returned with a handful of fresh mint, Brad had arranged the sliced tomatoes on a platter with a sprinkle of salt and cracked pepper. June was transferring the chicken salad to a serving bowl while Brad set out glasses for the tea.

"Perfect timing," he said, glancing up as she entered. "I was just telling your mom about summers in West Virginia when I was a kid."

"Oh?"

Brad nodded. "My parents would bring me camping near the New River Gorge for two weeks every summer. Dad would fish, Mom would sketch the scenery, and I'd spend days exploring trails and climbing rocks I probably shouldn't have."

"So that's why you chose Laurel Ridge," June said thoughtfully. "Childhood memories."

"Partly," Brad agreed, his expression softening with recollection. "I remember thinking these mountains were magical. When I was looking for somewhere to... start fresh, those memories kept coming back... and I just got lucky and found a listing online for the property I bought. It was meant to be."

"And how does the reality compare to your childhood memories?" Anna asked.

Brad's eyes met hers, his gaze steady and warm. "Better. Some things improve with age and understanding."

After washing the mint, Anna muddled it into the pitcher of tea. There was something about the quiet domesticity of the moment—three people moving around a kitchen together, preparing a simple meal—that felt both ordinary and a bit unsettling.

"Growing up in Lexington," Brad continued as he helped June set the dining table, "I experienced more city living than country. Those summer trips here were my introduction to what it meant to live close to the land."

"And now you own a hundred acres of it," June observed, setting out napkins. "Quite the commitment."

"When you know, you know," Brad said simply. "The moment I walked onto that property, I felt it. This was where I needed to be."

"Well, everything's ready," June announced. "Let's eat; I'm starved."

They settled around the oval oak table that had served the Mitchell family for generations. Brad waited until both women had served themselves before filling his plate. "This looks so good," he said appreciatively. "Thanks for including me."

"Our pleasure," June replied, passing him the tomatoes. "It's nice having company over for Sunday lunch. Usually it's just us and our thoughts."

"Or Katie, talking enough for five people," Anna added with a smile.

"She seems like a force of nature," Brad commented, taking a bite of chicken salad. "Mmm—this is delicious."

"Mom's secret recipe," Anna said. "Passed down from my grandma."

"Family traditions are special," Brad said thoughtfully. "My grandmother had a chicken salad recipe too—with grapes and walnuts. She'd make it every Fourth of July."

"Is she still in Kentucky?" June asked.

Brad's expression softened with a gentle sadness. "No, she passed about five years ago. But I still make her recipe sometimes, just to remember."

"I'm sorry," Anna said. Her hand almost moved across the table toward his before she caught herself, the instinct to comfort him both natural and startling.

He smiled at her, the expression genuine despite the touch of melancholy. His eyes lingered on hers for a beat longer than necessary. "It's okay. She lived a full life—always said the secret was to change when change was needed and hold fast when holding mattered. Pretty good advice, I think."

"Wise woman," June nodded. "Sounds like someone I would have enjoyed knowing."

"She would have loved your farm," Brad said, glancing out the window at the flower fields. "She kept the most incredible garden—not on your scale, of course, but impressive for a backyard plot. She could coax blooms from plants everyone else had given up on."

"That's a gift," Anna said. "Sometimes I think plants respond more to patience and attention than anything else."

"Like most living things," Brad agreed, his eyes meeting hers briefly.

The conversation flowed easily after that, moving from gardening to funny stories about Daisy's puppyhood adventures. Brad shared tales of his cross-country drive to West Virginia, describing a sunset in Kansas and the strange roadside attractions he'd stopped to visit. Anna laughed more than she had in months, drawn in by his storytelling and the way he listened so intently when she or June spoke.

"So there I was," Brad was saying, "standing in front of this ten-foot-tall concrete prairie dog in the middle of nowhere, when this tour bus pulls up and out comes an entire wedding party—bride, groom, bridesmaids, the works—for photos."

"No!" June exclaimed, laughing.

"Complete truth," Brad insisted. "The bride had grown up nearby and always joked she'd get married at the giant prairie dog. Turns out she meant it—kind of. They had the ceremony elsewhere, but she insisted on reception photos with this concrete rodent."

Anna laughed, shaking her head. "That's going to make for some interesting wedding albums."

"I thought so too, until I saw how happy they all were," Brad said, his expression softening. "They were having the time of their lives, completely unembarrassed about taking formal photos with this ridiculous concrete landmark. Made me think about what really matters in life—not how things look to others, but the joy you find in your own choices."

There it was again—that layer of thoughtfulness beneath the easy humor, Anna thought to herself as she noticed the tiny laugh lines at the corners of his eyes and the genuine warmth in his expression.

When lunch was finished, Brad stood to help clear the table. "Where do these go?" he asked, stacking plates.

"Oh, you don't have to—" Anna began.

"I insist," he cut in with a smile. "My mother would disown me if I didn't help clean up after being invited to lunch."

June beamed at him. "A man with good manners... how refreshing." She shot Anna a meaningful look that made her cheeks warm. "I'll wrap up the leftovers while you two handle the dishes."

"I'll wash, you dry?" he suggested, already pushing up his sleeves further.

"I—sure," Anna conceded, reaching for a clean dish towel.

They fell into a rhythm at the sink, Brad washing each dish thoroughly before handing it to her. Their fingers brushed with each exchange, small moments of contact that shouldn't have felt significant but somehow did. Anna noticed how his broad shoulders turned slightly toward her when he spoke. He stood just close enough that she could catch the clean scent of his cologne mingled with the fresh air that seemed to cling to him.

"You have a beautiful home," Brad said as he handed her a freshly rinsed glass. "It feels... lived in. Loved."

"Thanks," Anna replied, carefully drying the glass. "It's not fancy, but—"

"That's exactly what makes it special," he interrupted gently. "Every corner feels like it has a story. Like people have laughed and cried and lived real lives here."

Anna glanced up at him, surprised by how perfectly he'd captured what she loved about their farmhouse. "Uhhh... yeah... that's exactly it. This place has seen three generations of my family through all sorts of seasons. Good harvests, bad winters, celebrations, heartbreaks—it's all within these walls."

Brad nodded. "That's what I want for my place, eventually. Not just a house, but a home with a history I can tell my future grandkids."

"Your hundred acres has plenty of history already," Anna pointed out. "Just waiting for you to add your chapter."

His smile deepened at that. "I like that."

They worked in comfortable silence for a moment, the only sounds being the gentle splash of water and the distant ticking of the grandfather clock in the hallway.

"So," Brad said finally, handing her the last plate, "I was thinking..."

Anna raised an eyebrow, waiting.

"The weather is awesome outside... way too nice to spend it inside, and I remember you mentioning Sunset Point Trail." His voice carried a note of hopefulness, his eyes meeting hers with quiet anticipation.

Her pulse quickened slightly. "What about it?"

"Any chance you'd be interested in showing me that trail today? Take advantage of this perfect weather?" The way he asked made her breath catch slightly. Her fingers stilled on the dishcloth, and for a moment, she forgot the half-dried plate in her hand as their eyes met across the small space between them.

June reappeared, clearly having overheard. "That sounds like a wonderful idea. The trail's gorgeous this time of year."

"You wanna come with us?" Brad asked.

June waved a dismissive hand. "Oh, I think someone needs to stay home with Daisy. She gets lonely, don't you, girl?"

At the sound of her name, Daisy's tail thumped against the kitchen floor, completely undermining June's flimsy excuse.

"Mom," Anna said, giving her a pointed look.

"What?" June replied with exaggerated innocence. "It's too beautiful a day to spend indoors. Go."

Brad watched her, patient and unassuming. "No pressure," he said. "I just thought it might be nice to see some of that natural beauty you've been telling me about."

Looking at him—at the genuine interest in his eyes, the easy way he'd integrated himself into their Sunday—Anna felt something settle inside her. A quiet certainty that saying yes was the right choice.

"Alright," she said finally.

Brad's face lit up with a smile that reached all the way to his eyes. He tossed the dishtowel over his shoulder with a playful flourish. "So... you think you can keep up with me on this trail, or should I take it slow... no pressure?"

"I've been hiking these mountains since I could walk... even if it has been a while... you might just find yourself challenged to keep up with me."

"I welcome the challenge," he replied.

Chapter 9

Anna gestured toward the gravel turnoff ahead. "Take a left here—Sunset Point's about a mile and a half up that ridge."

Brad guided his truck onto the narrow access road, loose stones crunching beneath the tires. "This is probably not on any tourist maps."

"Nope, not that I'm aware of," Anna replied, rolling down her window to let the mountain air sweep through the cab.

The truck climbed steadily, leaving the valley's patchwork of fields and farms behind. Anna watched the landscape transform around them—open meadows giving way to thickening stands of oak, maple, and pine. The late afternoon light filtered through the canopy, dappling the road ahead with shifting patterns of gold and shadow.

"I used to hike up here with my dad when I was little," she said, the memory surfacing unexpectedly. "He'd pack peanut butter and honey sandwiches for our picnic lunch and tell me the mountains were sleeping giants and we needed to be still while we hiked so we didn't awaken them."

Brad glanced at her. "That's a good memory to have."

"It is," she agreed, though the sweetness came with its familiar edge of loss. "He left when I was ten. Those hikes are some of the clearest memories I have of him."

She hadn't meant to share that part—certainly not so plainly or so soon. But something about the enclosed space of the truck and the way Brad listened made the words feel safe once spoken.

"Sometimes the best gifts come from complicated people," he said, navigating around a pothole in the road.

Anna looked at him, struck by the quiet wisdom in his observation.

They rode in silence after that, Anna turning his words over in her mind longer than she wanted to admit. Her gaze drifted to Brad's hands on the steering wheel—steady, capable, relaxed. Not white-knuckling every curve like she'd expected on this narrow, winding road.

"The parking area's just ahead on the right," she said as they rounded a bend.

Brad pulled into the small clearing where three other cars were already parked. "Popular spot for a Sunday?"

"For locals, yes. Most tourists stick to the marked trails in the national park." Anna said as she grabbed the small backpack on the seat beside her that she'd packed with water bottles and trail mix. "We've got about a forty-minute hike ahead of us. Nothing too steep, but there are some rocky sections."

They set off side by side where the trail allowed, single file where it narrowed. Anna took the lead during the trickier portions, pointing out loose stones or exposed roots. The path wound through stands of towering trees, occasionally opening to reveal glimpses of the valley below.

"Look," Anna said, pausing to point at a cluster of tiny white flowers nestled beside the trail. "Nodding ladies' tresses. They're one of the last summer orchids to bloom before fall."

Brad crouched down for a closer look. "They're beautiful. Like tiny sculptures."

"Most people would walk right past them," she said. "But once you know what to look for, you start seeing them everywhere."

He straightened, his eyes meeting hers. "Isn't that true of most things in life?"

Anna nodded before they continued upward.

"The oaks are starting to show the tiniest hints of color already," she noted, pointing to where a few leaves were beginning to burnish slightly at their edges.

"Early for fall color, isn't it?" Brad asked, pushing a low-hanging branch aside for her to pass.

Anna nodded. "We had a long dry spell in June. Trees start preparing earlier when they've been stressed." She smiled wryly. "Nature's way of adapting to unexpected challenges, I suppose."

"Something we could all learn from," Brad replied, offering his hand as she navigated a particularly steep section of trail.

His palm was warm against hers, the grip secure but gentle. Anna accepted the help without comment, though she noticed he didn't immediately let go once they reached level ground. Neither did she at first. The rough calluses on his palm against her skin sent a whisper of awareness up her arm, his hand fitting against hers in a way that felt oddly right.

"How long has your family been in Laurel Ridge?" Brad asked as they rounded a bend in the trail. The genuine interest in his eyes made it clear this wasn't just polite conversation.

"Since 1920," Anna replied. "My great-grandfather bought the original acreage after coming back from World War I. He said that after everything he'd seen in Europe, all he wanted was a quiet place to grow things."

"Sounds like a smart man."

"He was from what my mom has said." Anna nodded. "He started with vegetables, then added a small apple orchard. My grandmother expanded into potted flowers she sold from a roadside stand at the end of our driveway. Then my mom took it even further—specializing in blooms that florists and event planners struggle to get from big distributors."

Brad nodded, thoughtful. "And you've always known this was your path too?"

"As I said before... not everyone needs to leave home to find themselves," she said, a bit sharply.

"I didn't mean anything by my question. I'm honestly just curious." His voice gentled, the expression in his eyes conveying a respect that caught her off guard.

"Sorry," Anna said, softening. "I guess I've had one too many people assume I'm just a country bumpkin with no ambition or education." She tucked a strand of hair behind her ear, momentarily breaking eye contact.

"Pretty sure those people don't matter," Brad replied, a smile tugging at the corners of his mouth, his eyes warm with understanding. The way he looked at her then made her feel seen in a way few people ever had—as though he recognized something in her worth knowing.

They continued upward; the trail steepened as they neared the ridge. Anna pointed out a stand of sassafras trees, their mitten-shaped leaves fluttering in the breeze.

"That's sassafras," she said. "The roots were used to make tea—or what my great-grandmother called a spring 'tonic.' Supposed to cleanse the system after a long winter."

Brad raised an eyebrow. "Did it actually work?"

Anna laughed. "Who knows? Later they figured out the root contains compounds that aren't so great in big doses. But it smells amazing—kind of like root beer and lemons had a baby."

As they climbed higher, the forest began to thin, allowing glimpses of the valley stretching out below. Brad paused at one such opening, his expression softening as he took in the view.

"This is just the preview," Anna said, nodding toward the trail ahead. "The overlook is another ten minutes or so upward."

When they finally emerged onto Sunset Point, even Anna, who had seen the view in the past, felt a quiet sense of awe. The late afternoon sun hung low over the mountains, casting the New River Valley in shimmering light. From this height, they could see for miles—the river winding like a silver ribbon through the landscape, farms, and forests creating a patchwork of textures across the rolling terrain, and in the distance, the faint outline of Laurel Ridge itself.

Brad stood perfectly still, his expression one of wonder. He took a slow breath, as if trying to absorb it all. For a moment, Anna watched him rather than the view, captivated by the play of emotions across his face—the widened eyes, the softened jaw, the slight parting of his lips in amazement.

"No words?" Anna asked, unable to keep the hint of pride from her voice.

"None that would do it justice," he replied.

They found a flat rock near the edge of the overlook and sat side by side. Anna unpacked water bottles and trail mix, offering them to

Brad. The day's heat was still heavy, but a gentle breeze softened it, carrying the scent of fresh, clean air and nature.

"Thanks for bringing me up here," Brad said after a while. "There are no words to describe this."

Anna nodded, her gaze following the river's meandering path through the valley. "I used to come up here when I needed perspective. Problems that seem huge down there look different from up here."

Brad was quiet for a moment, rolling a pine nut between his fingers. "What problems seem huge right now?"

Anna hesitated and thought about changing the subject to keep things light. But something about this place made her inclined toward honesty.

"My mom wants to step back from the farm," she said, the words feeling both heavy and relieving once spoken. "Not all at once, but gradually over the coming months. She wants to travel, to have a life beyond work."

"And that worries you?"

Anna turned the water bottle in her hands, watching condensation trail down its sides. "She handles all the business aspects—the accounting, the contracts, the marketing plans. I've always focused on the growing side, the creative part." She paused, gathering courage for the admission. "The quarterly reports for our wholesale accounts are due in two weeks, and I have no idea how to even start, and Mom asked me to take care of them this time."

The fear that had been sitting in her chest for days felt strangely diminished once spoken aloud.

Brad nodded, his expression thoughtful. "Financial systems can be intimidating," he said. "But they're learnable. Like anything else."

"Maybe for some people," Anna replied. "But every time I try to make sense of balance sheets or profit projections, my brain just... freezes."

She expected a typical response—that she wasn't trying hard enough, that she just needed to apply herself. Instead, Brad surprised her.

"Everyone's mind works differently," he said. "The way these systems are typically taught or shown doesn't work for everyone. I had a colleague once who couldn't make sense of spreadsheets until we translated everything into visual flowcharts. Then she could see the patterns instantly."

Anna looked at him, struck by this perspective.

"I'd be happy to help if you ever want another perspective," Brad offered, his tone casual but sincere. "I've set up more than my share of business systems and trained quite a few people in the past."

The offer felt natural, friendly even. No pressure, just a simple extension of support.

"I might take you up on that," she said finally. "Though I should warn you, it might be a lost cause."

"I very much doubt that."

As they continued to talk, Anna relaxed as the sun began its slow descent toward the mountain ridges. The valley below was transforming, shadows starting to lengthen across the landscape, the river catching fire with reflected light.

"Do you miss it?" Anna asked. "Your life before—in the tech world?"

"Parts of it," he admitted. "The creativity of it. The collaboration with people solving interesting problems." He paused. "But the constant pressure, the endless striving for more, bigger, faster? Constantly being in go mode. No. I don't miss feeling like I was always running out of time."

Something in his tone—a weariness beneath the words—made Anna wonder what he wasn't saying. What had driven this clearly knowledgeable and sophisticated man to leave behind a successful career for an Airstream and a hundred undeveloped acres?

"What about you?" Brad asked, turning the question back to her. "Ever wonder what life might have been like if you'd chosen differently?"

Anna watched a hawk glide in lazy circles above the valley, riding thermal currents with effortless grace. "Sometimes," she acknowledged. "Not because I regret staying, but just... curiosity, I guess. About roads not taken."

"That makes sense," Brad said. "It's the wondering without appreciation for what is that gets dangerous."

As the sun dipped a little lower, Anna reluctantly checked her watch. "We should probably start heading back. It gets dark quickly once the sun goes behind the mountains."

They packed up their small provisions and began the descent, the trail now bathed in the warm, golden light of the approaching sunset. The light caught in Brad's hair, turning the brown strands to copper and gold, and painted his profile in soft hues that made Anna miss a step when she glanced his way. He steadied her with a light touch at her elbow, his hand lingering a moment longer than necessary.

"I've been thinking about ways to get more involved in the community," Brad said as they navigated a rocky section. "Pastor Andrew mentioned the town is trying to increase tourism without losing its character or going into debt."

Anna nodded. "It's always a balancing act. We need the economic boost, but no one wants Laurel Ridge turning into just another tourist trap with chain stores and overpriced gift shops."

"What if there was a way to showcase what makes this place special, but in a way that preserves its authenticity?" Brad said. "Not changing Laurel Ridge to fit tourists' expectations, but inviting the right kind of visitors—ones who appreciate what's already here."

"That's sounds interesting. The question is how."

"I have some ideas," Brad said. "Nothing concrete yet, but I'm listening and learning."

By the time they reached the parking area, the forest had grown a little dimmer, evening shadows gathering beneath the trees. The air had cooled considerably, carrying the earthy scent of moss and fallen leaves.

As they approached Brad's truck, he turned to her, his expression quietly hopeful. "You free for breakfast tomorrow?"

She surprised herself by smiling. "Sure. Martha's Diner, 8 a.m. I'll drive myself—I've got errands afterward."

Brad nodded, clearly pleased. "I'll be there."

"Just so you know," Anna added as he opened the passenger door for her, "Martha will absolutely interrogate you. Consider yourself warned." She glanced up, caught by the golden evening light playing across his features.

Brad's laugh was warm and genuine. "I think I can handle it. Especially with you there for moral support." The way he said it—as though they were already a team facing the world together—sent a ripple of awareness down her spine. She ducked into the truck to hide the color that rose to her cheeks, her pulse quickening at the thought of tomorrow's breakfast.

Chapter 10

The bell above Martha's Diner jingled as Brad stepped in, pausing just inside the door to scan the cozy space. He spotted Anna in a booth near the window, and his face lit up when he smiled, his expression brightening in a way that made Anna's heart beat a little faster.

"Morning," he said, sliding into the seat across from her.

Anna looked up from her coffee, tucking a strand of auburn hair behind her ear. "Mornin'." She was surprised by how pleased she felt at the sight of him, as though his arrival had somehow made the familiar diner warmer and more inviting.

The morning sun streamed through the large front windows, highlighting the red vinyl booths and checkerboard floor tiles that had been part of Martha's since before Anna was born. The scents of coffee, bacon, and cinnamon rolls wrapped around them like a comfortable blanket.

"So this is the famous Martha's," Brad said, glancing around with appreciation.

"Wait until you taste the food," Anna replied, lifting her mug.

Brad picked up the laminated menu, studying it with genuine interest. "Any recommendations? What's the local specialty?"

"Depends on who you ask. The blueberry pancakes have a cult following. Martha's biscuits and gravy could probably end wars. And if you leave without trying her home fries, you've missed half the experience."

As if summoned by the mention of her name, Martha herself appeared beside their booth, coffeepot in hand. Her silver hair was neatly pinned back, and her blue apron had clearly seen its share of busy mornings.

"Well, well," she said, refilling Anna's mug and pouring one for Brad without asking. "The mysterious B. Knight finally graces my establishment."

"Martha Kincaid," Brad said with a warm smile, extending his hand. "I've heard so many good things about your diner that I feel like I know it already."

Martha's eyes twinkled as she shook his hand. "Flattery will get you everywhere, young man. But my cooking will earn your loyalty." She tilted her head, studying him with undisguised curiosity. "So, Brad Knight from Colorado. What brings you to our little corner of the world?"

Anna suppressed a smile. Martha had never been one for subtle interrogation.

To his credit, Brad didn't seem the least bit uncomfortable under her scrutiny. "A change of pace," he answered, his tone open and easy. "I used to vacation in these mountains as a kid. When I decided it was time for something different, this area was the first place that came to mind, and as luck would have it, I found a real estate that piqued my curiosity."

"Hmm," Martha nodded, as if filing away this information for later analysis. "Well, we're glad to have you. Now, what can I get you two this morning?"

They placed their orders—blueberry pancakes for Brad, veggie omelet for Anna—and Martha bustled away, already calling instructions to the cook.

"That wasn't so bad," Brad said, amusement in his voice. "From your warnings, I expected the Spanish Inquisition."

Anna laughed, the sound bright in the busy diner. "Oh, that was just the opening act. Trust me, she's gathering intelligence. The real questions will come with the food."

The bell above the door chimed again, and Pastor Andrew walked in with his wife, Lily. They spotted Anna and Brad immediately, and Andrew's face broke into a welcoming smile.

"Mind if we join you for a minute?" he asked, approaching their booth.

"Please do," Brad replied without hesitation, shifting to make room.

Andrew slid in beside Brad while Lily took the spot next to Anna. "Brad, this is my wife, Lily. Lily, this is Brad Knight, our newest Laurel Ridge resident."

"Wonderful to meet you," Lily said warmly. "I made those oatmeal cookies Andrew brought over."

"They were incredible," Brad told her with genuine enthusiasm. "I actually rationed them to make them last longer. I'm sorry I didn't get a chance to meet you at church this past Sunday."

Lily beamed. "High praise indeed! I'll have to make you another batch. And no worries about Sunday; I was busy discussing some upcoming activities we have at church, and next thing I know over half the congregation had left."

"So, Brad," Andrew said, leaning back comfortably, "how are you settling in? Getting everything you need for the Airstream living?"

"Pretty well," Brad replied. "Emma at the general store has been helpful. And your welcome basket filled some important gaps in my pantry."

Their conversation flowed easily, touching on Brad's property, the recent demolition of the old farmhouse, and his first impressions of Laurel Ridge. Anna found herself watching Brad with growing curiosity. There was no hint of the impatience or condescension she'd half-expected from someone used to city life. Instead, he listened to Andrew and Lily with genuine interest, asking thoughtful questions about the church's community outreach programs and Lily's work as a wedding planner.

"How long do you think you'll stay in the Airstream?" Lily asked.

"I'm not really sure," Brad answered. "I want to take my time and get to know the land before making any permanent decisions about building a home."

"Good idea," Andrew commented. "Most people would rush to put up a house right away."

Brad shrugged, his expression thoughtful. "I've done enough rushing in my life. I don't need to make any hasty decisions."

Martha arrived with their food, setting down plates piled high with blueberry pancakes and a side of crispy home fries for Brad. Anna's veggie omelet with home fries filled the entire plate.

"Don't let us keep you from enjoying this feast," Lily said, sliding out of the booth. "We just wanted to say hello."

After Andrew and Lily departed for their own table, Anna and Brad turned to their breakfast. Brad's eyes widened appreciatively at his first bite of pancakes.

"Delicious. This might be the best thing I've ever eaten in a restaurant," he declared. The childlike delight in his expression as he savored the pancakes made Anna smile—there was something endearing about a grown man taking such simple pleasure in good food.

Anna smiled, cutting into her omelet. "Martha will be thrilled to hear it. She takes her food very seriously."

They had barely made it through a few more bites when Mr. Taylor, the town's retired postmaster, stopped by their table.

"Just wanted to introduce myself," he said, extending a weathered hand to Brad. "Jim Taylor. Heard you bought the old Harmon place."

"Brad Knight," Brad replied, wiping his hand on his napkin before shaking Mr. Taylor's. "Nice to meet you, sir."

"There's lots of potential on that property," Jim observed. "My grandfather used to talk about the apple orchard that was there back in the day. Made the best cider in the county, he always said."

"I didn't know there was an orchard," Brad said, his interest clearly piqued. "Do you know where it is on the property?"

This launched Mr. Taylor into a detailed description of the northern edge of the property, where the old orchard had flourished until the 1950s. Brad listened attentively, asking questions that showed genuine curiosity about the history of his land.

Anna watched the exchange with growing amazement. Most newcomers would have politely nodded and waited for the old man to move on. Instead, Brad seemed genuinely fascinated, even pulling out his phone to make notes about the orchard's location.

"Might be some of those old varieties still growing wild up there," Mr. Taylor concluded. "Heritage apples, they call 'em now. Might even be a few June apple trees out there still. Worth looking for."

"I'll definitely check," Brad promised. "Thanks for telling me about this."

As Mr. Taylor ambled up to the counter, Martha reappeared to refill their coffee cups.

"I see you're getting the full Laurel Ridge welcome," she observed with a knowing smile. "How's the food?"

"Incredible," Brad replied. "Anna wasn't exaggerating about those home fries."

Martha's face softened with pleasure. "Family recipe, five generations old. My great-grandmother was frying potatoes for hungry miners when this town was just getting started."

"Really?" Brad's expression lit with genuine interest. "This diner goes back that far?"

"Goodness, no," Martha laughed, settling comfortably against the edge of their booth. "The diner building dates back to 1952. But the recipes—those go back much further. My family's been feeding Laurel Ridge since there was a Laurel Ridge to feed."

This launched her into a brief history of the diner, how her parents had opened it when the mining company built the original structure as a commissary. She'd taken over years ago and slowly transformed it into the community institution it is today.

"The red vinyl booths were my idea," she confided. "Everyone said I was crazy to spend that kind of money on decor, but years later, they're still here." She patted the booth seat with obvious pride.

"They're perfect," Brad said, glancing around the diner with appreciation. "The whole place feels like it couldn't—and shouldn't—be any other way."

Martha beamed at him. "You know, for a tech fellow from Colorado, you've got good sense." She glanced between him and Anna with barely concealed interest. "How was your hike yesterday? Anna knows all the best spots around here."

Anna felt heat rise to her cheeks. News traveled fast in Laurel Ridge, but this was impressive even by local standards. "Sunset Point was beautiful, as always," she replied, keeping her tone casual.

"Weather couldn't have been better," Brad added smoothly. "Though I'm still feeling it in my calves this morning."

Martha laughed. "Mountain trails will do that to you until you build up those hiking muscles. Keep at it—best way to see what makes this place special."

After Martha moved on to check on other customers, Brad leaned forward, his voice lowered conspiratorially. "How did she know we went hiking?"

Anna shook her head, amused despite herself. "Welcome to small-town life. Someone probably saw your truck with Colorado plates parked at the trailhead. Or my mom mentioned it to someone, and that person mentioned it to someone, and so on. Or Daisy told her dog friends, who told their owners."

Brad's laugh was warm and genuine. "I think I like it, actually. There's something reassuring about a place where people notice each other." His eyes met hers across the table, holding her gaze a moment longer than necessary. "Makes a person feel like they matter."

"It's nice until you're a teenager trying to get away with something," Anna replied wryly.

"I can imagine. Nowhere to hide."

"Not a chance. On my first date in high school, the boy picked me up at seven. By seven-thirty, Mom had received three phone calls reporting our whereabouts."

Before Brad could respond, Shirley from the bakery stopped by their table, a small white box in her hands.

"Morning, Anna!" she chirped. "And you must be Brad. I'm Shirley Gallagher from Taste of Heaven Bakery." She set the box on their table.

"Just a little welcome gift—cinnamon roll muffins, fresh from this morning's batch."

"That's incredibly kind," Brad said, clearly touched by the gesture. "Thank you."

"Not at all! Martha called and said you were here, so I boxed up some goodies and brought them over as quickly as I could. We're all just so pleased to have someone breathing new life into that beautiful property. Such potential there."

This led to several more interruptions as various townspeople stopped by to introduce themselves. Emma Talbot from the general store reminded Brad that the shipment of solar lights he'd ordered would arrive Wednesday. Earl from the hardware store wanted to discuss options for temporary power setups if he intended to live in the camper in the winter. Even Mrs. Henderson, in town to meet her husband for breakfast, paused to invite Brad to join the Historical Society.

Through it all, Brad remained attentive and chatted away as if he had always lived here. He remembered names, asked follow-up questions about people's families or businesses, and shared small pieces of information about himself. Yes, he'd worked in tech in Colorado. Yes, he was planning to stay in Laurel Ridge long term. No, he didn't have concrete plans for the property yet, beyond eventually planning to build a home and perhaps planting a small garden in the future.

When the flow of visitors finally ebbed, Anna shook her head in amazement. "You're a natural at this."

Brad looked up from his nearly finished pancakes. "At what?"

"Small-town integration. I kind of thought all the attention might get overwhelming for you."

"It's nice, actually," he said. "In Denver, I lived in the same building for years and didn't even know who my neighbors were. Here, I've been in town less than two weeks and already feel more connected than I did there."

The simple honesty in his voice struck Anna. There was no performative appreciation, just genuine gratitude for the welcome he'd received.

"So," Brad said, changing the subject. "What's on your agenda for today? Back to the farm?"

Anna shook her head. "Actually, I have a monthly contract with the town. I maintain the planters, hanging plants, and flower beds around town. Today's refresh day for the town square—replacing what's past its prime, adding new blooms for mid-summer color."

"Sounds interesting; gives you a break from working on the farm, I imagine."

"It does," Anna agreed.

"Would you like some help? I mean, if an extra pair of hands would be useful."

The offer caught Anna completely off guard. "You want to help plant flowers in the town square?"

"Why not?" Brad shrugged, his smile easy and open. "I've got nothing pressing on my schedule, and I could use the practice. My property will need plenty of planting eventually." There was something in his expression—an eagerness, perhaps, or a hopefulness—that suggested he was offering for reasons beyond just being helpful.

Anna studied him, trying to reconcile this offer with her lingering assumptions about city people. "It's not exactly glamorous work. Lots of digging in dirt, lugging water buckets..."

"After years of staring at screens and sitting in meetings, getting my hands in actual earth sounds like therapy." The honesty in his voice, the way his eyes sought her approval—it tugged at something inside her, making it impossible to refuse.

His sincerity was impossible to doubt. "Alright then," Anna said, smiling. "But don't say I didn't warn you; you're probably going to get filthy dirty."

"I'm not afraid of a little dirt," Brad assured her, finishing the last of his coffee.

As they paid their bill—Brad insisting on treating despite Anna's protests—Martha reappeared with a thermos.

"Coffee for the road," she said, handing it to Brad. "On the house. Consider it part of your welcome package... I heard you are one of those city slicker coffee snobs."

Brad laughed. "That's incredibly kind, thank you."

Martha waved away his thanks. "Just doing my part to make sure you know you're welcome here and that we want you to stick around." She gave Anna a meaningful look. "Some things are worth investing in."

Outside, the July morning had warmed considerably, the air thick with humidity that promised another scorching afternoon. Anna's truck was parked nearby, its bed loaded with flats of marigolds, petunias, and sweet potato vine.

"You sure you're up for this?" Anna asked as they approached the vehicle. "It's going to be hot, and those planters need a lot of work."

Brad looked at the truck full of flowers, then back at Anna, his eyes bright with genuine enthusiasm.

"Only one way to find out."

Chapter 11

Brad knelt beside the half-filled flowerbed, gently tamping down the soil around a blooming marigold. The sun beat down on the back of his neck, and droplets of sweat gathered at his temples. He'd shed his button-down an hour ago, working now in just his white t-shirt, which was already smudged with soil and grass stains. Anna noticed the contrast between his capable hands and the delicate blooms—strong yet careful, never crushing the tender stems.

"You have a lot of these yellow ones?" he said, reaching up to accept another plant from Anna.

"They're Mom's favorite this time of year," Anna replied, handing him a vibrant marigold. Their hands connected briefly in the exchange, his palm warm against her fingers. "She says they look like sunshine and make the town square sparkle."

Brad carefully nestled the plant into the hole he'd prepared, his fingers working the soil with surprising tenderness for their size. "Your mom has good taste. There's something inherently hopeful about yellow flowers. They just make a person... happy."

Anna paused, trowel in hand, to study him. Most men she knew approached planting with brute efficiency—get it done quickly, no fuss. But Brad handled each flower as if it mattered, taking care not to damage the delicate roots or crush the blooms.

"You're pretty good at this for a tech guy... Are you for real, or am I just imagining this?" she observed, reaching for a watering can.

Brad grinned up at her, squinting against the July sun. "I'm real as far as I know. I told you I wasn't afraid of dirt." He rocked back on his heels to survey their progress. "Besides, there's something satisfying about this kind of work. You see immediate results."

They'd been at it for nearly two hours, refreshing the flowerbeds that bordered Laurel Ridge's town square. The once-tired planters now burst with color—deep purple petunias cascading over the edges, coral begonias adding depth, and bright yellow marigolds providing cheerful focal points. White sweet alyssum created a delicate, fragrant border that softened the edges and unified the design. Anna realized she'd stopped several times just to watch him work—the focused concentration in his expression when handling each plant, the gentle precision so at odds with his strong build.

Anna handed Brad a water bottle from the small cooler she'd brought. "Drink. July heat and humidity in West Virginia doesn't mess around."

"Thanks," he said gratefully, accepting the bottle. As he tilted his head back to drink, his gaze caught on a family across the square—clearly tourists with their camera, map, and slightly disoriented expressions as they pivoted in place, looking in all directions.

"Are they lost?" he asked, nodding toward the family.

Anna followed his gaze. "Maybe." She noticed how Brad straightened slightly, the way his eyes tracked the visitors with analytical interest rather than mere curiosity.

The father approached an elderly man sitting on a bench nearby and pointed to something on his map. The local pointed vaguely toward the north end of town, his gestures animated.

Brad watched the interaction with interest. When the family moved on, still looking slightly confused, he turned back to Anna. The intensity in his expression made her pulse quicken—not because it was directed at her, but because she glimpsed a new facet of him: observant, strategic, and engaged. "Does the town get a lot of visitors year-round or more seasonally?"

"More and more visitors every year, and the season really doesn't matter. I'll admit summer and fall attract the most tourists, but winter is popular for all the skiing and ice skating in the area," she replied, kneeling beside him to plant a row of white alyssum. The delicate flowers released their honey-sweet scent as she worked. "The New River Gorge being designated as a national park two years ago brought in a massive wave of outdoor enthusiasts. And there was an article in a magazine that Greenbrier County puts out, and they recently labeled us the hidden gem of small towns."

"I can see why people would want to visit," Brad said, genuinely. "This place is like something from a storybook—but real, not manufactured."

He looked across Main Street, where red brick buildings housed family-owned businesses beneath striped awnings. He glanced back at the white gazebo in the center of the town square, which was surrounded by old maple trees, their broad leaves creating pools of dappled shade on the cobblestone walkways. Every corner spoke of care and history—from the antique replica lampposts to the wooden benches and rocking chairs worn smooth by generations.

"I've noticed most of the people that I'm guessing are visitors seem a bit... adrift," he added thoughtfully.

Anna glanced up from her planting. "What do you mean?"

Before Brad could answer, an older couple approached them hesitantly.

"Excuse me," the woman said, clutching a small travel guidebook. "Could you tell us where we might find a good lunch spot? Something local, not a chain?"

Anna straightened, brushing soil from her hands onto her jeans. "Martha's Diner is just down the block on Main Street. You can enjoy good home-cooked food there. If you want something lighter, Lily's Café is in the other direction on Main Street, and she has great sandwiches and homemade soups."

The couple thanked her and moved on.

"That's what I mean," Brad said, returning to their conversation as he reached for another marigold. "Beautiful town, friendly people, but visitors are left to wander and hope they stumble across the right information."

Anna considered this as she worked. "I guess I never really thought about it. When you grow up somewhere, you forget what it's like not to know where everything is."

"Does Laurel Ridge have a welcome center? Or a tourism board?"

Anna shook her head. "Not officially. The Chamber of Commerce has some brochures, but it's only open Tuesday through Thursday. Most people find out about local attractions through word-of-mouth or the businesses' social media pages, I would imagine. Others probably just come and wander around and discover things on their own."

"So there's no central place where visitors can get information? Learn about hiking trails, river access points, and local events?"

"Not really," Anna admitted. "Pastor Andrew puts together a community calendar that gets posted at the church, the library, and Martha's. But that's more for locals than tourists."

Brad nodded thoughtfully, continuing to work as he processed this information. They fell into a companionable rhythm, with Anna digging the holes and Brad following behind with plants and soil. The physical labor felt good—purposeful and grounding in a way his former work rarely had been.

Across the square, a young couple studied their phones, clearly trying to reconcile digital maps with their actual surroundings. A few minutes later, they approached a shopkeeper sweeping the sidewalk in front of his store, gesturing toward their phone screen with questioning expressions.

"It's a missed opportunity," Brad said quietly, almost to himself.

"What is?"

"This town has so much to offer—authentic businesses, incredible scenery, rich history—but there's no organized way for visitors to discover it all." Brad's voice took on a subtle energy, his entrepreneurial mind clearly engaged. "No central narrative that connects the town to the hiking trails or activities in the area... which should connect to the local crafts and festivals and events.... which should connect to farm experiences and other authentic things on the outskirts of town."

Anna sat back on her heels, studying him with growing curiosity. "You sound like you've thought about something like this before. You're rambling a little."

Brad hesitated, then offered a small smile. "Sorry... old habit. My brain never shuts down, though I'm trying to quiet it more these days. My background in tech focused on tourism applications."

"Applications?" Anna's brow furrowed slightly. "Like job applications?"

Brad's laugh was warm and genuine. "Sorry—tech speak. I meant apps. Software for phones and tablets. I developed a platform that helped travelers discover authentic local experiences instead of tourist traps."

"Wow. That makes sense now," Anna said, connecting the dots. "You're interested in the visitor experience in Laurel Ridge."

Brad nodded, placing another marigold in the prepared soil. "It's second nature to me—noticing the gaps between what a place offers and how accessible that information is to outsiders."

"So you built travel apps," Anna prompted, handing him a small bag of slow-release fertilizer. "For a company in Colorado?"

"I founded a company called LocalLens," Brad said, measuring the fertilizer carefully. "We created tools to help travelers experience destinations more authentically."

"Like TripAdvisor?" Anna asked, trying to understand.

"Similar concept, different approach," Brad explained. "Instead of focusing on reviews and ratings, we emphasized storytelling and connection. Helping visitors understand the soul of a place, not just its tourist attractions."

"That sounds... interesting," Anna said, genuinely impressed. She'd assumed his tech background meant coding in a cubicle or selling gadgets. "Did it work? Your company?"

Brad nodded, a small smile playing at the corners of his mouth. "It did. I eventually sold it and moved on to... this." He gestured to himself—dirt-stained clothes, kneeling in a flowerbed in a small West Virginia town.

Anna sensed there was more to the story, but she held back from asking. Instead, she handed him another plant.

"So what would you do differently here?" She asked, genuinely curious. "If you were responsible for helping visitors experience Laurel Ridge?"

Brad's expression brightened at the question. "I'd start with a physical welcome center—nothing elaborate, just a central hub where visitors could get oriented. Staffed by locals who know the area's history and stories, not just its data points." He gestured toward the end of town. "Maybe there, or an empty storefront on Main Street if there is one."

"Shirley's old place has been vacant for months," Anna mused, warming to the conversation. "Since she moved the bakery to the larger space."

"Hmmm... interesting," Brad nodded. "I'd include interactive maps of hiking trails, profiles of local businesses, and upcoming events and festivals. Maybe displays about the area's history and ecology."

"Like a museum?"

"More dynamic than that," Brad explained, his hands moving expressively as he spoke. "A launching point for exploration, not a destination itself. And I'd complement it with digital tools—a detailed and full app that lets visitors carry all that information in their pocket, updated in real-time."

A family with three children walked past their flowerbed, the youngest pointing excitedly at a butterfly that had landed on one of the freshly planted marigolds.

"Look how pretty!" the little girl exclaimed.

"It certainly is," her mother agreed. "I wonder what kind of flower that is?"

Brad caught Anna's eye and raised an eyebrow in silent question. Anna nodded, struck by how quickly they'd established this wordless communication, like musicians finding harmony without sheet music.

"It's a French marigold," Brad offered, smiling at the family. "They're pretty resilient from what my friend here tells me—good for home gardens. Nearly impossible to kill." The subtle pride in his voice when mentioning what she'd taught him made Anna bite back a smile.

"And butterflies love them," Anna added. "That's a Painted Lady visiting this flower."

The mother's expression warmed with appreciation. "Thank you! Are you the town gardener?"

"I'm just helping out; Anna here is the town gardening expert," Brad replied easily. "But if you're interested in local plants, her farm, Blooms Farm, just outside town, offers tours. They grow flowers you won't find anywhere else in the region." He glanced at Anna as he spoke, a hint of admiration warming his expression.

Anna blinked in surprise at the smooth promotion of her family business. No one had ever spoken about her work with such natural conviction, as though Blooms Farm were something remarkable rather than just her everyday life.

"Is there a brochure or website with information?" the father asked, phone already in hand.

"We're on Instagram and Facebook," Anna said. "Blooms Farm, all one word. The address and hours are listed there."

After the family moved on, Anna turned to Brad with a questioning smile. "Was that your tourism expertise in action?"

"Just connecting people with experiences they might enjoy," he replied with a shrug.

"Well, thanks for the free marketing."

They continued working, moving to the next flowerbed. The sun climbed higher, and the town square grew busier as lunchtime approached. Brad noticed more tourists appearing, drawn by the charm of the gazebo in the town square and all the interesting shops and inviting storefronts. Some took photos, others consulted their phones or asked passing locals for directions.

"I keep thinking about something Pastor Andrew mentioned," Brad said as they knelt together, preparing the soil for another set of plants. "About how the town wants to increase tourism without losing its character."

Anna nodded. "It's a real concern. No one wants Laurel Ridge turning into a generic tourist trap with souvenir shops selling mass-produced junk."

"That's exactly what good tourism development prevents. The goal isn't to change the town to attract visitors—it's showcasing what's already special in a way that respects its history and values."

"So no giant billboards advertising 'World's Best Apple Pie' or kitschy gift shops selling plastic mountains?" Anna teased.

Brad laughed, the sound warm and genuine. "Definitely not. The opposite, actually. Highlighting Martha's food. Connecting visitors to Leroy's handmade leather journals at the general store instead of imported keychains."

As they talked, Brad found himself seeing Laurel Ridge through dual lenses—appreciating its current charm while envisioning its potential. Not changes that would detract from its character, but thoughtful additions that would amplify what made it special.

"The town has everything it needs already," he continued, carefully placing a purple petunia in the prepared soil. "Incredible natural beauty, distinctive local businesses, rich history, and genuinely warm people. It just needs a way to tell its story."

Anna studied him, struck by the passion behind his words. The morning sun caught his profile, highlighting the determined set of his jaw and the intelligence in his eyes. "You really care about this stuff, don't you?"

Brad met her gaze, his expression earnest. "I believe places like Laurel Ridge matter. In a world where everything keeps getting more homogenized and algorithm-driven, real, down-to-earth communities become more precious, not less."

"Well, if you have more ideas about tourism, the town council meets every other Wednesday. They're always looking for fresh perspectives. I'll warn you though, it's not some hoity-toity meeting; we're all pretty laid-back. It's kind of like a family gathering on a front porch; we talk, share what's going on in our businesses... that sort of thing. We share upcoming events. Volunteers give updates on how planning is going or what they are working on. We voice our opinions on town matters."

"I might just look into that."

They worked together through the rest of the morning, completing the town square's flowerbeds just as the midday heat reached its peak. The results of their labor were evident in every direction—vibrant bursts of color framing walkways and surrounding the gazebo.

As they gathered their tools and empty plant containers, Brad paused to survey their work. "This looks spectacular," he said with genuine satisfaction. "Makes the whole square feel alive."

"That's why Mom accepts this contract every year... she loves these monthly refreshes," Anna said, loading the last of the equipment into her truck. "Small changes that make a big difference."

"I had fun. Thanks for letting me help today."

"You were actually pretty useful," Anna admitted with a small smile. "Most volunteers last about twenty minutes before they remember urgent appointments elsewhere."

"High praise indeed," Brad laughed as he closed the truck's tailgate.

They stood for a moment in the shade of a maple tree, drinking the last of their water and surveying the town square. The lunch crowd was thickening as they emerged from offices and shops, some heading toward Martha's Diner or Lily's Café, others claiming benches to enjoy packed lunches in the summer air.

Brad tossed his gloves into the back of Anna's truck and looked around the square one last time. "This town... it has heart. It just needs a louder voice."

Anna lifted an eyebrow, studying him. "You're really thinking hard about this, aren't you?"

Brad shrugged with a half-smile. "Just thinking—for now."

But Anna could see it was more than just thinking. There was a spark in his eyes, an energy in his posture that hadn't been there earlier. Whatever was taking shape in Brad's mind, it clearly excited him.

And despite her usual wariness of change, Anna found herself intrigued rather than alarmed.

"Well," she said, climbing into her truck, "when you're ready to share those thoughts, I'd be interested to hear them."

"I'll keep that in mind," he said. "And thanks again for today."

As Anna drove away, she glanced in her rearview mirror to see Brad still standing in the town square, hands on his hips, looking thoughtfully at the storefronts and the gazebo. For a moment, she tried to see Laurel Ridge through his eyes—not just as the familiar home she'd always known, but as a place with untapped potential.

The thought was both unsettling and oddly exciting, much like Brad Knight himself.

Chapter 12

Katie nudged Anna with her elbow as they worked side by side in the greenhouse. "So... will we be seeing the handsome new neighbor more?"

Anna's fingers stilled around the delicate seedling she was transplanting. She kept her eyes fixed on the work before her.

"Katie, he helped with the town square refresh yesterday. That's all. Don't read into it," she replied, carefully nestling the seedling into fresh soil.

"Don't play dumb with me, Anna Mitchell." Katie pressed, a smile lurking in her voice.

June looked up from where she was sorting through a flat of geranium seedlings. "He seems quite taken with the farm." She paused, her eyes twinkling. "And perhaps with its caretaker."

"Mom," Anna protested, heat crawling up her neck that had nothing to do with the July temperature.

Jake Williams, their steady and reliable field manager, chuckled as he hefted a bag of potting soil onto the workbench. His weathered face creased with amusement. "If y'all don't mind, I'm gonna head out and check those irrigation lines before this conversation gets any more uncomfortable. This is girl talk, and I don't want any part of it."

"Coward," Katie called after him good-naturedly as he slipped out the greenhouse door.

Anna jabbed her trowel into the soil with more force than necessary. "There's nothing to discuss. Brad is new here and looking for a friend, I suspect. That's completely normal."

"Normal, sure," Katie agreed, leaning closer. "But the way he looks at you isn't exactly what I'd call neighborly."

"He does not look at me in any particular way," Anna insisted.

"Keep telling yourself that, honey," June said.

Anna straightened, wiping her hands on her already soil-stained jeans. "He's clearly well-traveled and sophisticated. I'm sure he's just being friendly because we're his closest neighbors."

"Uh-huh," Katie nodded skeptically. "And I'm sure he spent four hours planting flowers in the town square yesterday just because he loves municipal beautification."

June laughed. "Katie, leave her be; she's just in denial."

"I am not in denial," Anna protested, reaching for another seedling. "I'm just being realistic. Brad's from an entirely different world. He's probably just passing through this phase of his life."

"All I'm saying," Katie continued, moving another tray of seedlings into position, "is that a man doesn't plant flowers for hours in July heat unless he's interested in more than gardening tips."

Anna tried to focus on the delicate work of transplanting a particularly fragile seedling, but her thoughts kept drifting to Brad. His laugh, his questions, the way he'd noticed small details about the farm or town that others might miss. She'd caught herself looking forward to seeing him again and wondering what he was doing on his property across the creek.

"Even if he is interested—which I'm not saying he is," Anna added hurriedly, "it doesn't matter. I've got enough on my plate with Mom's semi-retirement plans and the farm expansion ideas."

"Ah yes, the farm expansion," Katie seized on the subject change. "Speaking of which, I've been thinking about our social media presence."

Anna groaned. "Not this again."

"Hear me out," Katie persisted, her expression growing animated. "Posting more on Instagram alone could probably double our social media followers and increase revenue at the same time. And if we had more of an online presence showcasing all the farm experiences that we offer—the u-pick days, the flower arranging workshops, the seasonal events—we could attract a whole new customer base."

June nodded thoughtfully. "Katie's right. Most of our business comes from word-of-mouth and long-standing relationships. But there's a whole world of potential customers who find everything online nowadays."

"So let them find us the old-fashioned way," Anna grumbled, though without much conviction. She knew Katie was right; she just hated the thought of having to learn yet another technical system.

"I could handle it," Katie offered. "Create and schedule daily posts, develop a content calendar, that sort of thing."

Anna looked up. "You'd do that? You actually want to do that?"

"Of course," Katie replied. "I enjoy social media."

June moved closer, leaning against the potting bench. "That's a really good idea. I've been saying for years we need a stronger online presence."

"If you're serious, it's all yours. I hereby relinquish all social media responsibilities to you, Katie Reynolds," Anna said with a smile.

"I accept this sacred trust," Katie replied with mock solemnity, placing her hand over her heart. "I promise to post only the most flattering photos of your dirt-smudged face."

"Don't you dare," Anna warned, but she was smiling.

From outside the greenhouse, Daisy's bark interrupted their conversation—not her alert bark, but the friendly, excited one. The golden retriever had been sprawled in the shade of a nearby oak tree, but now she was on her feet, tail wagging furiously.

"Knock, knock," Brad called, stepping into the humid interior of the greenhouse. "Hope I'm not interrupting."

His arrival caught Anna off-guard, her heart performing an irritating little skip. He wore a simple blue t-shirt and jeans, his dark hair slightly damp at the temples, as if he'd been working outside already. Daisy pushed past him into the greenhouse, circled his legs before trotting over to Anna, tail still swinging like a metronome.

"Brad," June greeted warmly. "What brings you over?"

"Had the afternoon free and thought I might wander over, see if there was anything I could help with," he said, his eyes scanning the greenhouse before landing on Anna again. When their gazes connected, his expression brightened in a subtle but unmistakable way. "I figured I'd return the favor after Anna showed me around town."

Katie shot Anna a knowing look that she pointedly ignored, though she couldn't quite suppress the warmth that rose to her cheeks at his unexpected appearance.

"We're just finishing up some transplanting," she said, gesturing to the rows of seedlings waiting to be moved to larger pots. "Nothing exciting."

"Looks interesting to me," Brad replied, moving closer to examine the delicate plants. "What are these going to be?"

"Lisianthus," Anna explained, holding up a small seedling. "One of our signature flowers for late summer weddings. They're fussy to start, but worth the effort."

Brad's face lit with genuine interest. "Mind if I try my hand at a few? I'm still in that learning phase where everything about farming is fascinating." The genuine enthusiasm in his request reminded Anna of a child asking to help with a project—eager, unguarded, and authentic.

June and Katie exchanged a quick glance that Anna pretended not to notice.

"Sure. There's an extra apron on the hook." She watched as he crossed to retrieve it, noting how naturally he moved in their space, as though he belonged among the seedlings and soil rather than sleek offices and technology.

Anna was conscious of Katie's barely suppressed smile. She pointedly turned her attention back toward her but watched from the corner of her eye as Brad donned the spare apron.

"I wasn't expecting company today," Anna said as Brad settled at the workbench beside her. "Tell me the truth. What brought you over here today?"

"Honestly? I was going stir-crazy. I needed something productive to do with my hands and quiet my mind."

"And," he continued, "I've been curious about the operation you've got going here. Figured I might learn something I could apply to my land eventually."

His straightforward answer disarmed her skepticism.

Anna demonstrated the proper technique for handling the fragile seedlings, showing him how to support the delicate roots while transferring them to their new containers.

"Gentle but firm," she instructed, aware of how close they stood. The earthy scent of soil mingled with his clean cologne, creating a strangely appealing combination. "Too much pressure damages the roots, but too little and they won't establish properly."

Brad nodded, his brow furrowed in concentration as he carefully mimicked her movements. The intensity of his focus—as though this small task deserved his complete attention—struck Anna as oddly touching. His first attempt was clumsy, the seedling listing to one side, but by the third try, his technique had improved considerably.

"You're a quick learner," Anna observed, surprised.

"Good teacher," he countered with a smile that reached his eyes.

They fell into a rhythm, working side by side. Brad occasionally asked questions about soil composition or watering schedules, his interest evident in the thoughtful way he listened to her answers.

"Did you ever try gardening in Colorado?" June asked from across the greenhouse.

Brad looked up. "I didn't actually have property there. Just a condo in downtown Denver. Eighteenth floor, with a view of the mountains, but no garden space."

"No outdoor space at all?" Anna asked, trying to imagine it.

"A balcony," Brad replied with a rueful smile. "I managed to kill a few potted herbs out there. Turns out plants don't thrive on neglect and irregular watering schedules."

"Tell us more about your tech work," Katie chimed in. "Anna mentioned you worked in tourism technology?"

Anna shot Katie a warning look, but Brad seemed unfazed by the question.

"I did," he nodded. "Long hours, constant travel, always connected to devices. It was exciting and fun, but..." He trailed off, gently tamping soil around a newly planted seedling. "It wasn't sustainable. At least not for me."

For all his easygoing manner, Anna sensed that whatever had driven him from Colorado to West Virginia went deeper than a simple desire for change. She caught herself watching his hands as he worked, noting how they moved with deliberate care, as though each small action mattered.

"Well, you seem to catch on to new things easily," June observed, nodding toward the neat row of seedlings Brad had successfully transplanted. "Maybe there's a farmer hiding under that tech exterior after all."

Brad laughed, the sound warm and genuine. "I doubt that. But I am enjoying the chance to learn something completely new. There's something satisfying about work you can see and touch."

The openness in his confession—the willingness to embrace new experiences without pretension—struck Anna as rare. Most men she knew guarded their expertise carefully, reluctant to admit what they didn't know. Brad's approach to learning, his comfort with being a beginner, revealed a confidence that had nothing to do with ego.

"Unlike computer code?" Anna asked.

"Yep," Brad nodded. He held up a freshly potted seedling. "In a few months, this will be a flower someone carries down the aisle or gives to express love or places on a dinner table. That's a kind of magic technology can't replicate."

For the next hour, they all worked together, and Brad proved to be a willing and capable helper, following instructions and asking questions.

Anna found herself relaxing as time passed. There was something disarming about being around this man—who'd clearly succeeded in a fast-paced, high-tech industry—yet now patiently transplanted seedlings with soil-covered hands.

"That should do it for today," June announced, straightening with a hand pressed to her lower back. "I don't know about the rest of you, but this heat is getting to me. How about we call it quits and enjoy some lemonade on the porch?"

"That sounds heavenly," Katie agreed, wiping her forehead with her sleeve. "I'm melting in here."

"Lemonade?" Brad asked with exaggerated hope, setting down his trowel. "Because I think I've earned at least one glass with all these perfectly transplanted seedlings."

"Perfectly might be stretching it," Anna teased, nodding toward one listing slightly to the left. "But I suppose the effort deserves some reward."

Brad's eyes met hers, warm with amusement. "I'll take constructive criticism and lemonade any day."

As they cleaned up their workstations, Anna couldn't help but notice how easily Brad had integrated himself into their space. He washed the tools without being asked, stacked the empty trays neatly, and even helped her mom carry a box of supplies to the storage shelf. The thoughtfulness in these small actions revealed more about him than any conversation could have.

"Coming, Anna?" June called from the greenhouse door, where she, Katie, and Brad were already gathering to leave.

"Right behind you," Anna replied, untying her apron and hanging it on its customary hook.

She lingered for a moment, watching through the greenhouse's clear panels as Brad fell into step beside her mom and Katie on the path leading up to the farmhouse. Daisy trotted alongside him, occasionally looking back to see if she was following.

The scene made her wonder about the naturalness of it, as if Brad had always been part of their small circle. He was talking animatedly with her mom, his hands gesturing to emphasize whatever point he was making, while Katie laughed at something he said.

Three weeks ago, she hadn't known Brad Knight existed. Now he was walking toward her home like he belonged here, like the distance between stranger and friend had collapsed without her noticing.

Hmmm, I could get used to this.

Chapter 13

The porch boards creaked under Anna's bare feet as she set down a glass of lemonade beside Brad. "Careful," she warned with a teasing smile. "Mom makes it strong—might knock you out if you're not expecting it."

Brad reached for the glass. "Consider me warned."

The farmhouse porch stretched the entire width of the Mitchell home, wrapping around one corner to create a perfect evening sanctuary. Ceiling fans spun lazily overhead, stirring the humid July air into something almost comfortable. The late-day sun bathed everything in a honeyed glow that softened the edges of the world, turning the flower fields into a watercolor painting of oranges, purples, and pinks.

June settled into her favorite rocking chair, the wooden frame worn smooth from years of evening contemplation. "Nothing better than porch sitting after a long day," she declared.

"Especially when there are cookies involved," Katie added, helping herself to one of the oatmeal treats June had arranged on a blue ceramic plate. "Though I really shouldn't. I can't imagine how many calories are in these things."

"One or two cookies won't hurt," June assured her. "Besides, you've been working hard all day—you've earned it."

Daisy padded across the porch and flopped down with a contented sigh next to Brad's chair. The golden retriever's tail thumped against the wooden boards when Brad reached down to scratch behind her ears.

"Traitor," Anna murmured to the dog. "Two weeks ago, you wouldn't leave my side. Now look at you."

Anna sipped her lemonade, letting the tartness wake up her taste buds. The day's work had left her pleasantly tired, muscles humming with the satisfaction of labor well done.

"So, Katie," June began, leaning forward in her chair, "let's talk more about your social media ideas."

Katie's eyes lit up. "I've been doing some research, and I think we're missing a massive opportunity. Did you know that most flower farms of our size have at least triple our following online? If we created a consistent posting schedule—behind-the-scenes content, seasonal updates, customer features—we could expand our reach without spending a dime on traditional advertising."

"What would that look like day-to-day?" June asked, clearly intrigued.

"Maybe three posts a week to start and build up to daily posts as we gain more traction," Katie suggested. "Monday morning inspiration—a beautiful bloom or arrangement to start the week. Wednesday workshop—showing how we care for the flowers or create an arrangement. Friday feature—highlighting a customer or wedding that used our flowers."

Brad nodded, setting his half-empty glass on the small table between his and Anna's chairs. "That's smart. Consistent content creates anticipation. People start looking forward to specific posts."

"That's what I was thinking," Katie agreed eagerly. "And we'd use seasonal hashtags to reach new audiences. In the fall, we could showcase our dried flower arrangements with autumn-themed posts."

"What about a simple blog?" Brad recommended. "Nothing fancy—just semi-monthly updates about what's happening at the farm. It would improve your search rankings and give visitors more reasons to linger on your website."

Anna watched the exchange with a mixture of gratitude and mild amusement. The technical side of marketing had always made her brain fog over and hurt, but Katie and Brad spoke the same language, tossing ideas back and forth with enthusiasm.

"You all have fun with that," she chimed in, lifting her glass in a mock toast. "I'll stick to growing flowers and wrangling Daisy." She ruffled the dog's golden fur, earning a lazy tail thump in response.

Everyone laughed at her comment, but Anna's relief was genuine. The thought of learning yet another system, another platform, another technical skill made her want to hide in the flower fields indefinitely.

"I'll handle the online part," Katie assured her. "You just keep growing the gorgeous blooms we'll feature. And maybe start taking pictures with your phone while you're out and about. People love seeing behind the scenes of what businesses and people do in the world."

"That's a deal I can live with," Anna replied, helping herself to an oatmeal cookie. The first bite released hints of cinnamon and nutmeg, the comfort flavors her mom had baked into countless batches throughout her childhood.

The conversation drifted to other topics—the upcoming Laurel Ridge Founder's Day Festival, Katie's date plans, and a new variety of dahlia Anna wanted to try next season. The evening wrapped around them like a warm hug, rich with the sounds of birds beginning their nightly chorus and the distant clink of wind chimes from the garden.

Anna found herself studying Brad several times throughout the evening—the way he listened intently to whoever was speaking, how he answered questions thoughtfully rather than rushing to fill silence, and the genuine interest he showed in the details of their farm life. For someone who had clearly lived in a faster, more sophisticated world, he seemed completely at ease on their worn porch furniture, trading stories as the evening deepened around them.

"You've clearly got a head for business," June was saying, turning to Brad with a warm smile and casual curiosity. "So tell me a little bit more about Brad Knight before he transplanted to West Virginia. What possessed a successful businessman to move here?"

Anna watched Brad's expression shift slightly, a momentary hesitation crossing his features before he set down his glass and leaned forward in his chair.

"It's not a particularly dramatic story," he began, his voice quieter than before. "But I guess you could say it started with a wake-up call. Literally."

He drew a deep breath, his gaze focused on the darkening fields beyond the porch railing. "About eight months ago, I collapsed at work. My team called 911, and I woke up in a hospital room with a doctor telling me my heart was basically rebelling against the life I was living."

Anna felt something in her chest tighten at his words. The world seemed to hush, as if sensing the weight of his disclosure.

"Stress-induced cardiomyopathy," Brad continued, his fingers absently tracing patterns on the armrest of his chair. "A nurse called it 'broken heart syndrome,' which sounded almost poetic at the time until she explained what was happening to my actual heart. The doctors said if I didn't make significant changes, I wouldn't see forty."

"Oh, Brad," June murmured, her expression softening with maternal concern.

He offered a small smile that didn't quite reach his eyes. "It was the wake-up call I needed, honestly. I'd been working ten- and twelve-hour days for years, sleeping only four or so hours a night. I was building and running my company. I had the condo, the achievements, all the external markers of success—and a heart that was literally giving out under the strain."

The porch fell silent except for the gentle creaking of June's rocking chair and the rhythmic swish of the ceiling fans. Even Katie, usually quick with questions or comments, sat quietly, her expression thoughtful.

"When I told Michelle—my girlfriend at the time—that I had sold the company and bought land in West Virginia, she looked at me like I'd lost my mind. She said, and I quote, 'I signed up for a CEO, not a mountain man having a midlife crisis.'"

Anna felt a flare of indignation on his behalf. "She said that while you were recovering from a heart condition?" The words escaped before she could temper them, her voice sharp with a protective anger that surprised even her. The intensity of her reaction revealed something she wasn't quite ready to examine—how much she had come to care about this man in such a short time.

Brad nodded, meeting Anna's gaze briefly. "That's when I realized our relationship had never really been about me—just what I represented. Status, money, and a certain lifestyle." He shrugged, the gesture somehow both resigned and relieved. "Looking back, I can see our relationship was more like a business arrangement than a partnership. We looked good on paper, but there wasn't much substance beneath the surface."

"Her loss," Katie said firmly, reaching for another cookie.

"Maybe," Brad admitted. "But now? I'm grateful. If she'd stayed, I might have tried to compromise—keep one foot in my old life while pretending to change. Instead, I made a clean break. A fresh start in life."

"And here you are in Laurel Ridge," June prompted gently.

Brad's expression warmed, some tension leaving his shoulders. "When I found the listing for that hundred acres I bought, it felt... I don't know, like the universe was offering exactly what I needed. I can see now how everything just seemed to fall into place. My wake-up call started it all."

As he spoke, Anna watched the subtle changes in his expression—the way his eyes brightened when he mentioned the land and how his hands became more animated. This wasn't just a man running away from something; he was running toward a vision, a hope for a different kind of life. His passion for building something meaningful revealed depths that made him more compelling than any man she'd known before.

"So here I am," Brad concluded with a self-deprecating smile. "Living in an Airstream, trying to figure out what comes next." Despite his casual tone, there was a quiet dignity in his vulnerability that Anna found herself drawn to—the courage to embrace uncertainty after a lifetime of achievement.

"Well, I'd say you're doing just fine," June assured him. "Starting over takes courage, especially when you're walking away from success by most people's standards."

Brad glanced up, his gaze finding Anna's across the gathering twilight. "Some definitions of success aren't worth the price they demand." The words hung between them, weighted with meaning that seemed meant just for her.

Something in his direct gaze, in the quiet vulnerability of his words, reached into Anna's chest and settled there. She'd been so quick to categorize him as an outsider, a city person playing at country life. But the man before her wasn't playing anything. He was searching for something real—something she'd been blessed to have all her life without truly appreciating its rarity. Their eyes held for a moment longer than necessary, creating a private connection amid the shared conversation—as though they'd recognized something essential in each other that neither could yet name.

"I'm glad you shared that with us," Anna said softly. "It couldn't have been easy... what you went through and everything you left behind."

Brad held her gaze a moment longer. "Actually," he replied, his voice equally quiet, "it was easier than I expected."

The conversation gradually shifted to lighter topics as the last rays of sunlight faded from the horizon. June shared stories about Anna's childhood misadventures in the flower fields, making everyone laugh with tales of a determined five-year-old who insisted on "helping" with the spring planting.

Stars appeared one by one in the deepening blue above, pinpricks of silver against the vast canopy of night. The air grew heavy with the sweet scent of evening primrose that grew along the edge of the porch, their pale yellow blooms unfurling in the darkness.

"I should probably head back," Brad said eventually, setting his empty glass on the table. "Early start tomorrow."

"What's on your agenda?" June asked.

"Roy's crew is finishing the demolition cleanup and backfilling the basement area where the old house sat. I plan on searching for house plans online to see if I can find anything that fits my vision. Might run into town for groceries."

They all rose, stretching after hours of sitting. June gathered the empty glasses while Katie collected the plate with its few remaining cookies.

"I'll walk you down to the creek," Anna offered. "Daisy could use a quick evening stroll, anyway."

Daisy perked up at the mention of a walk, her tail immediately switching to high-speed wagging mode.

"That would be nice," Brad said, his smile visible even in the gathering darkness.

As they descended the porch steps together, Anna felt a flutter in her chest. The evening had shifted something between them—not dramatically, but perceptibly. Brad's willingness to share his vulnerability, to speak honestly about his failed relationship and future hopes, had touched her more deeply.

Daisy trotted ahead, occasionally glancing back as if to ensure they were following.

"Your mom is really a special person, and Katie too," Brad said after they'd walked a few yards in silence. "The way you all are together—it's special."

"They like you," Anna replied, then added with a small laugh, "which is saying something. Mom doesn't warm up to just anyone so quickly."

"Score for me," Brad smiled. "I enjoyed tonight. I'm glad I was included."

They reached the footbridge that spanned the creek, the water below a ribbon of silver in the moonlight. Crickets sang from the tall grasses along the bank, and somewhere in the distance, an owl called softly.

"I appreciate you sharing what you did about yourself," Anna said, leaning against the bridge railing. "About your health scare and everything after. I know that couldn't have been easy to talk about."

Brad stood beside her, close enough that she could feel the warmth radiating from him in the cool evening air. "Strangely, it felt right. Like I could trust you all with that part of my story."

"You can," Anna said simply.

They stood in silence for a moment, listening to the gentle gurgle of the creek beneath them. The night wrapped around them, intimate and vast all at once.

"I should let you get back," Brad said finally, though he made no move to leave.

"Probably," Anna agreed, equally stationary.

Their eyes met in the dim light, and Anna felt her heart quicken. There was something in his gaze—a question, perhaps, or an admission. His expression held an openness that invited her closer, even as the timing whispered, not yet.

Daisy broke the moment, splashing into the shallow creek with an enthusiastic bark at some night creature only she could detect.

"Daisy!" Anna called, laughing despite herself. "You're impossible."

Brad chuckled, the tension easing. "I'll see you soon?"

"Count on it," Anna replied.

As she watched him cross the bridge and make his way toward the silver gleam of his Airstream, Anna remained at the railing a little while longer. The space beside her felt strangely empty now, as though his presence had somehow become the natural state of things in just a few short weeks.

I like him, she admitted to herself. Not merely his smile or his kindness, but the deeper currents beneath—his courage to change course, his quiet thoughtfulness, the way he truly saw her and her family. *Goodness, I'm in trouble.*

Chapter 14

Brad took a sip of coffee, letting the complex flavors roll across his tongue. Sitting outside in the early morning stillness had become a ritual he cherished—-these quiet moments before the day began.

Movement across the creek caught his attention. Anna and Katie were carrying flats of flowers toward the farm stand near the edge of the property—a quaint wooden structure with a red metal roof that served as their retail shop. Even from this distance, he could see Anna's auburn ponytail swinging as she moved, her purposeful stride conveying the confidence of someone completely in her element. The morning light caught her hair, turning it to burnished copper against the green backdrop of the mountains in the distance. He paused mid-sip, his coffee momentarily forgotten as he watched her—the ease of her movements, the way she paused to adjust something in her arms, her animated conversation with Katie. A simple morning transformed into something captivating through her presence.

Brad watched them for a moment, noting how they worked in synchronized harmony, like dancers who'd practiced the same routine for years. He set his coffee down on the small side table and stood, stretching his arms overhead.

"What do you think? Should we go say good morning?" he asked the cardinal, who had landed on a nearby branch. The bird tilted its bright red head, regarding him with what Brad chose to interpret as encouragement before taking flight.

Decision made, Brad headed toward the footbridge. The morning dew soaked the edges of his boots as he walked across the lawn, and tiny droplets clung to the wildflowers that dotted his side of the creek.

As he approached the bridge, Daisy spotted him and immediately bounded over, tail wagging with unmistakable enthusiasm.

"Good morning to you too," Brad laughed, crouching to scratch behind her ears.

The golden retriever pressed against his legs, her warm weight familiar and welcome. He'd never considered himself a dog person before moving to Laurel Ridge, but Daisy's uncomplicated affection had quickly converted him.

When he looked up, Anna was watching them from beside a cart piled high with potted geraniums, a small smile playing at the corners of her mouth. The sunlight framed her against the farm stand backdrop, highlighting the strands of hair that had escaped her ponytail. His pulse quickened at the sight.

"Are you stealing my dog's loyalty with secret treats?" She called as he approached, hands on her hips in mock accusation.

"No bribery required. We just have an understanding."

"An understanding?"

"She recognizes quality companionship when she sees it."

Anna rolled her eyes, but her smile widened. "Is that what you're calling it?"

Katie emerged from the farm stand, hands full of empty plant markers. "Morning, Brad! You're up early."

"Old habits," he shrugged. He gestured toward the flats of flowers waiting to be unloaded. "Need another pair of hands?"

Anna exchanged a quick glance with Katie, something unspoken passing between them.

"You sure?" Anna asked. "This isn't exactly glamorous work."

"I've developed a taste for manual labor," Brad replied.

"Well, I'm not about to turn down free help. There's twenty more flats by the greenhouse that need to be brought over."

"Big day at the farm stand?" Brad asked as they walked toward the greenhouses.

Anna nodded. "Fridays are always busy. People stop by to pick up fresh flowers for the weekend or want to freshen up their flower beds. Our local customers like the variety we continually offer, and they keep coming back for more. I try to make sure the farm stand has a fresh look each week."

"Smart."

"I like to think so," she replied with a small smile.

They reached the staging area where flats of flowers waited in neat rows—vibrant clusters of color organized by variety. Marigolds, zinnias, petunias, and salvias created a living rainbow that perfumed the air with their mingled scents.

"These go to the stand," Anna explained, gesturing to the labeled sections. "Two flats of each for display; the rest will stay in back for quick restocking."

Brad picked up two flats of sunset-orange marigolds, their cheerful blooms bobbing slightly as he lifted them. "Lead the way."

They worked steadily, moving plants from the greenhouse area to the farm stand. Brad eventually took over transferring the inventory, including large pots of ornamental grasses, bags of specialty soil, and stacks of decorative containers, while Anna and Katie arranged displays and set up the cash register for the day.

The farm stand was larger than it appeared from a distance—a spacious, open-air structure with sturdy wooden shelving along three walls and a central island. Baskets of flowers hung from the rafters, filled with trailing vines and cascading flowers that created a lush, colorful canopy overhead. The entire space was designed to showcase the farm's bounty, from potted plants to freshly cut bouquets arranged in mason jars and vases of varying sizes.

"Those need to go up front," Anna directed as Brad carried in a flat of purple coneflowers. "They're this week's special."

He set them carefully on the designated table. "Like this?"

Anna stepped closer, adjusting the position slightly. "Perfect. Now we need to arrange the cut flowers in the cooler."

In the small walk-in cooler at the back of the stand, Anna showed Brad how to arrange the buckets of freshly cut blooms—zinnias, cosmos, snapdragons, and miniature sunflowers harvested that morning, their stems resting in nutrient-rich water.

"The key is to create a visual flow," she explained, demonstrating how to position the buckets so customers could easily see each variety. "People shop with their eyes first."

Brad watched her as she worked—confident, gentle, knowing exactly how to position each bucket for maximum impact. She was mesmerizing as she handled the flowers.

"You really love this, don't you?"

Anna looked up momentarily surprised by the question. "I do. There's something... I don't know, almost sacred about working with growing things. They're so honest—they either thrive or they don't. No pretense, no games."

"Unlike people," Brad added with a knowing smile.

"You nailed it." Their eyes met briefly, and something warm flickered between them before Anna turned back to the flowers.

As they worked side by side, Brad became acutely aware of Anna's presence—the soft scent of her shampoo mingling with the floral fragrances around them, the brush of her arm against his as she reached past him for another bucket, and the quiet concentration in her expression as she adjusted each display.

"Hand me that bucket of feverfew," she said, pointing to a container filled with delicate white blooms that resembled tiny daisies.

As Brad passed it to her, their fingers touched briefly, and he felt a small jolt of awareness race up his arm. From the slight widening of Anna's eyes, he suspected she'd felt it too.

"Thanks," she murmured, quickly turning her attention back to the display.

When they emerged from the cooler, Katie was arranging small succulents in decorative pots on the front counter, her quick fingers nestling the tiny plants into beds of colored stones.

"You two get everything set up in there?" She asked, a smile playing at the corners of her mouth.

"All set," Anna replied. "Just need to finish up a few more things, and we should be good to go."

Brad helped carry out a chalkboard sign announcing the day's specials, positioning it near the entrance where it couldn't be missed. As he straightened it, Anna appeared beside him with a stack of plant markers.

"I'll have to add you to the payroll if you keep this up," she teased, tucking a strand of hair behind her ear.

"What would my job title be?" Brad asked, pretending to consider the question seriously. "Professional flower carrier? Assistant plant mover?" He enjoyed this easy back-and-forth they'd developed, the rhythm of their conversations becoming as natural as breathing.

"How about 'City Boy in Training'?" Anna suggested with a grin that transformed her features, bringing a sparkle to her eyes that made it impossible not to smile back.

Brad clutched his chest in mock offense. "Harsh. And after I've been so careful with your precious blooms."

"Speaking of which," Anna said, glancing over at a display of potted herbs he'd arranged earlier, "I think those mint plants might need a little reorganizing. They look like they were arranged by someone who once saw plants in a magazine."

"Wow," Brad laughed, genuinely amused by her teasing. "Tell me how you really feel."

He moved to the herb display and began rearranging the plants under Anna's watchful eye. Her laughter when he deliberately placed a pot at a ridiculous angle made something warm unfurl in his chest.

"Here, let me show you," she said, stepping beside him and reaching for the pots. Her hands moved quickly, creating a natural, flowing arrangement that showcased each plant. "See the difference?"

"Night and day," Brad admitted. "Though I maintain my version had creative merit."

"Creative merit?" Anna raised an eyebrow, her blue eyes dancing with amusement.

Brad pulled out his phone. "Mind if I take a few pictures? This would make great content for Katie's social media plan."

"Go ahead," Anna replied, stepping back to give him a better view.

Brad moved around the display, capturing several angles. "These are perfect. The lighting in here is great—natural but soft."

"Is photography another hidden talent of yours?" Anna asked, watching him work.

"Hardly," Brad laughed. "But I've learned to appreciate good visuals. In my previous work, everything was about telling a story through images."

The first customers began arriving as they finished the final touches on the displays. Katie took over the register while Anna answered questions about plant care and helped customers select the perfect blooms for their needs.

Brad stepped back, content to observe the easy rhythm of the farm stand in operation. It was wonderful seeing the space come alive with customers exclaiming over arrangements and consulting Anna about their gardens.

An elderly woman with silver hair tucked beneath a wide-brimmed sun hat approached the herb section, examining the rosemary plants with careful deliberation.

"Mrs. Patterson," Anna greeted warmly. "How are you?"

"Just fine, dear," the woman replied, her voice as delicate as the lace collar on her blouse. "Looking for some fresh herbs for my window box."

"Let me introduce you to Brad Knight," Anna said, gesturing toward him. "He's our new neighbor. Brad, this is Mrs. Patterson. She makes the most delicious herb bread."

"The best around these parts," Mrs. Patterson added with a wink.

Brad shook her delicate hand gently. "It's a pleasure to meet you, Mrs. Patterson."

"You're the one who bought the old Harmon place, aren't ya?" she asked, studying him with bright, curious eyes. "My husband used to hunt on that land, back when old Jim Harmon still lived there. Beautiful property."

"It is," Brad agreed. "I'm still discovering all its secrets." As he spoke, his gaze drifted briefly to Anna, who was helping another customer select a hanging basket—her movements graceful and assured, her smile genuine as she offered advice.

"The best places keep their secrets close," Mrs. Patterson nodded sagely. "Reveal themselves slowly to those who pay attention." Something knowing flickered in the elderly woman's expression as she followed his gaze, a quiet understanding that made Brad wonder how transparent his growing feelings might be.

For the next fifteen minutes, Mrs. Patterson regaled Brad with stories of Laurel Ridge in decades past—how the Harmon family had hosted community barbecues by the creek each summer, the year lightning struck the old oak near the barn, and how her husband had once found a Civil War-era button while hunting on the land.

Brad listened attentively, genuinely fascinated by these glimpses into his property's history. When Mrs. Patterson finally selected her herbs—rosemary, thyme, and a pot of fragrant basil—he offered to carry them to her car.

"Aren't you sweet thang," she said, patting his arm.

As they walked slowly toward her sedan, Mrs. Patterson continued her stories, occasionally pausing to catch her breath. Brad matched his pace to hers, asking questions that prompted more details about the town's history.

"You know," she said as they reached her car, "you remind me a bit of my grandson. Same thoughtful way of listening." She fixed him with a direct gaze. "Anna's a special girl. You stick close to that one. Knows the land like it's part of her. Not many understand that kind of connection."

Brad blinked, surprised by the sudden shift in conversation. "She's certainly knowledgeable about farming," he replied.

Mrs. Patterson's smile was knowing. "That she is. Good day to you, Mr. Knight. I suspect we'll be seeing plenty of each other around town."

When he returned to the farm stand, the morning rush was in full swing. He helped where he could—retrieving additional stock from the back, carrying purchases to cars for customers who needed assistance, and answering basic questions about plants he was beginning to recognize.

Throughout the chaos, he remained aware of Anna's movements—how she pivoted seamlessly from arranging displays to advising customers to processing sales, never losing her patience or her smile. They developed an unspoken choreography, anticipating each other's needs without discussion. When she reached for a particular plant, he'd already be moving to restock that section; when a customer needed assistance to their car, he'd appear at her elbow before she could ask.

Around mid-morning, as the initial wave of customers subsided, Katie approached him with a bottle of water.

"You've earned this," she said, handing it to him.

Brad accepted the water gratefully, his eyes finding Anna across the stand where she was arranging a bouquet, her fingers deftly combining different blooms into a harmonious arrangement. There was something mesmerizing about watching someone perform a skill with such natural grace—like watching a musician or an artist completely absorbed in their craft.

"You know," Katie said casually, "there's a lot more to Blooms Farm than just the farm stand. Anna should show you around the rest of the property."

"That would be interesting," Brad replied, trying to sound merely interested rather than eager.

"I've got things covered here. You two should go—it's the perfect time of day for it."

Anna joined them, wiping her hands on a small towel.

"What's the perfect time of day for what?" she asked.

"For showing Brad the rest of the farm," Katie replied smoothly. "You should give him the grand tour."

Something flickered across Anna's face—surprise, followed by what might have been pleasure. "I suppose I could do that. If you're sure you've got things covered here?"

"Absolutely," Katie assured her as she looked at her watch. "Tyler and Beth are scheduled to work at noon, which just leaves me here alone for a little over an hour. If I need help, I'll message your mom."

Anna turned to Brad. "What do you say? Would you like a Blooms Farm tour?"

"Lead the way."

As they walked away from the farm stand, Brad glanced back at Katie, a satisfied expression on her face. Matchmaking, it seemed, was alive and well in Laurel Ridge.

Anna led him toward a large equipment shed where a side-by-side utility vehicle was parked. "Hope you don't mind riding in this," she said, grabbing a set of keys from a hook just inside the door.

"Not at all," Brad replied, watching as she seated herself behind the wheel.

"Hop in," she said, patting the space behind her. "And consider yourself warned... I love driving this thing around the property."

Chapter 15

Anna gripped the steering wheel of the utility vehicle with ease as they bounced along the dirt path that wound through the eastern fields. Wind whipped tendrils of auburn hair from her ponytail, and she tucked them behind her ear with one hand, never slowing their pace.

Brad braced himself against the frame, laughing as they crested the small hill. "I thought farmers were supposed to be slow, cautious drivers!"

"That's just a rumor we started to keep city folk off our roads," Anna replied with a grin, easing off the gas as they approached a sea of purple. "This is our lavender field. We grow three varieties—French, English, and Grosso. Each has different uses and bloom times, which helps us extend the harvest season."

She brought the vehicle to a stop at the edge of the field, where the sweet, herbal scent of lavender hung in the air like invisible clouds. Row upon row of silver-green plants stretched before them, topped with spikes of vibrant purple. Workers in wide-brimmed hats moved methodically between the rows, harvesting bundles of the fragrant stems.

"Wow," Brad said, stepping out of the utility vehicle. "I had no idea your operation was this extensive." He turned to face her, the sunlight catching the gold flecks in his eyes, his expression one of genuine admiration rather than merely polite interest.

"Most people don't," Anna replied, pride evident in her voice. "They see the farm stand and the fields visible from the road, but that's only about a quarter of what we do." She stepped beside him at the field's edge, their shoulders nearly touching. The way he looked at her land—with appreciation and understanding rather than just seeing dollar signs or pretty flowers—stirred something in her chest that had nothing to do with business pride.

A familiar bark interrupted them, and they turned to see Daisy racing toward them along the path, golden fur gleaming in the midday sun.

"How did she find us?" Brad asked, watching the dog's enthusiastic approach.

Anna shook her head, amused. "She knows every inch of this farm. Mom probably let her out of the house, and she tracked us down."

Daisy skidded to a halt beside them, tail wagging frantically. Without hesitation, she leapt into the back seat of the utility vehicle, settling in as if she'd been invited all along.

Brad burst out laughing. "Well, I guess we have another tour guide now."

"More like quality control. She inspects the farm daily. Very thorough."

They climbed back into the vehicle, Daisy panting happily behind them. Anna guided them through a winding path that cut between the lavender field and a section of vibrant zinnias that resembled a patchwork quilt of oranges, pinks, and reds.

"These are all for cutting," she explained, gesturing toward the zinnias. "They're workhorses—they keep producing all summer if you keep harvesting them. Great for bouquets because they last so long in a vase."

Brad nodded, taking it all in. "And these workers—are they all full-time?"

"Some are. Others are seasonal. During peak harvest, we might have thirty or so people working the fields. Right now, we have twenty in the fields, plus Katie, Jake, Mom, myself, and two part-time high school-age kids that work the greenhouses, the front fields, and the farm stand."

She navigated a sharp turn, and the landscape opened up to reveal a breathtaking sight—an entire hillside covered in miniature sunflowers, their cheerful colorful faces all turned toward the afternoon sun.

"This is incredible," Brad murmured, clearly awed by the scale and beauty.

Anna slowed the vehicle, allowing him to take in the view. She looked at his profile instead of the familiar landscape—the parted lips, the widened eyes, the unguarded wonder in his expression more captivating than the spectacular vista before them. "We plant these in succession, so they bloom continuously from July through September. Florists love them for late summer and fall weddings."

Brad shook his head in amazement. "I knew you grew flowers, but this is... an entire operation. A massive business with multiple moving parts."

"Yep," Anna said, a note of quiet pride in her voice. "Mom started the expansion from just a few acres. Now we're the largest specialty cut flower farm in the state."

They continued past fields of dahlias just beginning to form buds, past shaded areas where delicate ferns grew for greenery in arrangements. They also passed a section dedicated entirely to ornamental grasses that would be harvested in late summer for their feathery plumes.

At each stop, Anna shared details about growing conditions, harvest times, and market demand. Her knowledge was comprehensive, her passion evident in every explanation.

"How do you keep track of it all?" he asked as they paused beside a field of white cosmos dancing in the breeze. "The planting schedules, harvest times, employee hours, sales projections..."

"Mom handles the business side. I focus on the growing side and the creative aspects. We just make it work."

Brad nodded. "Playing to your strengths. That makes sense."

"I've been trying to learn more of the business side," Anna continued, staring out at the fields rather than meeting his eyes. "Mom wants to step back, travel more. And I want that for her; I really do. She deserves it after all these years of hard work."

"But?" Brad prompted gently.

Anna sighed, her fingers tightening slightly on the steering wheel. "But every time I sit down with the spreadsheets and profit projections, my brain just... freezes. Numbers have never been my thing, and marketing makes me want to hide in the greenhouse. I don't care for any of it."

She hadn't meant to be quite so honest, but something about Brad made the admission feel safe.

"That's completely understandable. Different brains work in different ways. The creative mind that can envision an entire hillside of perfect sunflowers doesn't necessarily think in columns and rows."

She turned to look at him directly. "Mom's been so patient, trying to teach me. But I worry I'll never get it, and then what? The farm's been in my family for generations. What if I'm the one who can't keep it going?"

"You won't be," Brad said with quiet confidence. "You know the heart of this business better than anyone—the plants, the rhythms, the quality that makes Blooms Farm special. The rest is just systems and tools."

"Easy for you to say, Mr. Tech Man," Anna replied, but there was no bite in her words.

He smiled. "I could show you a basic program that might help organize and simplify things. Something visual, intuitive—not just columns of numbers." He spoke without the slightest hint of condescension, offering expertise as one might offer a gift—with open hands and no expectations.

Anna hesitated. The offer was tempting, but accepting help with something so fundamental to the farm's operation felt like admitting a failing. Yet something in his expression—an earnestness, a genuine desire to share rather than show off—made the prospect less daunting.

"It wouldn't be a big deal," Brad continued, seeming to sense her reluctance. "Just a few tools that helped me when I was starting out. Things that make the business side less overwhelming." His eyes held hers, patient and steady, creating a bridge across her hesitation.

"You wouldn't mind?"

"I'd enjoy it, actually," Brad admitted. "Being useful again... feels good."

The simple honesty of his response decided her. "Okay. I'm willing to try."

A genuine smile spread across Brad's face. "Great. Whenever you're ready."

"How about after the tour?"

"Perfect."

They continued the tour, Anna guiding them to the far northwestern edge of the property, where a small orchard of apple trees stood. "These were my grandfather's," she explained. "We don't maintain them commercially, but they still produce enough for family use."

"Heritage varieties?" Brad asked, noting the gnarled, character-filled branches.

Anna nodded, impressed by his knowledge. "I see someone has been doing some research. Some of these trees are what we call June apples as well; they're over seventy years old. The apples aren't pretty enough for grocery stores, but they make the best pies you've ever tasted."

Their final stop was a secluded corner of the property where a small pond reflected the afternoon sky. Cattails swayed at its edges, and dragonflies skimmed across the surface.

"This is another favorite spot of mine," Anna admitted, cutting the engine. The sudden silence emphasized the natural sounds around them—the buzzing of insects, the rustle of leaves, and the distant call of a blackbird. Sharing this sanctuary with him felt significant, a revealing of something private she rarely showed to others.

"I can see why," Brad said quietly, taking in the peaceful scene. "It feels separate from everything else, like a little pocket of calm."

Anna nodded. "I come here when I need to think... when things get overwhelming. Occasionally I just ride out here to do nothing at all but sit. Something about water always helps clear my head."

"Nice. I like this out here."

"Anyway... we should probably head back. I've probably bored you enough for one day."

"Bored me? No… this has been rather eye-opening. Your farm is a lot bigger than I originally thought it was," he said as Anna started the engine and turned them toward home. The return journey took them along a different path, offering new views of the farm. The farmhouse came into view, its white clapboard exterior glowing in the afternoon sun.

"Thanks for the tour," Brad said as they pulled up beside the house.

"No problem. You impressed me… most people's eyes start glazing over after the first fifteen minutes when I get in flower talk mode."

"Their loss," Brad replied simply.

Inside the farmhouse, the temperature dropped noticeably thanks to ceiling fans and well-placed windows that caught the cross-breeze. Anna led Brad to the round oak table that sat beneath windows overlooking fields of flowers.

"Let me grab my laptop," she said. "Make yourself at home."

When she returned, Brad had filled two glasses with ice water from the pitcher in the refrigerator. "Hope you don't mind," he said, sliding one toward her.

"Thanks," Anna replied, setting her laptop on the table and taking a grateful sip.

She opened the computer, and her screen immediately displayed a spreadsheet—rows and columns of numbers that made her shoulders tense just looking at them.

"This is what Mom's been trying to teach me," she explained, turning the screen slightly so Brad could see. "Sales projections for next quarter, broken down by product category and sales channel."

Brad studied the spreadsheet for a moment, nodding thoughtfully. "This is good information, but I can see why it might feel overwhelming." He glanced at her. "Mind if I show you an alternative approach?"

Anna nodded, sliding the laptop toward him. "Please."

Brad's fingers moved efficiently over the keyboard, navigating to a website and logging into a demo account. "This is a program designed for small businesses, especially those with seasonal products," he explained. "Instead of just rows of numbers, it gives you visual representations of your data."

He demonstrated how to input basic information, explaining each step in clear, simple terms. Anna watched as columns of numbers transformed into colorful graphs and charts that suddenly made patterns visible—which products generated the most revenue, how sales fluctuated seasonally, and which expenses remained constant versus those that varied.

"The beauty of this system is that you input information once, and it generates all these different views automatically," Brad explained. "So you can see your business the way that makes sense to you."

Anna leaned closer, her initial resistance melting as she watched numbers become comprehensible patterns. "Interesting," she said, surprise evident in her voice.

Brad smiled. "Everyone processes information differently. Some people can look at rows of numbers and instantly see patterns. Others need visual representations. It doesn't make one approach better than the other—just different."

For the next hour, Brad guided her through the basics of the program, showing her how to set up categories that matched Blooms Farm's specific needs. He also showed her how to track inventory and employee hours and how to project future sales based on historical data. He never rushed, never used technical jargon without explaining it, and—most importantly—never made her feel inadequate for not understanding immediately.

"Can we set up different sections for the wholesale accounts versus the farm stand?" Anna asked, growing more engaged as her understanding increased.

"Absolutely," Brad replied, showing her how to create custom categories. "You can track them separately but still see the big picture when you need to."

Anna found herself leaning into the process, asking questions, and suggesting adjustments that would better reflect the farm's unique rhythm. The intimidating wall of numbers was gradually becoming a tool she might actually use.

"This is... actually helpful," she admitted. "I think I could work with this... the question is do I really want to? I worry I'll be spread too thin and not be able to do what I enjoy."

"I'm glad this is helpful. You know... you don't have to do it all. You could hire someone—."

June appeared in the kitchen doorway. "There you two are! Katie said you were giving Brad the grand tour." Her eyes landed on the laptop, curiosity evident in her expression.

"He's showing me a business management program," Anna explained. "Something that might make tracking everything easier for me to understand."

June's eyebrows rose in pleased surprise. "Well, isn't that nice! Brad, you might just accomplish what I've been trying to do for years."

Brad shook his head modestly. "I'm just recommending some tools. Anna's doing all the real work."

June's knowing smile suggested she saw more than either of them was saying. "Well... I'm going to head back to the farm stand and help Katie. Will you two be joining us later?"

Anna glanced at Brad. "Maybe later. Unless you need help now?"

"Not at all," June assured her. "You two carry on. Brad, will you stay for dinner? Nothing fancy—just grilled chicken and vegetables from the garden."

"Sounds good to me," Brad replied. "Thank you."

After June departed, they spent another thirty minutes working through the program. By the time they finished, Anna felt a new sense of confidence. The business side still wasn't her favorite aspect of running the farm, but it no longer loomed as an insurmountable obstacle.

"I can't thank you enough," she said as they closed the laptop. "You made something I've been dreading actually seem manageable... maybe, but don't hold your breath."

"Happy to help. You've got this, Anna. You know this business inside and out—these are just tools to organize numbers and data and spit out answers. So... I've been wondering..."

Anna looked at him questioningly.

Brad leaned forward slightly, eyes bright with enthusiasm. "You ever been whitewater rafting?"

The question caught her completely off guard. Anna blinked, then laughed. "Not in a few years. Why?"

"I booked a trip for two tomorrow on the New River," Brad explained. "Nothing too extreme—Class III rapids, perfect for a hot July day." He hesitated, then added, "I'd love the company, if you're interested."

Anna considered the invitation. The farmer's market was in the morning, but Katie, her mom, and the weekend staff could handle it. And the thought of cool river water on a scorching summer day was undeniably appealing.

"You're asking me to play hooky from work."

"Basically, yeah."

"I might be willing to go," she said finally, "if you promise to be patient with me. It's been a while since I've done anything like that."

"Deal," he laughed.

Anna felt a flutter of anticipation in her chest—not just for the rafting trip, but for the prospect of spending the day with him. Somehow, in the span of a few weeks, this man had gone from mysterious newcomer to... what, exactly? Friend seemed too simple a word for the connection that was forming between them.

"I should probably warn you," she said with a small smile, "I'm pretty competitive. Don't be surprised if I end up being better at rafting than you are."

Brad's laugh filled the kitchen, warm and genuine. "I wouldn't be surprised at all."

Chapter 16

Anna tightened her life jacket straps for the third time as Brad grinned beside her.

"Just being thorough," she said, tugging at the nylon straps once more. "Unlike some people."

Brad's life jacket sat perfectly adjusted across his broad shoulders and snug across his chest. He raised an eyebrow. "I've been rafting before, remember I once lived in Colorado... though it's been a few years since I've gone."

"Show-off," Anna muttered, but a smile tugged at her lips.

The July sun beat down on the loading area of Ridge Rush Adventures, where half a dozen colorful rafts waited at the river's edge. Other rafters milled about—a family with teenage children, a group of college-aged friends, and an older couple celebrating what Anna had overheard was their thirtieth anniversary. Everyone wore the same blue helmets and red life jackets, creating a strange uniformity among strangers about to share an adventure.

Anna glanced at the New River flowing beyond the staging area. The water looked deceptively calm here, but she knew that just around the bend waited rapids with names like "Surprise" and "The Grinder"—names that had seemed exciting but now stirred a flutter of anxiety in her stomach.

"Hey," Brad said softly, sensing her nervousness. "We can still back out if you want. No pressure."

Anna straightened her shoulders. "Absolutely not. I said I was going rafting, and rafting I shall go."

"That's the spirit," he laughed, the sound warm and rich against the background chorus of rushing water and excited chatter.

Their guide approached—a man in his early thirties with sun-bleached hair and arms tanned to leather. "Folks, I'm Jeff. I'll be taking you down the river today." He glanced at their life jackets with an experienced eye. "Looking good. Everyone ready for a wet and wild ride?"

The group responded with varying degrees of enthusiasm.

"Don't worry," Jeff said. "We haven't lost anyone yet." He paused dramatically. "This week."

Brad chuckled as Anna elbowed him in the ribs.

"All right then," Jeff continued, "quick safety briefing. When I say 'forward paddle,' you paddle forward. 'Back paddle' means exactly what it sounds like. 'Stop' means rest your paddle across your lap. And if I yell 'get down,' you duck into the center of the raft. Questions?"

A few hands went up, and Jeff patiently answered each one. Anna listened intently, committing every instruction to memory. Brad, meanwhile, stood relaxed beside her, occasionally nodding at information he clearly already knew.

"Last thing," Jeff said, "the most important command: 'high-side.' If I shout this, everyone moves to the high side of the raft—the side that's lifting out of the water. It prevents flipping. Got it?"

Everyone nodded.

"Great! Let's hit the water."

As they carried their raft toward the river's edge, Brad leaned close to Anna. "You've got this. Just follow Jeff's lead and remember—it's supposed to be fun."

"I know," she said, appreciating his encouragement despite her pride. "I've done this before... just not on rapids quite this... enthusiastic."

"Think of it as a farm tractor with attitude," Brad suggested, and Anna laughed despite herself.

The cold river water swirled around her ankles as they pushed the raft into the current. Anna climbed in, nearly losing her balance before Brad's steady hand at her elbow guided her to her seat. He followed with surprising grace for someone his size, settling beside her.

The slight rocking of the raft brought them momentarily closer, their shoulders touching. Anna was conscious of the minimal space between them and how they would be sharing this small craft for hours. Brad seemed equally aware, his eyes meeting hers with an unspoken acknowledgment of their proximity that made her heart beat a little faster than the adventure alone warranted.

Jeff took his position at the stern, paddle ready. "Forward paddle, folks! Let's get into the current."

Anna dipped her paddle into the water, matching Brad's rhythm. The raft moved smoothly away from shore, caught the main current, and began its journey downstream. The morning sun sparkled on the water's surface, and the forested canyon walls rose majestically on either side, creating a corridor of greenery that seemed to embrace the river.

"Not so bad, right?" Brad asked as they navigated the gentle current.

Anna had to admit it wasn't. The initial nervousness was fading, replaced by the simple pleasure of being on the water on a perfect summer day. "It's actually pretty peaceful."

"For now," Jeff called from behind them, with a mischievous glint in his eye. "First rapids coming up in about two minutes. Everyone ready to get wet?"

The current quickened. The smooth surface of the water began to ripple, then churn. Up ahead, Anna could see white foam breaking over submerged rocks—their first rapid.

"Forward paddle!" Jeff commanded, and everyone responded in unison.

The raft picked up speed, rushing toward the churning water. Anna's grip tightened on her paddle, her heart racing as they hit the first wave. Cold water splashed over the bow, drenching her instantly. She gasped at the shock, then laughed as they bounced through the rapids.

"Keep paddling!" Jeff shouted over the roar of the water.

Anna leaned into her strokes, working in perfect synchronization with Brad beside her. The raft danced through the remaining waves, each splash sending a thrill through her body. When they emerged into calmer water, she was breathless and grinning.

"That was amazing!" she exclaimed, pushing wet hair from her face.

Brad's smile matched hers, water dripping from his chin. "Toid you. And that was just a baby rapid."

The next hour passed in a blur of excitement. They tackled increasingly challenging rapids, each one washing away more of Anna's initial hesitation. Between the wilder stretches, the river opened into tranquil pools where they floated peacefully, catching their breath and absorbing the stunning scenery.

During one such calm section, Anna trailed her fingers through the cool water, watching ripples spread from her touch. The canyon had opened, revealing rolling mountains carpeted in dense forest. The July sun had climbed high overhead, warming her shoulders and drying her hair into wild, stiffened waves.

"I keep forgetting how beautiful this area is," she said, gazing at the landscape. "I've lived here my whole life, but sometimes I get so caught up in the day-to-day that I stop seeing it."

Brad nodded, his expression thoughtful. "That happens everywhere, I think. We get used to our surroundings, and they become invisible. It takes fresh eyes to remind us."

"Is that why you traveled so much with your app company?" Anna asked. "To keep your eyes fresh?"

"Not really, it was part of my job," Brad admitted. "I worked constantly when I traveled and never took the time to enjoy wherever it was I happened to be."

Before Anna could respond, Jeff's voice cut through their conversation. "Big one coming up, folks! This is 'Double Trouble'—two major drops back-to-back. Everyone ready?"

The peaceful moment evaporated as they gripped their paddles and faced forward. The roar of the approaching rapid grew louder, drowning out all other sounds. Anna could see the river dropping away ahead, white water churning violently.

"Forward paddle! Strong strokes!" Jeff shouted.

They hit the first drop with enough force to jar Anna's teeth. The raft bucked like a wild horse, sending water cascading over them in sheets. She barely had time to catch her breath before they plunged into the second drop.

"High-side left!" Jeff bellowed as the raft tilted dramatically.

Everyone scrambled to follow the command, but Anna's foot slipped on the wet floor. She felt herself sliding toward the churning water, paddle flying from her grasp. For one terrifying moment, she was certain she would be swept away.

Then a strong arm caught her around the waist, hauling her back into the center of the raft. Brad held her securely against him, his grip firm yet gentle as the raft righted itself and shot through the remainder of the rapid. The contrast between the chaotic water around them and the steadiness of his hold created a moment of stillness amid the turbulence.

"Got you," he said, his voice close to her ear, breath warm against her neck.

Heart pounding, Anna turned to find his face inches from hers. Water dripped from his dark hair, and his eyes held a mixture of concern and relief. His arm remained protectively around her waist, as though unwilling to risk letting her go too soon. Sparks sizzled between them, a current stronger than the river's, pulling her into the gravity of his gaze.

"Holy cow," she managed. "Thanks."

"Anytime," Brad replied, holding her gaze for a beat longer before reluctantly releasing her, his fingers trailing across her back as he withdrew—a touch so light she might have imagined it if not for the trail of warmth it left behind.

Jeff passed her the spare paddle he kept secured to the raft. "Nice save there! Everyone okay?"

Anna nodded, slightly dazed from the near-dunk in the river.

"That was the biggest rapid of the day," Jeff assured them. "Smooth sailing from here to our lunch spot."

As promised, the river calmed, allowing Anna to process what had just happened. The adrenaline from the rapid and Brad's rescue left her feeling oddly light-headed. She snuck a glance at him, finding him watching her with a small smile.

"What?" she asked, suddenly self-conscious.

"Nothing," he said, looking away. "Just glad you didn't go swimming in the middle of Double Trouble."

"Me too," Anna admitted. "Though it would have made a great tale to tell my future children."

Brad laughed as he scooped river water in his cupped hand and splashed it directly at her face. Anna gasped in surprise, then narrowed her eyes.

"Oh, it's on," she declared, immediately retaliating.

Their impromptu water fight ended only when Jeff announced they were approaching the lunch spot. A small, sandy beach came into view around a bend in the river, shaded by towering trees.

The guides expertly steered the rafts to shore, and everyone clambered out on slightly wobbly legs. Anna's muscles ached pleasantly from the morning's exertion as she helped drag their raft onto the beach.

"Lunch is served under the trees," Jeff announced, pulling waterproof coolers from the equipment raft. "We've got sandwiches, fruit, cookies, and cold drinks. Take what you like and find a spot to relax. We'll be here about an hour before heading downstream for the afternoon stretch."

Brad retrieved their lunch—thick sandwiches wrapped in waxed paper, apples, and bottles of water—and nodded toward a flat rock at the river's edge. "How about there? We can dangle our feet in the water."

"Perfect," Anna agreed, following him to the spot.

They settled side by side, unwrapping their sandwiches. The turkey and cheese on fresh bread tasted impossibly good after the morning's adventure. Anna hadn't realized how hungry she was until the first bite.

"So," Brad said between mouthfuls, "verdict so far? Was I right about this being fun?"

Anna pretended to consider the question seriously. "Well, I'm soaking wet, my arms feel like noodles, and I nearly fell into a rapid." She paused, then smiled. "And I'm having the best time I've had in years."

Brad's face lit up with genuine pleasure. "Really?"

"Really," she confirmed. "I needed this." She trailed off, watching the sunlight dance on the river's surface. "I forgot what it feels like to just play."

"Playing is underrated. Especially for adults."

"Says the man who literally moved across the country to start playing again."

Brad laughed. "Fair point. Though I prefer to call it 'recalibrating my life priorities.'"

"Is that what we're doing today? Recalibrating?"

"Nope." Brad shook his head firmly. "Today we're just having fun. No business talk, no farm concerns, no future planning. Just river, sun, and good company."

"I'll drink to that," Anna said, tapping her water bottle against his.

They finished their sandwiches and stretched out on the warm rock, letting the sun dry their clothes. Around them, other rafters chatted and laughed, but Anna felt cocooned in a private bubble with Brad, as if they'd carved out their own small corner of the world.

"Do you miss it?" she asked after a comfortable silence. "The excitement of your old life? Living in a big city, traveling everywhere, being at the center of it all?"

Brad considered the question, his gaze on the mountains rising beyond the river. "I miss the creativity, the problem-solving, and watching an idea become reality. But the pace was unsustainable. I was living for someday instead of today." He turned to look at her.

Anna drew her knees up, wrapping her arms around them. "You've made me start wondering a little... about what it's like—living somewhere else, doing something else. But then I think about not seeing the sunrise over our fields, or not seeing a thick fog hugging the mountains in the early mornings, or not knowing every inch of land under my feet..." She shook her head. "I really can't imagine living anywhere else."

"That's a gift from God; don't ever forget that," Brad said.

The simple sincerity in his voice touched Anna deeply. Before she could respond, he sat up and reached for a flat stone near his feet.

"Watch this," he said, standing and moving to the water's edge. With a practiced flick of his wrist, he sent the stone skipping across the river's surface—one, two, three bounces before it sank.

"Impressive," Anna said, joining him. "Let me try."

Her first attempt sank immediately. The second made two pathetic skips before disappearing.

"Here," Brad said, stepping behind her. "It's all in the wrist."

He positioned himself close enough that she could feel the warmth of his chest against her back, his presence enveloping her without overwhelming her. Time seemed to slow as his arms came around her, one hand settling lightly at her waist while the other gently clasped her wrist. His touch was careful yet confident, sending a cascade of awareness through her that had nothing to do with stone skipping.

His voice dropped to a lower register near her ear, the sound vibrating through her as he explained the technique. Anna found herself focusing less on his words and more on the sensation of being held in his arms, the scent of river water and sunshine on his skin, and the steady rhythm of his breathing against her back.

"Now try," he said, stepping back just enough to give her room, though his hands lingered a moment longer than necessary before releasing her, as if reluctant to break the connection.

Anna focused on the river, mimicking the motion he'd shown her. The stone left her hand and skipped beautifully—four times before sinking.

"I did it!" she exclaimed, turning to him with delight.

"Better than mine," Brad acknowledged, his smile warm and genuine.

They continued skipping stones, competing for the most bounces, and laughing when their attempts failed spectacularly. Anna couldn't remember the last time she'd done something so simple and joyful, with no purpose beyond the pleasure of the moment itself.

Eventually, they returned to their rock, pleasantly tired from the morning's exertions and the warm sun. Anna lay back, using her life jacket as a makeshift pillow, and closed her eyes against the bright sky. Beside her, Brad did the same, their shoulders nearly touching on the sun-warmed stone.

"We should do this again," Brad said, his voice relaxed and content.

Anna turned her head to look at him, taking in the profile of his face against the blue sky, the way the sun brought out hints of auburn in his dark hair. His features in repose held a quiet strength: the straight line of his nose, the curve of his mouth that seemed perpetually on the edge of a smile, and the tiny lines at the corner of his eye that spoke of laughter.

"Definitely," she replied, her voice carrying more meaning than the single word could convey.

Brad turned to face her then, their eyes meeting in a gaze that held questions and possibilities neither had voiced. Slowly, deliberately, he reached across the small space between them. His hand found hers on the warm stone, hovering for just a moment above her fingers—an unspoken question. Anna answered by turning her palm upward in silent invitation. His fingers gently interlaced with hers, the connection deliberate and unhurried.

The simple touch sent a ripple of warmth through Anna's chest, more powerful than any rapid they'd navigated. She squeezed his hand lightly, a confirmation that needed no words, and was rewarded with an answering pressure that seemed to speak volumes in the language they were just beginning to learn together.

As they lay there, hands linked and faces turned to the summer sun, Anna realized she'd gained more than just a fun day on the river. She'd rediscovered a part of herself that had been buried under responsibilities and worries—the part that knew how to laugh freely, take risks, and live fully in the moment.

And she had Brad Knight to thank for it.

Chapter 17

Anna squinted at her laptop screen and muttered, "What do you mean, internal server error?" She clicked again. And again. The website's admin panel—which had been working perfectly just moments ago—now displayed nothing but an ominous red message.

The gentle Appalachian morning that had started with such promise now felt like a cruel joke. Birds still sang in the maple trees surrounding the farmhouse porch, and the July sunshine still painted golden patterns across the weathered floorboards, but Anna's determination had crumbled into dismay.

"This can't be happening," she whispered, clicking refresh for the fifth time. Nothing changed—just the same error message staring back at her like a digital accusation.

From her spot beside Anna's rocking chair, Daisy lifted her golden head. The dog let out a sympathetic whine, as if sensing her owner's rising distress.

"It's fine, girl. I'm fine. Everything's fine," Anna insisted. "I just need to... figure this out."

She'd been doing so well. She'd updated pricing and photos on their website in the past. This morning's goal had been simple: update the farm's website with summer offerings and adjust some online store prices. For nearly an hour, she'd successfully navigated the content management system, proudly updating photo galleries and crafting product descriptions for their specialty cut flower packages.

The sense of accomplishment had been intoxicating. *Look at me actually doing this business stuff. Girl... you've got this!* She'd thought triumphantly after publishing a particularly compelling description of their sunflower bouquets. Her confidence had grown with each small victory.

Until she'd tried to change the pricing tier structure in the online store.

One click—that's all it had taken. One innocent click, and everything had collapsed. The entire website had gone from functional to frozen in the blink of an eye.

"Breathe," Anna reminded herself, running her fingers through her auburn hair. "Just breathe and think."

But thinking was undoubtedly the problem. The digital landscape of websites and servers and code had always been like a foreign country to her—one where she didn't speak the language and couldn't read the signs. She glanced toward the distant fields where she could see her mother and Katie moving between rows of flowers, already deep into their morning work routine.

The thought of interrupting them made her stomach clench. June had been delegating more responsibilities, trusting Anna to handle aspects of the business on her own. Calling for help now felt like confirmation of what Anna had secretly feared: that she wasn't capable of managing the farm's business side after all.

Daisy nudged Anna's hand with her cold nose, pulling her from the spiral of self-doubt. The golden retriever tilted her head, offering silent canine encouragement.

"I know," Anna sighed, scratching behind the dog's ears. "Panicking won't fix this."

She considered her options. She could keep clicking randomly and hope for a miracle. She could call the website hosting company and wait forever for a human to respond, which would further her frustration. Or...

Anna reached for her phone, hesitated, then typed a quick message:

Hey. Are you around? I may have accidentally crashed the farm website. Please don't laugh.

The reply came almost instantly:

On my way.

Relief and embarrassment warred in Anna's chest as she set the phone down. Mr. Tech Man was undoubtedly the person she needed right now. But admitting her digital helplessness to him felt like showing weakness in a way that unnerved her.

She spent the next ten minutes alternating between refreshing the error page and pacing the length of the porch, Daisy trailing faithfully at her heels. When the sound of tires on gravel announced Brad's arrival, Anna drew a steadying breath and tried to compose herself.

He climbed the porch steps two at a time, dressed in a simple navy t-shirt and jeans. His expression held concern rather than amusement. Even in her distressed state, Anna couldn't help noticing how the fabric stretched across his shoulders, or how quickly he'd come to her rescue—as though her problems mattered to him as much as his own.

"That was quick," Anna said, attempting lightness in her tone.

"I was already in my truck, heading into town for supplies," Brad explained. His eyes met hers, warm and reassuring, making the technological crisis feel suddenly less overwhelming. "What happened with the website?"

The kindness in his voice—the complete absence of judgment or condescension—loosened the tightness in Anna's shoulders. She showed him the laptop still displaying the error message.

"I was just trying to update our summer prices, and then... this. Everything's gone. The whole site is down." Her voice cracked slightly. "Our online orders come through that system, Brad. Without it..."

"Hey," he said, as he guided her to sit on the porch swing, his hand resting lightly at the small of her back. The gentle pressure of his touch steadied her in a way that had nothing to do with physical balance. "First rule of technology: nothing is ever as broken as it seems. Let's take a look."

Anna nodded, expecting him to take the laptop from her. Instead, Brad shifted closer on the swing, his thigh pressing lightly against hers as he angled the screen so they could both see it. The swing swayed slightly with his movement, creating a gentle rhythm that somehow calmed her racing thoughts.

"Walk me through what you were doing before the crash," he suggested.

"I was in the store section," Anna explained, her finger hovering over the screen. "I wanted to adjust our pricing tiers for the summer bouquet subscriptions. I clicked on this settings icon, and then—boom. Digital apocalypse."

A small smile curved on Brad's mouth at her dramatic description. "Definitely not an apocalypse. More like a temporary roadblock." He pointed to the error message. "This actually tells us exactly what went wrong. See this part about 'database connection'? That means the website lost its link to where all your information is stored."

Anna frowned. "But I didn't do anything to any database. I was just changing prices."

"Sometimes in these simple website builders, changing certain settings can trigger bigger system processes," Brad explained. "Think of it like how shifting one small support beam can affect an entire structure."

He guided her through a series of steps—accessing the website's control panel through a different URL, navigating to a section called "database connections," and verifying settings that looked like meaningless combinations of letters and numbers to Anna.

"This part is like the root system of your website," Brad explained as they worked. "You know how flowers need healthy roots before they can produce blooms? Websites are the same way. The pretty part—the design, the photos, the text—that's what everyone sees. But underneath, there's a whole structural system that makes everything work."

The farming analogy clicked in Anna's mind, creating a bridge between what she knew intimately and this digital landscape that had always seemed so alien.

"So the database is like the soil?" she asked, gaining interest despite her frustration.

"Exactly," Brad nodded, clearly pleased by her understanding. "And what we're doing now is basically checking the soil pH and nutrient levels—making sure everything's balanced so your digital garden can thrive."

Working together, they followed a logical sequence—Brad explaining each step as Anna's hands performed the actions. He leaned in closer to point at specific areas of the screen, his shoulder brushing against hers, bringing with it a subtle scent of his cologne. He never tried to take over the laptop and never made her feel incompetent for not knowing. Instead, he framed each task as a simple problem with a clear solution, connecting it to concepts she already understood.

Occasionally their fingers would brush as he guided her to the right section of the screen, each brief contact sending a small current of awareness up her arm. Anna found herself noticing the contrast between his strong, capable hands and the gentle patience in his voice—how he could possess such technical expertise yet explain it without a hint of condescension.

"Now we're going to reconnect the database," he explained, pointing to a specific field on the screen. "Think of it like grafting a broken stem back onto the main plant."

Anna carefully typed in the string of characters Brad dictated, her confidence growing with each keystroke. When she finally clicked "Save Changes" and received a confirmation message rather than an error, the knot in her chest began to loosen.

"Now let's refresh the main site," Brad suggested.

Anna held her breath as she clicked over to the Blooms Farm homepage and hit refresh. For a moment, nothing happened—then the familiar layout appeared, complete with the photo updates she'd made earlier.

"It worked!" she exclaimed, turning to Brad with unfiltered delight. In her excitement, she grabbed his hand where it rested on the swing between them. "Everything's back!"

"Of course it worked," he said with a smile that creased the corners of his eyes, his fingers gently squeezing hers before she realized she was still holding his hand. "You fixed it."

Anna scoffed, reluctantly releasing her grip, though the warmth of his hand lingered on her skin. "With you telling me exactly what to do every step of the way." She held his gaze, struck by how his eyes reflected genuine pride in her accomplishment rather than pride in his own ability to help.

"That's just guidance," Brad countered. "Your hands did the work. And next time, you'll remember some of these steps yourself."

"Next time, I'm staying far away from that pricing section," Anna declared, only half-joking.

"Actually," Brad said, "let's fix that now. I think I know what happened."

He guided her back to the store section, explaining that some systems required administrator approval for price changes above a certain percentage. Sure enough, when they checked the settings, they found that Anna had inadvertently triggered a security protocol by trying to change multiple prices at once.

"It's actually a good feature," Brad explained. "It prevents accidental big changes that could cost you money. But the error message could definitely be more helpful."

Together, they adjusted the settings to allow for the changes Anna needed to make, then successfully updated the summer pricing. Each small victory built Anna's confidence, transforming what had started as a technological disaster into a valuable learning experience.

"Try changing the featured bouquet price now," Brad suggested, pointing to an item on the screen.

Anna made the adjustment, clicked save, and let out a small, victorious "Ha!" when the system accepted the change without complaint.

"See? You've got this," Brad said, his voice warm with genuine pride.

Anna scrolled through the updated website, loving how the changes she'd made earlier that morning showcased their summer offerings. The photos she'd uploaded captured the vibrant colors of their field-grown zinnias and sunflowers, making them almost jump off the screen.

"It actually looks pretty good," she admitted.

"You have a natural eye for visual balance," Brad observed. "The way you arranged those product images creates a beautiful flow down the page. That's not something you can teach—it's instinct."

The compliment made Anna smile. Brad wasn't flattering her; he recognized a skill she hadn't even realized she possessed.

For the next half hour, they continued working on the website. With Brad's patient guidance, Anna created a new section highlighting their dried floral arrangements and set up an automatic email response for online inquiries. With each task becoming less intimidating under his tutelage, the digital world gradually transformed from enemy territory into simply another tool she could learn to use.

As they worked, the space between them seemed to shrink, their shoulders touching more often than not. Anna found herself increasingly aware of each shared glance, each approving nod, each small smile when she mastered a new skill. At one point, when she successfully added a particularly complex form, Brad's hand came to rest briefly on her shoulder in congratulation—a casual touch that somehow felt more significant than it should have.

"I think that covers everything you wanted to update," Brad said eventually, leaning back as Anna published the final changes.

Anna closed the laptop, feeling a sense of accomplishment that had seemed impossible two hours earlier. The morning sun had climbed higher, bathing the porch in golden light, catching in Brad's dark hair and illuminating the kindness in his eyes as he watched her. In the distance, she could see June and Katie heading toward the greenhouse, unaware of the crisis that had been averted and the quiet intimacy that had developed on the porch during those two hours.

"Thanks," Anna said, turning to face Brad fully. "Not for fixing the mess I created—for showing me how to fix it. I appreciate your patience more than you know."

"That's what neighbors are for... and friends."

He stood, stretching slightly before heading toward the porch steps. "I should get going. Those supplies won't buy themselves."

Anna walked him to his truck, Daisy trotting alongside them. The morning's frustration had evaporated, replaced by a quiet gratitude that extended beyond website repairs.

"Brad," she said as he opened his truck door. He turned, eyebrows raised in question. The morning sunlight framed him perfectly, highlighting the strong lines of his profile in a way that made her pulse quicken. "I really mean it. Thank you."

He smiled—that genuine smile that seemed to start in his eyes before reaching his mouth. "Anytime, Anna... and I mean that."

As she watched him drive away, the word he'd used echoed in her mind. Friends. It seemed simultaneously too simple and too loaded to capture what was developing between them.

Neighbors? Friends? Anna thought as Brad's truck disappeared down the driveway. *I think this... whatever this thing that is going on between us is way more...*

Chapter 18

Anna glanced at her phone, double-checking that the text had sent before sliding it into her back pocket. A flutter of nerves danced in her stomach as she packed the wicker basket, nestling the food between cloth napkins to keep it from shifting.

Be ready at 5. I'll pick you up. Don't eat dinner.

She'd added a smiley face at the end, trying to keep the message light.

Daisy watched with bright eyes from her spot near the kitchen door, head tilted in anticipation. The golden retriever always seemed to know when something out of the ordinary was happening.

"Yes, you're coming too," Anna assured her, tucking a quilt under her arm.

After Brad had helped her with the website that morning—his patience, his ability to guide without taking over, and the way he'd made complex technology accessible through farming metaphors—it had touched her deeply. He'd seen her frustration and met it with kindness rather than condescension.

The least she could do was treat him to dinner.

Anna checked her watch—4:45. She loaded the basket, quilt, and a small cooler into the utility vehicle she'd parked behind the house. Daisy hopped into the back seat without being prompted, settling in with the contentment of a dog who knew an adventure was coming.

"All set, girl?" Anna asked, scratching behind the retriever's ears. "We're going to our special place today."

Anna drove slowly toward the creek, savoring the familiar landscape. When she reached the creek that marked the property line, she guided the vehicle through a shallow section. The water splashed beneath the tires, sparkling in the late afternoon sun. On the other side, Brad's land stretched before her—wild and untamed compared to the cultivated order of Blooms Farm, but beautiful in its own way.

She spotted him waiting outside his Airstream, one hand shielding his eyes as he watched her approach. He wore the same navy t-shirt and jeans and a ball cap shading his face from the slanting sunlight. As she drew closer, a smile spread across his features—warm, genuine, and tinged with curiosity.

Anna pulled up beside him, cutting the engine. "Your chariot awaits," she called, patting the passenger seat.

Brad laughed, his eyes crinkling at the corners. "So mysterious. Should I be worried?"

"Depends on how you feel about surprises."

"I'm learning to appreciate them," he replied, climbing in beside her. "Hey, Daisy," he added, reaching back to scratch the dog's head. Daisy responded with an enthusiastic tail thump against the seat.

"Buckle up," Anna advised as she started the engine. "The terrain gets a little rough."

Brad complied, his shoulder brushing against hers in the confines of the vehicle. "So, are you going to give me any hints about where we're headed?"

"Nope," Anna replied, navigating back through the creek crossing. "But I promise it's worth the suspense."

They crossed the creek and followed it upstream, away from both houses and deeper into the property. The cultivated flower fields gradually gave way to wilder growth—meadow grasses dotted with wildflowers and stands of oak and maple creating patches of dappled shade. The path narrowed, becoming little more than twin tracks worn into the earth from Anna's weekly visits.

"I didn't realize your property extended this far," Brad commented, taking in the changing landscape.

"This corner of the farm holds plenty of memories for me." She paused, then admitted, "Actually, I like that it's a bit secluded and untouched. Makes it feel more special somehow."

The utility vehicle climbed a gentle rise, the engine working harder against the incline. As they crested the top, Anna slowed to a stop and cut the engine.

"We can walk from here," she said.

Brad followed her lead, climbing out and waiting as she gathered the basket and quilt from the back. Daisy bounded ahead, clearly familiar with the routine and excited to be on an adventure.

"Here, let me carry something," Brad offered.

Anna handed him the quilt. "This way," she said, nodding toward a path that wound between two large boulders. "Just another minute or two."

They walked in comfortable silence, the only sounds their footsteps on the soft earth and the increasingly audible murmur of water. The path curved around a cluster of ancient oaks, their massive trunks creating a natural gateway. Anna paused, watching Brad's face.

"After you," she said, gesturing ahead.

Brad stepped through the trees and stopped abruptly, his expression transforming from curiosity to wonder.

Before them lay an impressively sized clearing. A natural spring tumbled down a series of rock formations, creating a gentle waterfall that fed a crystal-clear pool. The pool, not over fifteen feet across, connected to the creek through a narrow channel. Wildflowers dotted the grassy area around the pool—black-eyed Susans, Queen Anne's lace, and purple coneflowers swaying gently in the early evening breeze. The setting sun cast everything in a warm glow, like a scene from a storybook brought to life.

"Wow," Brad breathed, his voice hushed with appreciation. "This is incredible."

She moved to stand beside him, a quiet pride warming her chest. His expression of genuine awe meant more than she'd anticipated—as though seeing her special place through his eyes made it even more magical. "This is my place," she said simply. "Has been since I was a kid."

"It's like a little piece of heaven tucked away."

Anna led him to a flat area of soft grass near the pool, spreading the quilt. Daisy had already made herself at home, lapping water from the edge of the pool before settling on a patch of sun-warmed grass to watch them.

"How did you find this spot?" Brad asked as he helped her arrange the quilt.

Anna set the basket down and sat, tucking her legs beneath her. "I was ten," she said, her voice softening with memory. "It was right after my dad left. Mom was working around the clock to keep the farm afloat, and I started wandering further and further from the house, just... filling the hours in the day, I guess."

"I followed the creek one day," Anna continued, "mad at the world and determined to run away, at least for an afternoon." She smiled at the childish drama of it. "I heard the waterfall before I saw it. It was like discovering a secret world. A place where nothing bad could touch me."

She gazed at the waterfall, its gentle cadence as familiar to her as her heartbeat. "I thought it was magic, honestly. My own personal fairy tale setting where everything was perfect and homes didn't break and parents didn't leave."

Brad's gaze never left her face as she spoke, his expression thoughtful and tender.

"And now?" he asked. "What is it to you now?"

Anna drew her knees up, wrapping her arms around them. "My sanctuary. My Sunday thinking place. Every Sunday morning, before anyone else is awake, I pour a thermos of coffee and come here to watch the sunrise. It's... where I feel closest to God, I guess. Where I can say thank you for everything good in my life and be reminded of how lucky I am to have this life he's given me."

"That's inspiring... it sounds like a special time each week that really means something to you."

Anna's throat tightened unexpectedly. She busied herself with opening the basket, unpacking their dinner to hide the rush of her emotions.

"Hope you don't mind chicken salad sandwiches again," she said, handing him one wrapped in waxed paper.

"I don't mind at all," Brad replied, accepting it gratefully.

They ate as the sun continued its slow descent, casting longer shadows across the clearing. The food was simple but perfect for the setting—sandwiches, fresh strawberries, and slices of pound cake for dessert. Conversation flowed easily between them, touching on her memories of other childhood hideaways here on the farm and their favorite summer foods.

Anna noticed how Brad's eyes would occasionally linger on her face when she spoke, how his smile seemed to deepen whenever she shared something personal. There was an intimacy to this picnic that had nothing to do with the secluded setting and everything to do with the man beside her. His presence made even simple food taste better and familiar stories feel new in the telling.

As they finished the strawberries, Anna leaned back on her elbows, watching as a family of goldfinches flitted between the trees at the edge of the clearing. Brad mirrored her position, their shoulders nearly touching as they traced the birds' flight paths together.

"Can I ask you something?" Brad said after a comfortable silence.

"Sure."

"When you look at this place, what do you see for its future? Does it always stay your private retreat, or have you ever imagined something else here?"

"Funny you should ask that," she said, sitting up fully. "I've actually been thinking about this spot a lot lately. Not this exact clearing—I'd want to preserve this—but the surrounding area."

Brad nodded encouragingly, waiting for her to continue.

"Mom had this idea years ago," Anna said, warming to the subject. "She thought this part of the property would be perfect for a barn-style venue. For weddings, community events, church gatherings, and that sort of thing." She gestured toward another level area beyond a few trees. "Over there, where it's naturally flat but still has a view of the creek."

"An event venue," Brad repeated thoughtfully. "Okay, I can see it."

"Think of the photo opportunities." Anna's voice quickened with enthusiasm. "Ceremonies by the waterfall, receptions in a beautiful timber-frame barn with big windows and string lights. I could create garden paths, maybe another separate ceremony area with an arbor overlooking the valley."

She paused, suddenly self-conscious about her excitement. "Sorry. I've never told anyone about this idea."

"No, keep going," Brad encouraged, his expression genuinely interested. "This sounds like more than just a passing idea."

Anna hesitated, then admitted, "It's been on my mind a lot lately. I've been thinking about approaching Mom with the idea instead of expanding the flower fields as we'd originally planned this year. It could be another extension of Blooms Farm—one that would bring in money year-round, not just during the growing season."

"Your flowers for decorating and landscaping... grow more in one of the greenhouses with climate control during the off-season for weddings or events in the winter," Brad said. "Built-in vertical integration."

"Yep. I could handle all the floral decorating and landscaping," Anna continued, her confidence growing as Brad nodded. "I'd hire help to manage the business side of the venue itself—I want nothing to do with that part."

She stood, walking toward the edge of the clearing where the land opened up to a wider view of the valley below. The setting sun painted the mountains in shades of pink and gold—the kind of tableau that would make a perfect backdrop for wedding photos. For any type of photography purposes, actually, engagements, anniversaries, and family photos.

"Mom wants to step back from the daily physical labor on the farm and the management aspects," she continued, gesturing toward the landscape before them. "But this could be something she'd enjoy taking part in—the perfect semi-retirement project that would let her stay involved in the farm and socialize with people, all while doing something new that won't eat up every hour of every day."

Brad had joined her at the edge of the clearing, standing close enough that she could feel the warmth radiating from him in the cooling evening air. The slight breeze carried his familiar scent—a blend of soap, sunshine, and something uniquely him that she'd begun to recognize and anticipate.

"What made you start thinking about this more seriously?" he asked, his voice lower in the twilight stillness. His gaze on her profile was intent, as though her answer mattered deeply to him.

"A few things," she admitted. "Watching how many couples come to the farm placing orders for their wedding flowers but continually have problems finding somewhere to get married. Not everyone wants to get married in a church anymore. People today are searching for an experience. Something different. And honestly..." She took a deep breath. "Seeing Mom dream about travel and new experiences made me think about dreams she and I both have been putting off for far too long."

Brad was quiet for a moment, his gaze thoughtful as he scanned the landscape. When he finally spoke, his voice carried an energy that caught Anna's attention.

"I can see it," he said, his eyes bright with possibility. "Not just the structure, but what it would mean for the community. For couples looking for something real, not manufactured. For local vendors who'd benefit from the events." He turned to her, his expression animated. "It's brilliant, Anna."

"You really think it could work?" She asked, her voice quieter now. "It's a huge investment, and I don't know the first thing about starting something like this."

"That's just details," Brad said with a certainty that made her smile. "The vision is solid. And think about it—Laurel Ridge doesn't have anything like this."

He gestured toward the pool, now reflecting the deepening colors of sunset. "I could see people booking a place like this for the view alone. I can clearly see opportunities for businesses that are already established in town. And if you designed it right, you could host numerous events like holiday markets, community gatherings and family reunions, and workshops."

Anna watched his face as he spoke, struck by how clearly he could envision what had been only half-formed thoughts in her mind. He wasn't just being supportive—he was adding dimensions she hadn't considered, expanding the possibilities beyond what she'd imagined.

"You make it sound so achievable," she said, a small laugh escaping her. "When I think about it alone, all I see are the obstacles."

"That's because you're looking at it from inside the challenge," Brad replied. "Sometimes you need an outside perspective to see the full picture."

They returned to the quilt as twilight deepened around them. The first fireflies appeared, tiny lanterns winking in and out of existence among the trees. Crickets began their evening symphony, their rhythmic chirping rising from the tall grass.

Anna leaned back on the quilt, propping herself up on her elbows, watching the emerging stars above them. "You're pretty good at this."

"At what?"

"Seeing potential. Turning vague ideas into concrete possibilities."

Brad smiled, with a hint of self-deprecation in his expression. "Years of practice. It's the entrepreneurial side of my brain I can't seem to shut off."

Daisy wandered over and settled between them, her warm weight a comfortable presence against Anna's side. The dog sighed contentedly, clearly at home in this peaceful spot.

"If you ever decide to build that barn. I'd love to help you make it happen."

Anna looked over at him—surprised, hopeful, and quietly moved. "You really think people would come? You think it could work?"

Brad met her gaze, his expression earnest in the fading light, as he placed his hand over hers. The warmth of his palm against her skin sent a current of awareness up her arm. "I do. I think you and your mom's dream could become a reality that would benefit not only you both but the entire area."

The fireflies danced around them, tiny lights mirroring the stars beginning to appear overhead. Brad's eyes held hers for a moment longer, then dropped to their joined hands. With gentle deliberation, he turned her hand over in his, his thumb tracing a light pattern across her palm before bringing her hand slowly to his lips. The kiss he placed there was soft, respectful—a gesture from another time that somehow felt perfectly right in this moment.

"Thank you," Anna whispered, her voice barely audible above the gentle sounds of the waterfall.

"For what?" Brad asked, still holding her hand in his.

"For seeing possibilities I couldn't see on my own."

As twilight deepened around them, neither seemed in a hurry to leave this moment or this place, where possibilities seemed as abundant as the stars now appearing above them.

Chapter 19

Anna's fingers moved instinctively through the cosmos, selecting the strongest stems with practiced precision. The morning dew had long since evaporated under the July sun, leaving the flowers warm to the touch as she gathered a bundle of pink and white blooms. The familiar rhythm of cut, bundle, repeat usually cleared her mind, but today her thoughts kept drifting like pollen on a breeze.

Back to yesterday evening and Brad.

The memory of their evening by the spring felt almost dreamlike in the harsh daylight—the way he'd listened so intently to her ideas, the quiet understanding in his eyes when she'd shared her childhood sanctuary, the way his hand had covered hers as they'd watched fireflies and stars emerge against the twilight. The gentle pressure of his lips against her hand lingered in her memory, a gesture so old-fashioned and respectful yet somehow more intimate than any kiss she'd ever received. None of it had been overtly romantic, and yet it was deeply significant to her in ways she was only beginning to understand.

She paused, resting on her haunches amid the dancing cosmos. The field stretched before her in waves of multiple colors, punctuated by the distant silhouette of mountains that cradled Laurel Ridge.

What would it be like to share this view with someone like him every day? The unbidden thought slipped past her defenses, conjuring images of Brad beside her in these fields, of quiet evenings on the porch with his shoulder pressed against hers, and of his laugh mingling with the morning sounds of the farm. Of strong, capable hands working alongside her own, of knowing glances across a dinner table, of a presence that somehow made even ordinary moments feel special.

The possibility made something warm unfurl in her chest, a sensation both foreign and familiar at once. It also terrified her, this longing for something she hadn't allowed herself to want in a very long time.

"You're hopeless," she muttered to herself, reaching for another stem. The last time she'd allowed herself to imagine a shared future had ended with Ryan, her ex, taking a job in California without even discussing it with her. He'd called it "an opportunity too good to pass up." She'd called it what it was—choosing a career over her and thinking only of himself.

Brad isn't Ryan. The thought arose with a quiet certainty that surprised her with its strength. Where Ryan had seen her farm as a quaint hobby, Brad saw its potential and value. Where Ryan had dismissed her attachment to this land as provincial, Brad understood it as part of who she was. Where Ryan had expected her to fit into his life, Brad seemed to consider how they might build something together.

But that certainty itself was alarming. How could she be so sure about a man she'd known for barely a month? And yet, in some ways, she felt she'd known Brad's heart from the first day they'd met.

The sound of approaching footsteps pulled Anna from her reverie. She glanced up to see Katie making her way down the row, a determined set to her shoulders. Something in her friend's expression—a mixture of resolve and sadness—made Anna set down her pruning shears.

"Don't freak out, but we need to talk," Katie said, crouching down beside her. "I love you. I love my work here. But..." She drew a deep breath. "I need to find a job that pays more."

The words landed like a stone in still water, sending ripples of surprise through Anna's chest.

"What? Where is this coming from?" Anna asked, straightening to face her friend fully.

Katie sank to her knees. "My landlord raised my rent a hundred dollars, and I need benefits, Anna. I can't keep living paycheck to paycheck, especially with my student loans coming due again soon."

"How long have you been thinking about this?" she asked quietly.

"A couple of weeks," Katie admitted, her fingers absently tracing the edge of a cosmos petal. "I was hoping to figure something out without having to bring it up. I've been looking at positions in Fayetteville. There's an office manager job that would pay almost thirty percent more than I make here, plus health insurance."

The thought of losing Katie—not just her assistant but her friend, the person who made the long days lighter with her humor and unfailing support—sat like a weight on Anna's chest.

"You'd have to commute almost an hour each way," Anna said, searching for objections.

"I know. I love working with you and our mom. And I'd hate leaving all this." Katie gestured toward the flower fields stretching around them. "But I have to be practical. I'm turning thirty-one next month, Anna. I should have savings by now, not just enough to cover rent and groceries."

Anna nodded slowly, understanding the position Katie was in. They'd talked about finances before—how Katie had put herself through college, how she'd supported her mother during a difficult illness a few years back, depleting what little savings she'd managed to accumulate.

"When would you need to give them an answer?" Anna asked.

"I haven't even applied yet," Katie said. "But they're accepting applications until the end of the month. I wanted to talk to you first."

Anna's mind raced, sorting through implications and possibilities. The timing couldn't be worse with her mom's semi-retirement plans looming. Losing Katie now would leave a massive gap in their operations, especially with the summer season in full swing and fall on the horizon.

But as she considered the problem, a new thought unfurled, like a tightly closed bud suddenly blooming.

What if?

What if this wasn't just a challenge, but an opportunity?

What if Katie could step into a different role at Blooms Farm?

The idea crystallized with surprising clarity. Katie's strengths—her organizational skills, her ease with technology, and her head for numbers—were exactly the abilities Anna herself lacked and dreaded using. They were also the skills that had defined June's role in the business, the role her mom was eager to step back from.

"What if you didn't have to leave?" Anna said slowly, the words forming as the idea took shape.

Katie raised an eyebrow. "I'm listening."

"What if we created a new position for you? Business Manager for Blooms Farm. More responsibility, better pay, and healthcare benefits."

"What exactly are you thinking?"

Anna set down her flower shears, turning to face her friend. "Mom wants to step back from the day-to-day management. You know I've been dreading taking over all her responsibilities because, let's be honest, I'm terrible with the business side. And quite honestly, I don't want to."

"You're not terrible," Katie interjected. "You just—"

"Hate it with every fiber of my being?" Anna finished with a wry smile. "Let's call it what it is. I don't enjoy it, I'm not good at it, and it stresses me out. But you? You're amazing with organization, social media, customer relations, and the financial stuff."

Katie's eyes widened as she followed Anna's train of thought. "Are you serious? You'd trust me with all that?"

"I trust you way more than I trust myself with it," Anna said honestly. "You'd manage the business operations—the contracts, the marketing, the books. I'd continue overseeing the growing side, the creative decisions. We'd be partners in a way, both reporting to Mom while she transitions into retirement."

"But could the farm afford it?" Katie asked, practical as always.

"Oh, honey, I'm sure the farm could afford it. We'd have to run some numbers, I imagine," Anna admitted. "I know we could make it work. Plus, with you handling the business growth side full-time, I bet we could increase revenue through the ideas you've already been suggesting."

Katie's expression grew animated. "Like the expanded online store and the flower arranging workshops we talked about. And the subscription service for local businesses."

"Yes," Anna nodded. "All those ideas we never seem to have time to implement properly."

They fell silent for a moment, both contemplating the possibility.

"I'll create a detailed proposal," Katie said, her voice cautious but hopeful. "Figure out exactly what the role would entail, the salary, and how we could structure the transition."

"Could you put something together by tomorrow evening?" Anna asked. "I'm thinking we could take Mom out to dinner before the town council meeting and present it to her then."

"Tomorrow?" Katie's eyebrows shot up. "That's ambitious."

"Is that a no?"

A slow smile spread across Katie's face. "It's a challenge accepted."

"This could actually work," she said, half to herself.

"I think it really could. I could put my degree in business to good use. Your mom already trusts me, and with you focusing on what you do best and me handling the stuff you hate."

"We'd make a great team. Better than we already do."

Katie reached over and squeezed Anna's hand. "I love this farm, Anna. I wasn't exaggerating about that. The thought of leaving has been making me sick to my stomach."

"Then let's make sure you don't have to."

"What made you think of this now?" Katie asked as they gathered their bundles of cut flowers. "We've worked together for a couple of years now. You could have suggested this arrangement before."

Anna considered the question, clipping a particularly perfect stem of white cosmos. "Honestly? I think I needed to be pushed."

"Pushed how?"

Anna secured her bouquet with a twist tie, choosing her words carefully. "I've always assumed that running the farm meant becoming Mom—handling every aspect the way she does. It never occurred to me that leadership could mean something different."

She thought of Brad, how naturally he'd recognized her strengths rather than focusing on what she lacked. How he'd shown her that systems and tools existed to compensate for the things she found challenging. How he'd helped her see possibilities rather than limitations.

"Brad helped me realize I don't have to do it all myself," she admitted, unable to keep a softness from entering her voice at the mention of his name. "That it's okay to lean on other people's strengths. He has this way of seeing solutions instead of obstacles—of making challenges feel manageable instead of overwhelming."

A knowing smile tugged at Katie's lips. "Brad, huh? So things are progressing there." She studied Anna's face with the practiced eye of someone who'd known her for years. "You light up when you talk about him, you know."

Heat rose to Anna's cheeks as she realized how transparent her feelings must be. "We're friends," she said, though the word felt inadequate for the connection that had formed between them.

"Friends who go on hikes, have Sunday lunches together, go white water rafting..."

"None of which were romantic," Anna protested, though memories of fireflies, quiet conversations, and a gentle hand over hers suggested otherwise.

Katie's laugh was light and knowing. "Sure. And I'm the Queen of England."

Anna shook her head, unable to stop her smile. "Fine. Let's just say we're friends, and I'm hoping for more." The admission felt both terrifying and liberating, putting into words what her heart had been trying to tell her for days. "He makes me see possibilities I wouldn't have considered on my own. And not just for the farm." She straightened, brushing soil from her hands. "But can we please focus on the actual business plan here? Tomorrow night. Martha's Diner. We pitch it to Mom."

Katie loaded the last of the cut flowers into the harvest basket. "You really think she'll go for it?"

"I think she'll love it."

As they lifted the heavy basket between them and began walking back toward the processing shed, Anna felt hope, not just for the farm's future, but for her own. A sense that maybe, just maybe, everything was falling into place exactly as it should.

And if her thoughts drifted occasionally to a certain pair of warm brown eyes that seemed to see her more clearly than anyone ever had, to the gentle strength in his hand that had held hers under a canopy of stars, to the quiet understanding in a voice that made her feel both heard and valued—well, that was simply another possibility blooming on the horizon. Perhaps the most beautiful one of all.

Chapter 20

Brad pushed his coffee mug aside and stared off into the distance, the soft whir of crickets rising behind him as he muttered, "Now where would a welcome center even go…?"

The question lingered in the still morning air, unanswered but persistent, as he sat at the picnic table beside the Airstream and surveyed his property. Birds called to each other from the trees that edged his clearing—chickadees, cardinals, and wrens creating a layered symphony that never failed to soothe him.

Brad took another sip of coffee, savoring the rich flavor as he returned his attention to the laptop, where a browser tab displayed real estate listings for commercial properties in Laurel Ridge. Nothing appropriate jumped out. Most were either too large, too run-down, or poorly positioned.

"Maybe not an existing building," he murmured, reaching for his sketchbook.

His pencil moved across the blank page, rough lines forming the outline of a small, cabin-like structure. A wide covered porch wrapped around the front, dotted with rocking chairs. Large windows would invite natural light and showcase views of the mountains beyond. Inside, he envisioned an open floor plan with rustic beams, local artwork, and interactive displays.

"Natural materials," he wrote in the margin. "Stone foundation, timber frame, metal roof." Then: "Local craftsmen for construction."

Another thought struck him, and he flipped to a fresh page, sketching a floor plan. One side would feature a large touchscreen map of the area, highlighting hiking trails, kayaking spots, and scenic overlooks. The other would showcase local businesses and events.

"Not a museum," he reminded himself aloud. "A launching point."

Brad continued sketching, adding details as they came to him—a coffee corner serving local blends, a small retail section featuring handcrafted souvenirs from town artisans, pamphlets sorted by interest. He imagined visitors entering, orienting themselves, and then setting out to experience Laurel Ridge with purpose and understanding.

The concept excited him in a way he hadn't felt since the early days of LocalLens. That familiar creative energy bubbled up—the desire to solve a problem, to create something useful and beautiful that didn't exist before.

But this time, it felt different. Healthier. He wasn't driven by the frantic need to disrupt an industry or capture market share. This wasn't about building an empire or proving himself. It was about contributing to a place that already felt more like home than anywhere he'd lived in years.

Brad set his pencil down and stretched, his back popping after nearly an hour hunched over the table. The sun had climbed higher, warming his shoulders through his t-shirt. He opened another tab on his laptop and began researching tourism statistics for the broader region.

The numbers confirmed his observations. Tourism in the New River Gorge area had increased steadily since its designation as a national park. Visitors were flooding into nearby towns, seeking authentic experiences beyond just outdoor activities.

"But they need guidance," he muttered, typing notes into a document. "Context. Connection."

He opened another document and began drafting features for a complementary app:

- Interactive trail maps with difficulty ratings and real-time updates
- Local business listings with rich profiles and seasonal offerings
- Community calendar with direct ticket purchasing options
- Storytelling features highlighting local history and lore
- Photo spots with suggested angles and lighting conditions
- Accessibility information for trails and attractions
- "Hidden gem" recommendations from locals

Brad tapped his fingers on the table, considering how to make the digital and physical experiences work in harmony. The Welcome Center would be the tangible heart of the system, while the app would extend its reach, allowing visitors to carry Laurel Ridge in their pockets.

His thoughts inevitably drifted to Anna and her vision for an event venue that she had shared with him yesterday evening by the waterfall. How perfectly it would complement what he was imagining—another authentic experience anchored in the land and community. People who discovered Laurel Ridge through the app and welcome center he was envisioning might celebrate their most precious moments at her venue—weddings, anniversary celebrations, and family reunions. He could picture locals gathering there for birthday parties beneath string lights or seasonal festivals that would bring the entire town together.

Each vision seemed to strengthen the other, creating something neither would be able to achieve alone.

The connection between their visions felt natural, effortless—much like the way he and Anna had begun to fit together in each other's lives. Without trying or planning, they seemed to complement each other in ways he'd never experienced before.

The realization startled him. In his former life, he'd evaluated potential partners with the same clinical assessment he'd used for business acquisitions—compatible goals, complementary skills, mutual benefits. But with Anna, the connection transcended such calculated thinking. When they were together, ideas flowed more freely, challenges seemed more manageable, and the future appeared brighter. Their strengths and weaknesses balanced each other in a way that felt almost deliberately designed.

Brad smiled, remembering their evening the day before. The way her eyes had lit up as she described her vision, the passion in her voice when she spoke of creating something new. She'd been so focused on what the venue would mean for her mother, for the farm, and for couples seeking a perfect setting. Not once had she mentioned personal profit or prestige.

He remembered how the fading sunlight had caught in her auburn hair, turning it to copper and gold. How her hand had felt beneath his—warm and strong, with calluses that spoke of honest work and dedication. The quiet vulnerability in her voice when she'd shared the childhood memory of discovering the waterfall. The way her smile had appeared, genuine and unguarded, when he'd expressed belief in her vision.

That authenticity was what drew him to her—that and a hundred other qualities he was discovering day by day. Her unwavering integrity. Her quiet strength. The way she moved through the world with purpose and grace. The unexpected flashes of mischief that brightened her blue eyes when she teased him. The careful way she considered new ideas, neither dismissing them outright nor accepting them without thought. The gentle patience she showed with everyone from her mother to Katie to the farm's customers.

When he'd taken her hand and brought it to his lips that evening—an impulse he hadn't planned but couldn't regret—he'd seen something shift in her expression. A recognition perhaps, that whatever was growing between them deserved to be nurtured.

He'd come to Laurel Ridge seeking solitude and healing. Finding Anna had been an unexpected gift—one he was increasingly unwilling to take for granted.

Brad scrolled through his notes, adding a section about wedding tourism: "Coordinate with local venues—specifically Blooms Farm potential development—to create seamless experiences for wedding parties and guests."

He paused, wondering if he was getting ahead of himself. Anna hadn't even presented the idea to her mother yet or fully fleshed out the idea. And here he was, already integrating it into his own ideas.

Still, the potential was undeniable.

A notification popped up on his screen—a calendar reminder that the utility company would be visiting tomorrow to discuss installing new power poles, upgraded power lines, and a permanent power installation for his future home. The word "permanent" caught his attention, making something shift in his chest.

Months ago, permanence had been an alien concept. His life had been defined by momentum and change—always pushing forward, always reaching for the next milestone. Now, he found himself craving roots, connection, and continuity.

The more time he spent here, the more right it felt. Not just as a place to recover, but as a place to build a life—a real life, with meaning and balance and joy. A life that, increasingly, he hoped would include Anna. Not just as a neighbor or a friend or even a business partner, but as something more profound, more lasting.

The thought should have terrified him. In Denver, none of his relationships had lasted—each one shallow, fleeting, built more on convenience than connection. Yet here, just a few weeks after meeting Anna, he was already imagining something deeper. A life where their paths didn't just cross—they ran alongside each other, steady and entwined, like the native vines curling along the creek between their properties.

What would that life even look like?

The question lingered, warm and unsettling in equal measure, as Brad refocused on his laptop. He opened a new browser tab and typed: Laurel Ridge town government. The results were modest—just a basic site with contact information, ordinances, and a few meeting announcements.

One line caught his eye: *Town Council Meeting—Wednesday, July 24th, 7:00 PM—City Hall; Public Welcome.*

Tomorrow night.

Anna had mentioned the meetings—low-key, open to all, part business and part neighborly gathering. She'd encouraged him to attend once he felt more settled in.

Brad drummed his fingers on the table, considering. He wasn't ready to present any proposals yet—his ideas were still taking shape, and he wanted to understand the community dynamics better before suggesting changes. But attending as an observer would give him valuable insights.

Plus, Anna might be there. The thought brought a warmth to his chest that had nothing to do with the July sun.

He added the meeting to his calendar, then closed his laptop and gathered his sketches. As he slid everything into his messenger bag, a sense of purpose settled over him—different from the driving ambition of his past, gentler and more patient, but no less real.

This wasn't about building another empire or making a name for himself. It was about finding the sweet spot where his skills could serve a community he was growing to love, where success would be measured not in dollars or downloads, but in connections strengthened and experiences enriched.

And if those connections included a certain auburn-haired flower farmer with a sharp wit and a generous heart? Well, that would be the most meaningful success of all.

Brad tucked his bag into the Airstream and grabbed his work gloves from the hook by the door. The morning was still young, and the land called to him—there were trails to clear, wood to split, and a hundred small tasks that kept his hands busy while his mind processed all he'd been planning.

Physical labor had become a balm for his restless spirit, the perfect counterpoint to the mental work that still energized him. Finding that balance—between thinking and doing, between creating and being present—was at the heart of the new life he was building.

As he headed toward the barn, a flash of gold caught his eye—Daisy, racing along the creek bank, her exuberant barking carrying across the property. Where Daisy went, Anna usually followed, and sure enough, a moment later he spotted her, auburn hair catching the sunlight as she called to the dog.

She hadn't seen him yet, absorbed in whatever morning task had brought her to the creek's edge. Brad paused, his heart performing a familiar skip that happened whenever she appeared. He watched her move with that characteristic purpose and grace that had captivated him from the beginning—the confident way she navigated the uneven ground, the gentle authority in her voice as she called to Daisy, the easy way she belonged to this landscape as if she'd grown from it like one of her flowers.

He simply watched for a moment, savoring the unexpected joy her presence brought him. There was something quietly miraculous about these unplanned glimpses of her—Anna unaware of being observed, completely herself, moving through her world with an authenticity that made his former life seem like an elaborate performance in comparison.

From this distance, he couldn't see the exact blue of her eyes or the constellation of freckles across her nose that he'd begun to memorize. But he could see the silhouette that had become more familiar to him than his own—the proud set of her shoulders, the way she tucked her hair behind her ear when concentrating, and the graceful strength in every step.

He smiled, hands resting on his hips, and thought, This is what happiness feels like.

Chapter 21

Martha's Diner hummed with the gentle clatter of silverware against plates and the murmur of Wednesday evening conversations. The scent of fresh-baked apple pie mingled with the savory aroma of meatloaf and gravy, creating that distinctive comfort-food perfume Anna had known since childhood.

Anna slid into the worn red vinyl booth, the familiar creak of the seat oddly reassuring as her stomach twisted with nervous anticipation. Katie settled across from her, while June took the spot beside Anna, her reading glasses perched on top of her head in their usual resting place.

"My three favorite customers," Martha announced, approaching with a pitcher of sweet tea. Her silver hair was pulled back in its usual neat bun, and her blue apron bore the evidence of a busy day in the kitchen. "What brings you ladies in on a Wednesday? Are you going to the town council meeting tonight?"

"We are," June confirmed. "Just thought we'd grab dinner first."

Martha filled their glasses with sweet tea, ice cubes clinking against the sides. "The special tonight is meatloaf with mashed potatoes and green beans. Made the potatoes with extra butter, just how you like them, June."

"You know me too well," June smiled.

"Three specials, then?" Martha asked, her pencil poised above her order pad.

They nodded in unison, and Martha gave them a wink before heading back toward the kitchen, pausing briefly to check on the Henderson family in the corner booth.

Anna took a long sip of her tea, the sweetness coating her tongue as she gathered her courage. Katie caught her eye across the table and gave a small, encouraging nod.

"So," June said, arranging her napkin in her lap, "what's this mysterious dinner about? You two seem rather nervous about something."

Anna set down her glass, condensation cool against her fingertips. "There's something we want to talk to you about, Mom."

"Sounds serious," June replied, her expression curious.

Martha returned with a basket of warm cornbread and a small crock of honey butter. "To tide you over," she said with a smile before moving on to another table.

Anna broke a piece of cornbread in half, the steam rising with the sweet, nutty aroma. The familiar comfort food steadied her nerves as she gathered her thoughts.

"Okay," she said, heart thudding against her ribs, "I want to talk through something. Katie, please jump in whenever you want."

Katie nodded, her expression a mixture of excitement and apprehension that mirrored Anna's own feelings.

"You want to step back from the farm," Anna began, meeting her mother's gaze directly. "And I've been... worried about taking over everything, especially the business side."

June's eyes softened. "And..."

"Well," Anna continued, "I think we have a solution." She drew a deep breath. "Katie needs a better salary and benefits. The farm needs someone who actually enjoys and understands business operations. And I need to focus on what I do best—growing things and working with customers—not staring at spreadsheets until my eyes cross."

The beginning of understanding dawned in June's expression. "Go on."

"I want to restructure," Anna said, her voice growing steadier with each word. "Katie would become Blooms Farm's business manager, handling operations, marketing, and finances—all the parts that I..."

"Hate with a fiery passion?" June supplied with a small smile.

"You nailed it," Anna laughed, relieved by her mother's perceptiveness. "I'd continue managing the growing side, design, and customer relationships. And you could stay involved with whatever aspects you enjoy most, without the pressure of day-to-day operations."

Katie leaned forward, pulling a neatly organized folder from her bag. "I've put together some projections," she said, opening the folder to reveal color-coded charts and detailed tables. "With the increase in tourism and expanded local business accounts, the farm can afford a competitive salary for the position. And with more focused management, I believe we can increase revenue by at least fifteen percent in the first year."

June's eyebrows rose as she examined the documents. "This is impressive, Katie."

"I've outlined specific growth initiatives," Katie continued, confidence evident in her voice as she pointed to a section of her proposal. "Expanding our online presence, formalizing our subscription service for local businesses, and developing winter workshops when field work is slower."

Anna watched her mother's face, searching for any sign of hesitation. "What do you think, Mom? I know it's a lot to absorb at once."

June was quiet for a moment, her fingertips resting lightly on Katie's meticulously prepared documents. The diner's ambient sounds seemed to fade as Anna waited, her pulse quickening with each passing second.

"I think," June said finally, looking up with clear eyes, "that this may be the smartest idea either of you has ever had."

Relief washed through Anna in a dizzying wave. "Really?"

"Really," June confirmed. "Katie's financial acumen is undoubtedly what the farm needs. And you—" she turned to Anna with a tender expression, "—you were never meant to be chained to a desk running payroll. Your gift is out in the fields, creating beauty and connecting with people."

Martha arrived with their meals, steaming plates of comfort food that momentarily paused their conversation. The aroma of home-style cooking filled the surrounding air—savory meatloaf, creamy mashed potatoes with butter pooling in the center, and green beans flecked with bacon.

Once Martha moved away, June picked up her fork and continued, "I've been worried about how to step back from the farm and enjoy life a little more. Not because I don't trust you, Anna, but because I know how much you dread the administrative side."

"I've tried," Anna said, stirring her potatoes absently. "But every time I sit down with QuickBooks, I want to run screaming into the fields."

"And every time I try to design a flower arrangement," Katie added with a laugh, "it looks like a five-year-old did it. It takes me twice as long to create one than it does Anna. I do love working in the fields and the greenhouses though, I'll admit. But we all have different strengths, and if we concentrate more on those, I think in the end it will benefit Blooms Farm the most."

June nodded thoughtfully. "The farm needs both of you—your vision and growing expertise, Anna, and Katie's business mind. It's actually perfect."

Anna felt the tension she'd been carrying for weeks begin to unravel. She took a bite of meatloaf, savoring the blend of spices as relief settled in her chest.

"There's something else," she said after a moment, setting down her fork. "This restructuring isn't just about the farm. It's also about... having more of a life beyond it for myself."

June's expression was expectant, open. "What do you mean?"

Anna traced the condensation on her tea glass with one finger, gathering her courage. "I love our farm. You know that. But lately, I've realized I want more balance. I want time for... other things. Other people."

A knowing smile tugged at June's lips. "Other people like Brad?"

Heat rose to Anna's cheeks as she met her mother's gaze and nodded. "I don't know what's happening between us, but... I want to find out."

"About time you admitted it," Katie said, her tone gently teasing.

Anna rolled her eyes but couldn't suppress her smile. "The point is, this plan gives all three of us what we need and want. Mom gets to semi-retire and travel without worrying about the farm falling apart. Katie gets a position that uses her talents and pays her what she's worth. And I get to focus on what I love without feeling like I'm failing at what I don't."

"There will be challenges," Katie acknowledged, returning to the practical aspects. "We'll need to hire someone to take over my current responsibilities, especially with Tyler and Sarah going back to school soon."

"I was thinking about Lily Johnson's granddaughter," Anna suggested. "She just graduated from college and moved back home, and she's looking for full-time work."

"She's a good possibility," June agreed. "Smart girl, works hard."

They continued discussing logistics as they ate. The conversation flowed naturally, all three women contributing ideas, their excitement building with each resolved question.

As they finished their meals, June set down her napkin and looked at them both with shining eyes. "I am so proud of you two. This plan shows real maturity and foresight."

She reached for Anna's hand, squeezing it gently. "Especially you, sweetheart. You've always been so determined to handle everything yourself in regard to the farm... well, not the business aspects. But seeing you recognize that leadership sometimes means delegation—that's the growth I've been hoping to see. And I'm glad that you notice you need time away from the farm... to live a little."

The simple praise brought unexpected tears to Anna's eyes. "I had a good teacher," she said softly. "Watching you all these years, seeing how you built this business while still being present as a mom... you made it look effortless, even though I know now how hard it must have been."

June's smile was tinged with emotion. "It wasn't always easy, especially after your father left. But the farm gave us both roots when we needed them most." She looked between Anna and Katie. "Now it's evolving again, into something that can sustain all of us in different ways. That's how living things should grow."

Martha approached their table, coffeepot in hand. "Dessert tonight, ladies? Just pulled a fresh apple pie from the oven."

"Absolutely," Katie said without hesitation. "We're celebrating."

"Oh?" Martha raised an eyebrow, pouring coffee into the mugs she'd brought. "What's the occasion?"

"New beginnings," June replied. "Katie's been promoted to business manager at Blooms Farm."

Martha's face lit up. "Well, isn't that wonderful! Dessert is on the house, then. Can't have a celebration without proper sustenance."

As Martha bustled away, June turned back to Anna. "Now, about this 'other people' situation... Brad seems like a good man. Thoughtful. Respectful."

"He is," Anna agreed, warmth spreading through her chest at the mention of his name. "He sees me—really sees me. Not just as a farmer or your daughter, but... me. And he helps me see possibilities I might have missed on my own."

"Like restructuring the farm?" June asked perceptively.

Anna nodded. "Partly. He showed me that asking for help isn't a weakness—it's wisdom. That I don't have to become you to honor what you've built."

"Hmmm, I like him more and more every day," June said with approval. "And he's handsome too, which doesn't hurt."

"Mom!" Anna protested, though laughter bubbled beneath her embarrassment.

"What? I may be in my fifties, but I'm not blind," June quipped, her eyes twinkling. "Seriously though, Anna. Life is too short not to follow your heart. The farm will always be there, but opportunities for real happiness... maybe even love... well, those don't come along every day."

Katie nodded in agreement. "I agree. And with this new structure, you'll actually have time to see where things might lead with Brad."

"We're not... I mean, we haven't... let's just say we haven't labeled ourselves as a couple yet," Anna stumbled over her words, the memory of Brad's lips against her hand by the spring suddenly vivid in her mind.

"You haven't yet," June supplied gently. "But there's something there worth exploring."

Martha returned with three generous slices of apple pie, steam rising from the flaky crust, cinnamon, and sugar glistening on top. "Here we go, ladies."

June reached for her sweet tea glass, lifting it with a gentle smile. "I think this calls for a toast," she said, her eyes shining with pride and emotion.

Katie raised her glass immediately, and Anna followed, the ice clinking softly against the sides.

"To new beginnings," June said, her voice warm and steady. "To a farm that will continue to grow and flourish under your care. To Katie's well-deserved promotion." She paused, her gaze settling on Anna with motherly intuition. "And to following your heart wherever it may lead."

"To new beginnings," Katie echoed, her smile bright with promise.

"To new beginnings," Anna repeated.

As they turned their attention to the apple pie, savoring the perfect balance of tart fruit and sweet cinnamon, Anna felt a sense of peace settle over her. She no longer felt she had to become someone she wasn't.

And Brad? The thought of him brought warmth to her cheeks that had nothing to do with the steam rising from her pie. Whatever was growing between them deserved the chance to blossom—just like the carefully tended flowers in her fields, with space to stretch toward the sun and time to develop strong roots.

As they finished their dessert and prepared to head to the town council meeting, Anna found herself looking forward rather than backward, anticipating what might grow from the seeds they'd planted today. New beginnings indeed—for the farm, for her friendship with Katie, and for the quiet hope taking root in her heart.

Chapter 22

Brad pressed the tip of his pen to the attendance sheet, signing his name with a deliberate stroke. The practical motion grounded him, a small anchor in this unfamiliar setting. City Hall was nothing like he'd expected. The building itself was impressive but a little less formal inside than he expected. The room where the meeting was to be held had more of a community gathering space feel than a structured governmental-type meeting feel, with its honey-colored wood-paneled walls and rows of mismatched chairs arranged in a loose horseshoe shape.

"Mr. Knight, welcome." Mayor Wilson extended his hand, his weathered face crinkling into a genuine smile. At sixty-something, the mayor wore his position with the casual dignity of a man who'd known most residents since birth. His plaid shirt and khaki pants spoke of a leader who saw no need for performative formality. "Glad you could join us tonight."

"Thanks for having me," Brad replied, returning the firm handshake.

"You picked a good night to join us. Nothing too controversial on the agenda," the mayor said with a wink. "Just our usual updates and community business. Feel free to grab a seat anywhere—we don't stand on ceremony here."

An older gentleman with steel-gray hair approached, his posture military-straight despite his age. "You must be the new owner of the old Harmon property," he said, extending a hand. "Walter Harrison, a fifth-generation Laurel Ridge resident and long-serving council member."

Brad shook the offered hand. "Brad Knight. Pleasure to meet you, sir."

Mr. Harrison studied him with keen eyes that had likely witnessed decades of newcomers passing through their mountain town. "Hope you're settling in well," he said, his tone measured but not unwelcoming. "Takes time to understand how we do things here."

The words carried a subtle caution beneath their surface—not hostility, but the natural wariness of a community protective of its character.

"I've got a lot to learn about Laurel Ridge, which is undoubtedly why I'm here tonight."

Something in his response seemed to satisfy the older man, who gave a short nod. "Good answer, son." He gestured toward the chairs. "Grab a seat and settle in... and welcome to Laurel Ridge."

"Thank you, sir," Brad said, moving toward the indicated chair.

As he settled in, he took a moment to observe the room filling with townspeople. The atmosphere was relaxed, more reminiscent of a family gathering than a government proceeding. Neighbors greeted each other with easy familiarity, their conversations punctuated by laughter and the occasional good-natured ribbing. Several people nodded in his direction, their curious glances friendly rather than suspicious.

Brad had arrived fifteen minutes early, a habit from his corporate days that now served a different purpose. Rather than positioning himself for boardroom dominance, he'd come to observe—to understand the heartbeat of Laurel Ridge. The gentle hum of conversation around him carried snippets of local concerns, personal updates, and community plans.

"...still trying to find someone to fix that leak at the library..."

"...Martha's apple pie won first place at the county fair again..."

"...thinking of extending Friday hours at the shop through fall..."

He pulled out his phone, opening a notes app where he'd already jotted down observations about local businesses, potential opportunities, and gaps in services. The tactile process of making notes helped organize his thoughts while maintaining the low profile he wanted for this initial meeting.

The door opened, bringing with it a fresh wave of evening air and three familiar figures. Brad's attention immediately shifted, drawn like a compass finding north. Anna stepped into the room flanked by June and Katie, her auburn hair loosely gathered at the nape of her neck, a few escaped strands framing her face. She wore a simple blue sundress that brought out the color of her eyes—casual, feminine, and more dressed up than her usual work attire.

He watched as she scanned the room, exchanging warm greetings with neighbors. When her gaze finally landed on him, surprise registered in her expression before blooming into a smile that reached her eyes.

Brad stood and made his way toward her.

"Evening, ladies," he greeted them. "Fancy meeting you here."

"Brad," Anna said. "I didn't expect to see you tonight."

"Thought it was time I learned how things work around here," he replied. "You mentioned that these meetings were important to the town."

"And here I thought you were just missing Anna after not seeing her today," June teased lightly.

"Mom," Anna protested, a flush creeping up her neck.

"That too," Brad admitted with a small grin, enjoying the blush that deepened on Anna's cheeks. "Is this seat taken?" he asked, indicating the empty chair beside where they'd set their belongings.

"It is now," Katie replied before Anna could speak.

They settled into place just as Mayor Wilson called the meeting to order with three taps of a small wooden gavel.

"Evening, everyone," the mayor began, his voice carrying easily through the modestly sized room. "Thanks for coming out tonight. We'll keep this moving so you can all get home at a decent hour."

A ripple of appreciative chuckles moved through the audience.

"First up, Pastor Whitman has an update on the church fundraiser," the mayor continued, gesturing toward Andrew in the front row.

As the meeting progressed through its agenda items—library repairs, the summer reading program, and planning for the annual Founder's Day celebration—Brad found himself drawn into the rhythm of the proceedings. This wasn't the rigid parliamentary procedure of corporate boardrooms or the performative politics of larger cities. Instead, it had the organic flow of a community conversation.

He made notes as people spoke, capturing not just the content but the connections between residents. Mrs. Patterson, whom he'd met at the farm stand, apparently also headed the historical society. Earl, who owned the hardware store, seemed to be the unofficial fixer of all town emergencies. The librarian and the elementary school principal worked closely on educational initiatives.

Each revelation added another thread to the tapestry of Laurel Ridge that was slowly taking shape in his mind—a community where roles overlapped, where business wasn't separated from personal, and where the strength came from interconnection rather than isolation.

Beside him, Anna listened attentively, occasionally leaning toward her mother to whisper a comment or jotting something in a small notebook. The casual grace of her movements, the intent focus in her expression when someone spoke about community needs—these details captivated him as much as the meeting itself.

"Next up," Mayor Wilson announced, consulting his agenda, "June Mitchell has an update on Blooms Farm's participation in the fall festival."

June rose, elegant and assured. "Evening, everyone. As most of you know, Blooms Farm has handled the floral decorations and autumn displays for the festival for the past fifteen years. This year, we'll continue that tradition, but with a change in leadership."

She turned slightly, her gesture encompassing both Anna and Katie. "Anna and Katie will be taking over the planning and execution this year as part of some exciting changes at the farm."

A murmur of interest rippled through the audience.

"Katie has been promoted to business manager, handling all operations and financial aspects of Blooms Farm," June continued, pride evident in her voice. "Anna will continue leading our growing and design work, focusing on what she does best. And I'll be transitioning to a more advisory role, which means more time to help with community projects—and take that vacation I've been putting off for a decade. In other words... I'm finally going to start enjoying a semi-retirement stage of life."

Gentle laughter and a smattering of applause followed this announcement. Brad turned to Anna, finding her watching her mother with a mixture of pride and relief that made his heart tighten with understanding.

"Congratulations," he whispered, reaching for her hand. His hand found hers and gave a gentle squeeze.

Anna's fingers curled around his, returning the pressure. The simple weight of her hand in his felt right, and she made no move to withdraw hers.

"That's quite an undertaking," Brad said softly to Anna as the meeting moved to the next agenda item. "The festival displays. I imagine that will be a huge job."

"It's a lot of work," she agreed, her thumb absently tracing a small circle against his knuckle in a way that made it difficult to focus on her words. "But worth it. It's my favorite festival of the year."

"I'd like to help if you could use an extra pair of hands," he offered. "I'm getting pretty good at following directions."

Her smile warmed her entire face. "You're hired."

The meeting continued, with updates from various community members. The owner of Talbot's General Store reported on summer tourist traffic and that sales have increased. The librarian outlined plans for expanding its local history section. A debate—friendly but spirited—arose about whether to allow food trucks during the fall festival or stick with only local restaurant vendors.

Through it all, Brad remained acutely aware of Anna's hand in his, of the subtle shifts in her posture when topics interested her, and of the occasional glances she cast his way. Their physical connection anchored him to the moment in a way that felt profoundly different from his observer's stance at the meeting's start.

When Mayor Wilson opened the floor for new business, a brief silence fell over the room. Brad felt a momentary urge to speak—to share the ideas taking shape in his mind about tourism development and community resources. But the timing wasn't right. He felt he needed to understand more and build relationships to earn the right to offer suggestions in this close-knit community.

After a few more announcements—a reminder about the upcoming blood drive, a call for volunteers to help paint the elementary school fence—the mayor tapped his gavel lightly.

"If there's nothing else, we'll adjourn for tonight. Thanks for coming, everyone. As always, we've got coffee and cookies in the back courtesy of Martha's Diner."

As the formal meeting dissolved into casual socializing, Brad made no move to release Anna's hand. Neither did she attempt to withdraw either. They sat for a moment in the gentle chaos of neighbors greeting each other in the aisles, a small island of quiet connection.

"So," Anna said finally, turning slightly to face him, "what did you think of your first Laurel Ridge town council meeting?"

Brad considered the question, his thumb brushing lightly over her knuckles. "It's nothing like the city council meetings in Denver," he said. "There, everything was formal presentations and political positioning. This felt more like..."

"A family discussion?" Anna suggested.

"Yeah... even the disagreements had this underlying sense that everyone ultimately wants what's best for the town." He glanced around at the groups of people chatting in the aisles, the easy laughter, and the genuine interest as neighbors caught up on each other's lives. "This is a special town, Anna. Something worth preserving while it grows."

Her eyes searched his face. "You're thinking about how you fit into all this, aren't you?"

The perceptiveness of her question surprised him. "I am," he admitted. "I came here looking for peace, for a chance to heal and figure out what's next. But being here tonight, seeing how this community works…" He gestured with his free hand toward the room. "I keep thinking about what I could contribute. How my skills might serve a place like this."

Anna's expression softened. "Something related to tourism, I'm guessing, based on our previous conversations?"

"Maybe," he nodded. "But I'm still figuring out the shape of it. Tonight helped me see more clearly how interconnected everything is here—how a change in one area affects everyone."

She squeezed his hand gently. "That's why it matters that you came tonight. That you're taking time to understand before jumping in with big plans."

"I've learned the hard way that the fastest way isn't always the best way," Brad said, thinking of his former life where speed and disruption had been valued above all else. "Some things deserve patience."

His gaze held hers, the double meaning in his words hanging between them. She didn't look away.

June approached them, Katie close behind. "Hey, you two," June said, her knowing glance falling to their still-joined hands before rising to their faces. "We're heading over to the ice cream shop; I'm craving some strawberry ice cream. Care to join us?"

Brad looked to Anna, letting her decide.

"Sounds perfect," Anna replied, her smile including them all but lingering on Brad.

As they gathered their things and moved toward the door, Brad kept Anna close, their hands finding each other again naturally once they stood. The rightness of it all—her hand in his, the warmth of her presence beside him, the gradual acceptance he felt from the townspeople who nodded in greeting as they passed—settled over him like dawn after a long night.

Laurel Ridge wasn't just a quiet place to heal anymore. It was becoming something more—a place where he could build something meaningful on his terms, where his skills and passions might serve a purpose beyond profit, and where connections ran deeper than transactions.

And Anna? Her presence beside him, strong and graceful and rooted in this place he was coming to love, felt increasingly essential to whatever future he might build here.

Chapter 23

Anna wiped her forehead with the back of her gloved hand, leaving a smudge of potting soil across her skin. The July heat pressed against the greenhouse glass, transforming the space into a steam bath despite the whirring fans overhead. Her t-shirt clung to her back as she crouched between rows of celosia, their crimson and gold plumes nodding in the artificial breeze.

"Just a few more trays," she murmured to herself, gently separating the seedlings before transferring them to larger containers. The methodical work usually cleared her mind, but today her thoughts kept circling back to last night's town council meeting—to Brad sitting beside her, his hand warm around hers, his quiet presence somehow both calming and exhilarating.

The buzzing of her phone startled her. She peeled off one glove and fished the device from her back pocket, expecting a message from Katie about lunch plans. Instead, Brad's name lit up the screen.

Free this afternoon? I've got an idea I want to run past you. Adventure included.

Her stomach performed a ridiculous little flip. She stared at the message, reading it twice more as if the words might rearrange themselves. After a moment's hesitation, she typed back:

Depends on the adventure. Should I be concerned?

His response came immediately: Only if you're afraid of brilliant ideas and good food. I'll pick you up in an hour?

Anna bit her lip, glancing at the remaining seedling trays. She could finish them tomorrow; they weren't urgent.

I'll be ready.

She pressed send before she could overthink it, then stared at the phone for a moment longer, a smile tugging at her lips. Tucking the device back into her pocket, she surveyed the greenhouse with new eyes. The remaining work that had seemed so pressing now appeared perfectly postponable.

"Sorry, little ones," she told the waiting seedlings. "I've got an adventure to prepare for."

She finished the tray she'd been working on, cleaned her tools, and hung up her apron with efficient movements. After a quick check of the irrigation system, she stepped outside, the difference in temperature making her skin prickle despite the summer heat.

In the farmhouse, Anna showered quickly, washing away the greenhouse grime and changing into her favorite dark denim jeans and a light blue blouse that Katie always said brought out her eyes. She quickly fixed her hair, applied a touch of tinted lip balm, and dabbed on a hint of the floral perfume she reserved for special occasions.

Daisy padded into the bathroom, tail wagging hopefully.

"Sorry, girl. Not this time." Anna crouched to scratch behind the dog's ears. "You've got to stay and keep Mom company."

The sound of tires on gravel drew her attention. She peered through the window to see Brad's truck pulling up, right on time. He stepped out, wearing khaki pants and a forest-green polo that emphasized the breadth of his shoulders. Even from this distance, she could see the easy confidence in his stance, so different from the restless energy he'd carried when they first met.

Anna gave herself one final glance in the mirror, took a steadying breath, and headed downstairs. June looked up from her book as Anna passed through the living room.

"Going somewhere?" her mother asked.

"Brad's taking me to lunch. And...something else. He mentioned an adventure."

June's eyebrows rose. "Mysterious. Have fun, honey. Don't rush back."

"It's probably just lunch and...I don't know, maybe a hike or something."

"Mm-hmm," June hummed, returning to her book. "Tell Brad I said hello."

Anna stepped onto the porch, and Brad was waiting on the bottom step for her. His smile—that genuine, unguarded smile that never failed to catch her breath—spread across his face.

"Hi," he said simply.

"Hi yourself," she replied, suddenly shy despite all they'd shared. "So...adventure, huh?"

"That's the plan... nothing major." He gestured toward his truck. "Your chariot awaits, madam."

Anna laughed, the sound breaking the momentary tension. "Very gallant. Where are we headed?"

"Martha's first. I'm starving, and we need fuel for the rest of our expedition."

"Martha's it is," Anna agreed, falling into step beside him.

Brad opened the passenger door for her, his hand briefly touching the small of her back as she climbed in. The casual contact sent a ripple of warmth up her spine. She buckled her seatbelt as he rounded the hood and slid into the driver's seat.

"You look beautiful," he said as he started the engine.

"Thanks," Anna replied, feeling heat rise to her cheeks. "You clean up pretty well yourself. Must be a special adventure."

"It could be," Brad said, with a hint of something in his voice she couldn't quite name. "I hope so, anyway."

The drive to Martha's Diner passed quickly, filled with easy conversation about the previous night's town council meeting and Katie's excitement about her new role at the farm. Brad asked thoughtful questions about the transition plans, showing genuine interest in the details.

"She's already created a spreadsheet tracking all our fall plantings and harvest projections," Anna said as they pulled into a parking space near the diner. "Mom's thrilled."

"That's the beauty of partnering with someone whose strengths complement yours," Brad replied, cutting the engine. "You can each focus on what you do best."

The mid-afternoon lull meant Martha's was only half-full when they entered. Martha herself stood behind the counter, her silver hair neatly pinned back, her eyes lighting up when she spotted them.

"Well, well," she called, wiping her hands on her apron. "If it isn't my two favorite people."

"Hello, Martha," Anna smiled, settling onto a stool at the counter. Brad took the seat beside her.

"What brings you two in this afternoon?" Martha asked, setting two glasses of sweet tea before them without being asked.

"We're fueling up for an adventure," Brad explained, with a sidelong glance at Anna. "And nobody does fuel like you, Martha."

Martha's eyes twinkled as she looked between them. "Adventure, is it? Well, aren't you two just the picture of summer romance?" Before either could protest, she continued, "What'll it be today? The special is turkey club sandwiches with my homemade potato salad."

"Sounds good to me," Brad nodded.

"Make that two," Anna added.

As Martha moved away to place their order, Brad turned slightly on his stool to face Anna more directly.

"So," he said, "I've been thinking a lot since last night's meeting."

"That sounds dangerous," Anna teased.

"Potentially," he admitted with a smile. "But in a good way, I think." He took a sip of tea before continuing. "You know I've been trying to figure out what's next for me—how I can contribute here in Laurel Ridge."

Anna nodded. "You mentioned something about tourism."

"That's where it started," Brad agreed. "But it's evolved into something more specific." His eyes lit up with a spark she'd come to recognize—the one that appeared whenever his creative mind was fully engaged. "I'm thinking more and more about developing an app specifically for Laurel Ridge and the surrounding area."

Martha returned with their sandwiches, each cut diagonally and accompanied by a generous scoop of potato salad flecked with dill.

"Here you go, dears. Enjoy," she said, giving them a wink before moving to check on an elderly couple in a corner booth.

Brad picked up his sandwich but paused before taking a bite. "The idea for this app is to highlight experiences for people visiting here, not just tourist traps. The kinds of places locals actually value and want others to experience."

"Like Martha's," Anna suggested, gesturing with her sandwich.

"Exactly like Martha's. And Talbot's General Store. And the trails only locals know about." He took a bite, his enthusiasm momentarily contained by the practical necessity of chewing. After swallowing, he continued, "The app would offer itineraries based on interests—outdoor adventure, local history, arts and crafts, and seasonal activities. It would connect people with guides, workshops, and events."

Anna listened, oddly moved by the passion in his voice. This wasn't just idle brainstorming; he'd clearly been developing this idea seriously.

"That sounds...really thoughtful," she said finally. "Different from typical tourism apps."

"That's the goal," Brad nodded. "I don't want to turn Laurel Ridge into a commercial destination. I want to help visitors connect with what's already here—the authentic heart of the town." He set down his sandwich, his expression growing more serious. "And here's where it gets interesting—I think it could tie in perfectly with your venue idea."

Anna's eyebrows rose. "My venue idea? How so?"

"Picture this," Brad said, leaning slightly closer. "A couple visits Laurel Ridge using the app. They fall in love with the town, the mountains, and the whole experience. When they get engaged a year later, where do they want to have their wedding? At that magical place in the mountains where they felt so connected."

"Blooms Farm... the event venue."

"Yes. Your venue would be featured on the app—not just as a wedding location, but as a place to experience the natural beauty of the area. You could offer photography sessions too—not just for weddings but also engagement photos, family portraits, and seasonal mini-sessions against the amazing landscapes you can design. You could collaborate with a local photographer."

Martha appeared with the coffeepot, refilling the cups of nearby diners before approaching them. "Everything taste alright?"

"It's wonderful, Martha," Anna assured her, though she'd barely tasted her food, so engrossed was she in Brad's vision.

"Good," Martha said, her perceptive gaze taking in their intense conversation. "You two are looking mighty serious for people planning an adventure."

Brad laughed. "Sometimes the best adventures start with good planning."

"And sometimes they start with throwing plans out the window," Martha countered with a knowing smile. "But what do I know? I'm just an old woman who's seen half the town fall in love over my counter." She moved away before either could respond, leaving another charged silence in her wake.

Anna took a bite of her sandwich to give herself a moment to process. The food was delicious as always, but her mind was racing too quickly to fully appreciate it.

"This is serious for you, isn't it?" she asked finally. "You're really thinking about building something here. Not just carving out a quiet new way of life."

Brad's expression softened. "I came to Laurel Ridge looking for peace, yes. But I'm discovering that true peace isn't about absence—it's about presence. Being fully engaged in a place that matters, with people who matter." His gaze held hers, the implication clear in his warm brown eyes.

"But what about the slower pace you wanted?" Anna pressed gently. "If you're not careful, your vision could grow into something that demands just as much from you as your previous life did."

It was a valid concern, one she'd been mulling over since he first mentioned his tourism ideas. Brad had come to Laurel Ridge to escape the crushing pressure of his former career. Would these new plans eventually recreate the very stress he'd fled?

Brad considered her question, thoughtfully chewing a bite of sandwich before answering. "That's something I've been thinking about a lot," he admitted. "The difference is intent and control. In my previous life, growth was the only metric that mattered—more users, more features, more markets, more profit. It was never enough."

He set his sandwich down, brushing crumbs from his fingers. "This would be different. It would be about quality, not quantity. About being useful on my terms, not chasing endless expansion." His voice grew more certain as he continued. "I need purpose, Anna. I'm learning that about myself. I can't just sit around and watch the sunset every day, as nice as that is. But I can choose a purpose that aligns with my values and respects my limits."

Anna nodded, understanding blooming in her chest. "Balance."

"Exactly," Brad smiled, relief evident in his expression. "Finding meaningful work without letting it consume me. Creating something valuable without sacrificing my well-being to do it."

"I get that. The farm gives me purpose too. I just want to make sure you're not setting yourself up to burn out again."

"I appreciate that," Brad replied, his voice warming. "More than you know."

After finishing their lunches, Martha returned to clear their plates, sliding two forks and a single slice of apple pie between them.

"On the house," she announced. "Can't send you off on an adventure without proper sustenance."

"Thanks, Martha," they said in unison, then laughed at the synchronicity.

"So," Anna asked as they shared the pie, their forks occasionally clinking against each other, "what's the next step in your plan?"

Brad's expression brightened. "Actually, that's part of today's agenda. I was really impressed by Ben Turner at the council meeting last night—the man who runs Adventure Tours? I'd love to speak with him about the tourism landscape here, maybe explore potential partnerships."

Anna nodded in recognition. "Ben's a great person. His business is quite popular with tourists here."

"You know him well?" Brad asked.

"Well enough." Anna took another bite of pie, savoring the perfect balance of tart apples and sweet cinnamon. "I could introduce you."

"That would be amazing," Brad said, with genuine appreciation in his voice. "Having a local connection would make a huge difference."

"Happy to help," Anna replied, warmth spreading through her chest at his obvious gratitude. "Is that our adventure destination? Adventure Tours?"

"That's stop number one," Brad confirmed with a mysterious smile. "The rest unfolds as we go."

They finished the pie, and Brad paid their bill. As they stepped outside into the afternoon sunshine, the heat had softened slightly, though humidity still hung in the air like an invisible veil. Without hesitation or fanfare, Brad reached for her hand, his fingers sliding between hers with natural ease.

Anna's pulse quickened at the simple contact. His palm was warm against hers, his grip firm but gentle. They walked in silence to his truck, no words needed in this quiet acknowledgment of something deepening between them.

At the passenger door, Brad paused, still holding her hand. Then, with deliberate gentleness, he raised their joined hands and pressed his lips to her knuckles.

"What was that for?" Anna asked.

Brad's eyes crinkled at the corners, his smile reaching all the way to their warm brown depths. "No reason. Just because I'm thankful. For this day."

Anna laughed softly, the sound carrying more joy than humor. "You're too charming for your own good, Brad Knight. Keep looking at me like that, and I might start thinking this is more than just a friendly outing to discuss business ideas."

"Would that be so terrible?"

"Not at all," Anna replied.

Chapter 24

The crunch of gravel under tires mingled with the distant rushing of the New River as Brad steered his truck down the winding access road. Anna pointed toward the wooden bridge stretching across a narrow section of the creek.

"Just over there," she directed. "Adventure Tours is right on the other side."

Brad eased the truck onto the bridge, the weathered planks rumbling beneath it. Through his open window, the scent of river water and summer-warmed nature filled the cab. He stole a glance at Anna, who was leaning slightly forward in her seat, fingers tapping lightly against her thigh—a subtle tell he'd noticed whenever she was anticipating something.

As they crossed the bridge, a large hand-carved wooden sign appeared between two towering oaks: "Adventure Tours—Explore. Experience. Remember." An arrow pointed toward a clearing where a substantial log building stood nestled against the backdrop of emerald mountains.

"That's impressive," Brad remarked, taking in the rustic yet well-maintained structure. Expansive windows reflected the afternoon light, and a wide porch wrapped around the front, dotted with wooden rocking chairs that invited visitors to pause and absorb the surroundings.

"Ben's worked really hard to build this business up over the past several years," Anna said, pride for her friend evident in her voice. "He's very well known in the area, and his tours stay booked."

Brad parked beside a row of mud-spattered SUVs emblazoned with the Adventure Tours logo—a stylized mountain peak with a river running beneath it. As they stepped out of the truck, a wind chime crafted from polished river stones and driftwood sang a gentle melody from the porch eave, its notes floating on the mountain breeze.

The scent of cedar grew stronger as they approached the entrance. Brad held the door for Anna, the solid weight of it speaking to the building's sturdy construction. Inside, the space opened into a welcoming great room where exposed beams stretched overhead and large windows framed postcard-worthy views of the mountains.

The practical beauty of the place immediately struck Brad—this wasn't a tacky tourist trap, but a thoughtfully designed gateway to authentic experiences. Wooden racks held kayak paddles and life vests along one wall, while topographical maps and trail guides lined another. Glass display cases showcased local handcrafted souvenirs: woven baskets, carved wooden animals, and jars of honey from Laurel Ridge apiaries.

What captured Brad's attention most, however, were the photographs covering the central wall—hundreds of them showing people of all ages engaged in river rafting, mountain biking, hiking, and fishing expeditions. Each image radiated genuine joy, not posed tourist smiles but the authentic happiness that comes from meaningful connection with nature and others.

"Anna Mitchell!" A deep voice called from across the room.

Brad turned to see a tall, broad-shouldered man approaching them with long, purposeful strides. He wore hiking pants and a faded blue shirt with rolled sleeves that revealed forearms tanned and strengthened by years of outdoor work. His sandy brown hair had sun-bleached streaks, and laugh lines framed hazel eyes that held both warmth and careful assessment.

"Ben," Anna greeted, accepting his quick, affectionate hug. "Busy day?"

"Just sent out the afternoon rafting group," Ben replied, his voice carrying the gentle cadence of Appalachian roots. "They'll be back around sunset." His gaze shifted to Brad, curious but not unwelcoming.

"Ben Turner, this is Brad Knight," Anna said, completing the introduction. "Brad recently moved here from Colorado. He bought the old Harmon property next to our farm."

Ben extended a hand, his grip firm and steady. "Welcome to Laurel Ridge. Heard about you at the council meeting last night." His direct gaze held Brad's for an extra beat—not challenging, but certainly taking his measure.

"Thanks," Brad replied, matching the firm handshake. "Anna speaks highly of your operation here. I can see why."

A slight smile warmed Ben's expression. "Anna's good people. Her opinion carries weight around here." He gestured toward the hallway off the main room. "Why don't we head to my office? Grace just made a fresh pot of coffee."

He led them past a small retail area where hiking boots and outdoor clothing were displayed alongside field guides and nature-focused children's books. The walls here featured framed newspaper articles about Adventure Tours and various conservation efforts in the region.

Ben's office reflected the man himself—practical, unpretentious, and connected to the outdoors. A large desk crafted from reclaimed barn wood dominated the space, while the bookshelves held titles on local ecology, business management, and wilderness first aid. Through the window behind his desk, Brad could see kayaks stacked near the riverbank, ready for the next expedition.

"Have a seat," Ben offered, indicating two comfortable chairs opposite his desk. "Coffee?"

After they'd settled with steaming mugs, Ben leaned back slightly in his chair. "So... what brings you out here today?"

Brad appreciated the direct approach. He took a sip of coffee—rich and strong, exactly what he needed—before responding.

"I've been thinking about how to contribute to Laurel Ridge," he began, setting his mug down. "I want to be useful here, but in a way that preserves what makes this place special rather than changing it."

Ben nodded slightly, his expression attentive but reserved.

"I was in tech before moving here," Brad continued.

"Something about an app company... someone mentioned it last night at the meeting," Ben confirmed, glancing briefly at Anna.

"Yes. I founded LocalLens—a travel app that helped people discover authentic local experiences instead of tourist traps."

Recognition flickered in Ben's eyes. "I've used that app before when Grace and I took a trip out to Colorado. Pretty solid platform."

"Thanks," Brad said. The simple acknowledgment warmed him more than he'd expected. "I built it because I saw how traditional tourism was failing both visitors and communities. Visitors weren't finding the real heart of places, and communities were being transformed by mass tourism in ways they never wanted."

Anna watched him speak, a small smile playing at the corner of her mouth as though she was seeing something in him that pleased her.

"After selling the company, I came here looking for a new way of life... I wanted a little more peace, not so fast-paced as I had in Denver," Brad continued. "What I found instead was a community worth investing in." He leaned forward slightly, enthusiasm coloring his voice. "I've been developing an idea for Laurel Ridge—a custom app that would connect visitors with authentic local experiences. Not just hiking trails and white water, but Anna's flower arranging workshops at Blooms Farm, Martha's Diner, Earl's hardware store collection of mining artifacts, the local trails, events here locally..."

"The full Laurel Ridge experience," Ben supplied, his posture shifting as interest replaced caution.

"Exactly. Not trying to reinvent the town for tourists, but helping them discover what's already here—the places and experiences locals value."

Ben rubbed his jaw thoughtfully. "You're talking about controlled tourism growth. Quality over quantity."

"Precisely," Brad nodded, pleased by the quick understanding. "No one wants Laurel Ridge turning into a crowded tourist trap with chain stores and overrun trails. But thoughtful growth could help local businesses thrive, create opportunities for the next generation to stay rather than leave for cities, and preserve what makes this place special by making it economically sustainable."

Anna placed her mug on the corner of Ben's desk. "I think what Brad's proposing would complement what you're already doing with Adventure Tours, Ben. Your guided experiences could be featured prominently."

Ben tapped his fingers on the desk, considering. "What would this look like practically? An app where visitors browse local attractions?"

"Much more than that," Brad explained, pulling out his phone and opening a sketch he'd made. "Interactive trail maps with difficulty ratings and real-time updates. Local business listings with rich profiles. A community calendar with direct booking options for events and tours. Storytelling features highlighting local history." He swiped to another screen. "But the technology is just a tool. The real value would be the curation—featuring experiences that represent the authentic Laurel Ridge, not just whatever pays for placement."

"And the business model?"

"Initially, I'd fund development myself. Long-term, it could be sustained through a small commission on bookings made through the platform, plus premium placement options for businesses that want extra visibility." He set his phone down. "But profitability isn't my primary goal here. I want to create something valuable for the community."

Ben's eyebrows rose slightly. "That's... refreshing to hear."

"I've already had the 'chase every dollar' phase of my career," Brad said with a wry smile. "It nearly killed me—literally. I'm looking for purpose now, not just profit."

Something in Ben's expression shifted at that, a recognition passing between them. "I get that."

The conversation flowed more easily after that, with Ben asking thoughtful questions about implementation timeline, technology requirements, and community involvement. Brad found himself impressed by the outdoor guide's business acumen—beneath the rugged exterior was a sharp mind that grasped both practical details and larger implications.

"The key," Brad emphasized as their discussion deepened, "is that this needs to be a true community asset, not just my project. I'd want input from business owners like you, from town leadership, and from longtime residents who understand what should be highlighted and what should be protected."

"You're thinking about this the right way," Ben said, leaning back in his chair. "Too many people come in with big ideas but no understanding of what we value here." He studied Brad for a moment longer. "I'd back something like this. Could introduce you to some key people, maybe even consider investing down the road if you open it up."

The offer—so straightforward and genuine—caught Brad by surprise. He'd hoped for advice and perhaps some local insights, but Ben's immediate willingness to support the concept suggested he'd passed some unspoken test.

"I appreciate that," Brad replied, the simple words carrying more weight than elaborate thanks. "Your endorsement would mean a lot."

Ben nodded, a small smile breaking through his typically reserved expression. "Small towns run on trust, Brad. Anna bringing you here tells me you're worth listening to. What you've shared confirms it."

Anna, who had been quietly observing their exchange, looked pleased but not surprised by this outcome, as though she'd anticipated the connection that would form between the two men.

Ben glanced at his watch. "I should check on our afternoon groups soon, but before you go—" He opened a drawer and pulled out a flyer, sliding it across the desk. "Community potluck dinner tomorrow night at the church hall. Best way to meet folks if you're serious about putting down roots here."

Brad picked up the colorful paper announcing the monthly community dinner. The casual invitation felt significant somehow—another small step toward belonging.

"I completely forgot that was tomorrow," Anna said, shaking her head. "I need to figure out what dish to bring."

"Your mother's peach cobbler would be welcome," Ben suggested with a smile. "Grace still talks about it from last month's dinner."

"No pressure," Anna laughed.

They wrapped up their meeting with handshakes and promises to connect again soon. As they followed Ben back through the main area, Brad noticed how employees and customers alike greeted him with genuine respect—not the deference commanded by title or wealth, but the natural regard earned through character and contribution.

Outside, the late afternoon sun had begun its slow descent. The air had cooled slightly, carrying the scent of water from the nearby river.

Before they reached Brad's truck, he slowed his steps, turning to face Anna. Her auburn hair caught the golden light, framing her face with a soft glow that made his chest tighten with an emotion too new to name.

"Thank you for that," he said, gesturing back toward Adventure Tours. "For the introduction. For vouching for me."

Anna's smile reached her eyes, crinkling the corners. "I didn't say anything that wasn't true."

The mountain breeze stirred the treetops above them, a gentle rustling that seemed to emphasize the quiet moment stretching between them. Brad took a deep breath, suddenly feeling like a high school boy about to ask for his first date.

"About the potluck tomorrow," he said, his voice steady despite the unexpected flutter in his stomach. "Would you do me the honor of being my date?"

"I'd like that."

"Good," Brad replied, relief and happiness warming his voice. "Are you up for a hike this afternoon?"

"Sure, why not."

"I found a trail near here... nothing crazy, just a nice easy hike to enjoy nature... and spend more time with you. And no more business talk for the rest of the day either... just you and me enjoying the day."

"You're a charmer for sure, Brad Knight... keep it up," she said with a grin.

Chapter 25

Anna gazed up at the wooden steeple of Laurel Ridge Community Church, golden in the setting sun as Brad pulled his truck into the gravel parking lot. Already, the parking lot overflowed with familiar vehicles—Mrs. Patterson's blue sedan, the Miller's minivan with its "My Child is an Honor Student" bumper sticker, and her mom's pickup.

"Looks like most of the town is here already," Anna said, smoothing her sundress nervously. She'd chosen the yellow one with tiny white flowers, a favorite she usually saved for special occasions. The soft cotton felt comfortable against her skin, though her stomach fluttered with anticipation that had nothing to do with hunger.

Brad cut the engine and turned to her, his expression warm. "Ready for this? I hear the potluck competition gets pretty cutthroat in Laurel Ridge."

"Oh, it does. Mrs. Patterson and Martha have had a decades-long rivalry over whose potato salad is superior." Anna tucked a strand of hair behind her ear. "But I think we're safe. Mom's peach cobbler is legendary, and you..." She glanced at the covered dish beside them on the seat. "What did you bring again?"

Brad lifted the dish with exaggerated care. "My grandmother's oatmeal chocolate chip cookie recipe. Do you know how hard it is to bake in an oven in the Airstream?"

The image of Brad in his kitchen, sleeves rolled up and flour dusting his forearms as he struggled to perfect a family recipe for this community gathering, made something warm unfurl in Anna's chest.

"I can't believe you baked cookies," she said.

"Why not?"

"I don't know." Anna shrugged. "It's just... unexpected."

"I'm full of surprises, Anna Mitchell." Brad winked before opening his door. "Come on. Let's go enjoy the evening together."

They walked together along the stone path that curved around the whitewashed church. The evening air carried the layered scents of summer—freshly cut grass, distant honeysuckle, and the promise of rain hovering just beyond the mountains.

Brad's hand found hers as they rounded the corner, his palm warm and sure against her skin.

Behind the church, the community hall nestled into a grove of oak trees. Its broad wooden porch spilled over with people chatting in clusters, their laughter carrying across the dusky air. Strings of white lights crisscrossed overhead, casting a gentle glow on the gathering.

At the bottom of the steps, Brad paused. "So, a community potluck." He adjusted his grip on the cookie dish, looking suddenly, endearingly uncertain. "Are there rules I should know? Special handshakes?"

Anna squeezed his fingers. "Just be yourself. That's more than enough."

"In that case, shall we?" He gestured toward the porch with a small bow that made her laugh.

As they climbed the steps, familiar faces turned toward them with waves and calls of greeting. The warmth of the welcome wrapped around Anna like a favorite quilt—the same comfort she'd known all her life, now extended to include Brad beside her.

"Anna! Brad!" Pastor Andrew approached, his welcoming smile crinkling the corners of his eyes as he greeted them. "So glad you could make it tonight."

"We wouldn't miss it," Anna replied, accepting his quick, one-armed hug. "Brad's first community potluck—a true Laurel Ridge initiation."

"Is there a ceremony?" Brad asked with mock seriousness. "Do I need to recite the town charter or something?"

Pastor Andrew laughed. "Nothing so formal. Though Martha might quiz you on any number of things as the evening progresses." He turned toward the crowded hall behind him. "Come on in. We're just about to bless the food."

They followed him inside, where the mingled aromas of comfort food wrapped around them—savory casseroles, fresh-baked bread, and the sweet perfume of at least a dozen desserts. Long tables lined with dishes stretched along one wall, while round seating tables filled the open space.

Brad surveyed the scene, his expression brightening with genuine pleasure. "This is exactly what I hoped it would be," he murmured to Anna, his voice warm against her ear.

Katie appeared at her elbow. "Finally! I was beginning to think you weren't coming. Your mom's already here—she saved seats for you both at our table."

"Thanks, Katie," Anna said.

They made their way to the dessert table, where Brad placed his cookie tray next to a chocolate layer cake. Anna placed her dish of potato salad nearby. As they moved through the room, Anna watched with quiet pride as Brad greeted people they passed. He remembered names from their previous encounters.

"Brad! Come meet my husband," called Mrs. Patterson, waving from where she stood with a tall, silver-haired man near the punch bowl.

"Be right there," Brad answered, his hand resting lightly at the small of Anna's back as they changed direction. The casual possessiveness of the gesture, so natural and unforced, sent a pleasant shiver across her skin.

Mrs. Patterson beamed as they approached. "This is my Harvey. Harvey, this is Brad Knight, the young man who bought the old Harmon place. And you know Anna, of course."

"Indeed, I do," Harvey said, extending a weathered hand. "She's always grown the prettiest flowers in the county, this one, even when she was knee-high to a grasshopper."

As Brad and Harvey fell into an easy conversation about property boundaries and the best time to plant apple trees, Anna felt a gentle tap on her shoulder. She turned to find Martha, her sharp eyes taking in the scene before her.

"Well, well," Martha said softly. "Your young man seems to be making quite an impression."

"He's not my—" Anna began, then stopped herself, suddenly unsure of how to define what Brad was to her. Not just a neighbor anymore. More than a friend.

Martha's knowing smile cut through her confusion. "Honey, I've been watching people fall in love for forty years. I know the signs. You two are meant to be."

Before Anna could form a response, Pastor Andrew's voice rose above the din. "If I could have everyone's attention, please! Let's gather for the blessing before we eat."

The crowd quieted, forming a loose circle as Pastor Andrew stepped to the center of the room. Brad returned to Anna's side and reached for her hand.

"Let's bow our heads," Pastor Andrew said, his voice warm and inclusive. "Lord, we thank You for this beautiful evening and the blessing of community. For the hands that prepared this food, for the fellowship we share, and for the seasons of growth You provide. Bless this meal and the hearts gathered here. Amen."

A chorus of "Amens" rippled through the room, followed immediately by good-natured jostling as people lined up at the buffet tables.

"Quite the spread," Brad commented as they joined the line, plates in hand. "I think I counted at least four different types of potato salad."

"Five," Anna corrected with a laugh. "Mrs. Patterson and Martha each brought their own, plus there's mine, Lily Whitman's German version, and whatever that one with the bacon is."

"A serious potato salad community."

"You have no idea. There was almost a schism in the church three years ago over whether sweet relish belongs in potato salad."

Brad's laugh, rich and genuine, drew glances from those around them. "And where do you stand on this critical theological issue?"

Anna leaned closer, pitching her voice to a dramatic whisper. "I'm firmly in the 'no relish' camp. Don't repeat that to anyone."

"Your secret is safe with me," he promised, his eyes crinkling with mirth as he spooned a helping of her potato salad onto his plate.

They moved down the buffet line, filling their plates with home-cooked offerings—June's fried chicken, Earl's wife's green bean casserole, Pastor Andrew's cornbread, and thick slices of honey-glazed ham from Emma Talbot. The abundance reflected the generosity of the community, each dish representing not just food but tradition, care, and connection.

When they reached the table where June and Katie had saved them seats, Anna found Ben Turner and his wife, Grace, already settled across from her mother.

"Saved you a spot," June said, patting the empty chairs beside her.

Brad pulled out Anna's chair before taking his seat, the simple courtesy drawing an approving grin from her mom that Anna pretended not to notice.

"This is wonderful," Brad said, surveying his heaping plate. "I don't think I've seen this much homemade food in one place since I attended potlucks at church when I lived in Lexington."

"Wait till you taste it," Ben said, pointing his fork at Brad's plate. "June's fried chicken will ruin you for all others."

Grace Turner, elegant even in casual clothes, smiled warmly. "Ben's right. June's fried chicken is literally heaven on earth. I'm Grace, by the way, Ben's better half. It's nice to finally meet you."

"Nice to meet you as well, Grace," Ben responded.

Conversation flowed around the table as they ate—stories of past community events, updates on local families, and good-natured debates about everything from the best fishing spots to whether the Founder's Day parade should include the high school marching band this year. Brad listened attentively, asking thoughtful questions and laughing at the right moments, his genuine interest in their town evident in every response.

"So, Brad," Ben said as they scraped up the last bites of their dinner, "have you figured out what you're going to do with all that land yet? A hundred acres is a lot of opportunity."

Brad set down his fork and dabbed his mouth with a napkin before answering. "I know I want to build a house eventually—Airstream living's not a forever plan—but beyond that? I'm still thinking it through."

"Well, when the time comes, let me know. I've got a buddy who owns a construction company—solid work, reasonable pricing."

"I'd appreciate that," Brad said, then turned as Mayor Wilson approached their table with an easy smile.

"Evening, everyone," the mayor greeted warmly. "Figured I'd come join the liveliest crowd in the room."

"Good to see you again, Mayor," Brad said, offering his hand.

"Call me Bill tonight," the mayor added with a wink as he settled in. "None of that formal stuff at a church potluck."

"Brad," Ben said, "why don't you tell Bill more about the idea you proposed to me yesterday."

"I'd actually enjoy that, but how about I set up a time with you, Mayor... I'm sorry, Bill. I'd like to run a few ideas by you, but tonight let's just enjoy an evening of no business talk. I'm here to get to know folks, eat too much banana pudding, and enjoy some good company." He glanced toward Anna with a quiet smile. "So far, I'm hitting all three."

Mayor Wilson clapped Brad on the shoulder. "I like your way of thinking, young man. How about ten o'clock at my place tomorrow? Bring Anna along with you; she knows where I live."

"Perfect. We'll be there."

As dinner transitioned to dessert, Brad excused himself briefly to fetch coffee for them both. The moment he was out of earshot, Katie leaned across the table.

"Okay, spill. What's happening with you two?"

Heat rose to Anna's cheeks. "We're... figuring it out."

"Figuring what out?" June blurted out. "The man looks at you like you hung the moon, Anna."

"Mom," Anna protested.

Anna traced the pattern on her napkin. "It's new. Something's there. Something good. I can feel it."

"He seems like a genuinely good man, and he's bringing out the best in you, my friend," Katie said.

Brad returned with two steaming mugs of coffee. "What did I miss?" he asked, setting one in front of Anna.

"Nothing important," she assured him, accepting the mug gratefully. "Just Katie being nosy."

"As is my sacred duty as best friend," Katie replied cheerfully.

As the evening progressed, more people stopped by their table to chat. Anna noticed how Brad engaged with each person—remembering details from previous conversations, asking follow-up questions about children or projects mentioned at the town council meeting, and offering genuine compliments on dishes they'd brought. He wasn't performing or networking; he was simply present, interested, and kind.

When the first notes of guitar music drifted in from the pavilion outside, Anna saw several couples rise from their tables and head toward the door.

"They do this every month when the weather's nice outside," June explained to Brad. "After dinner, whoever brought instruments plays for a while. People dance, children run around and have fun, and everyone lingers until the mosquitoes drive us home."

Brad's expression brightened. "That sounds great."

They joined the flow of people moving outside, where the evening had cooled to a comfortable temperature. Strings of lights illuminated the pavilion where three musicians had set up—an older man with a guitar, a middle-aged woman with a fiddle, and a teenage boy tentatively strumming a mandolin. The melody they created was simple but heartfelt, filling the dusky air with gentle harmony.

Brad led Anna toward a wooden bench near the edge of the gathering, where they could watch children darting across the lawn in pursuit of fireflies, their laughter punctuating the music like joyful percussion.

"This reminds me of summers at my grandparents' farm in Kentucky," Brad said, his voice soft with nostalgia. "We'd sit on the porch after dinner, listening to my grandfather play the harmonica while fireflies lit up the fields."

Anna smiled, picturing a young Brad, eyes wide with wonder as he watched the night fill with tiny, living lights. "Did you catch them in jars?"

"Of course. But my grandmother always made us release them before bedtime. 'They need to find their way home too,' she'd say."

The simple memory, shared in the quiet space between them, felt like a gift—another piece of himself offered without expectation. Anna found herself collecting these fragments, building a more complete picture of the man beside her with each one.

"I'm glad you agreed to be my date tonight," Brad said after a moment. His eyes, warm and sincere in the golden light, held hers.

The music shifted to a slower tune, a wistful melody. Several couples moved to the center of the pavilion, swaying together beneath the string lights.

Brad stood and extended his hand to her. "Dance with me?"

Anna hesitated only briefly before placing her hand in his. "I should warn you, I'm not very good at this."

"Neither am I," he replied with a smile that crinkled the corners of his eyes. "We can be awkward together."

He led her to a quiet corner of the pavilion, away from the main cluster of dancers but still within the gentle pool of light. His hand settled at her waist, while the other held hers against his chest. Anna rested her free hand on his shoulder, acutely aware of the solid warmth beneath her palm.

They began to move together, finding a rhythm that felt natural despite their lack of formal skill. The fiddle's mournful voice wrapped around them as they swayed.

"I'm glad I moved here," he said, his breath warm against her hair.

Anna tilted her face up to his. "I'm glad too. Though I wouldn't have believed it when you first arrived."

"No?" His smile held a hint of teasing. "You mean you weren't immediately charmed by the city boy moving in next door?"

"Not exactly," she laughed softly. "I was worried you'd change everything."

"And now?"

Anna studied his face in the gentle light—the earnest eyes that saw her so clearly, the curve of his mouth that so often quirked with humor or softened with understanding, and the quiet strength in his features that had become a source of comfort rather than concern.

"Now I think maybe some change is good," she admitted. "The right kind of change, with the right person."

"Anna," he said, her name like a prayer on his lips.

She knew what was coming—had perhaps been waiting for it since that moment by the waterfall when he'd pressed his lips to her hand with such reverence. Now, beneath a canopy of lights with the music surrounding them like a blessing, it felt inevitable.

Brad's hand released hers to gently cup her cheek, his thumb brushing across her skin with feather-light tenderness. "May I?"

Anna nodded, unable to form words past the swell of emotion in her throat. She closed her eyes as he leaned down, his breath mingling with hers for one suspended moment before his lips found hers.

The kiss was gentle, almost tentative—a question asked with reverent care. Anna answered by pressing closer, her hand sliding from his shoulder to the nape of his neck, fingers threading through the short hair there. The contact deepened between them, still sweet and unhurried, a perfect first verse in what felt like the beginning of a longer song.

When they parted, Brad rested his forehead against hers, his eyes remaining closed as though savoring the moment. Anna watched him, memorizing the peace in his expression, the slight curve of his smile, and the way his lashes fanned against his cheeks.

"I've been wanting to do that for a while now," he confessed, opening his eyes to meet her gaze.

"I'm glad you finally did," Anna admitted.

Around them, the music continued, and couples danced, and children laughed as they chased fireflies across the darkening lawn. But for Anna, the world had narrowed to just this—Brad's arms around her, the lingering warmth of his kiss on her lips, and the certainty blossoming in her heart that whatever was growing between them was worth nurturing.

Chapter 26

Anna clung to the door handle as Brad's truck rounded another hairpin curve. The mountain road stretched before them like a ribbon laid carelessly across the hills, its edges dropping away to reveal breathtaking glimpses of the New River valley below. Sunlight filtered through maple and oak canopies, casting shadowed patterns across the dashboard as they climbed higher into the hills surrounding Laurel Ridge.

"Mayor Wilson really lives all the way up here?" Brad asked as they approached yet another bend.

"He does, calls it his 'thinking place,'" Anna replied, her gaze catching on a patch of black-eyed Susans waving in the breeze beside the guardrail. "Says he needs the distance from town to gain perspective."

Brad hummed thoughtfully. "Interesting."

The road narrowed as they continued their ascent; the pavement giving way to well-maintained gravel that crunched beneath the tires. Anna rolled down her window, letting the mountain air rush in—cool and fragrant with pine and wild mint growing along the roadside. The familiar scents grounded her, calming the flutter of nerves that had accompanied her since waking.

Last night's potluck kiss lingered in her memory: the gentle pressure of Brad's lips against hers and the way his hand had cradled her face with such reverence. They hadn't talked about it afterward—hadn't needed to.

And now here they were, driving to meet the mayor about Brad's tourism ideas—business mixed with the personal in that particular small-town way that was so uniquely Laurel Ridge.

"It's just around this next bend," Anna said. "There's a wooden gate with a metal eagle on top."

The truck rounded the curve, and Brad whistled low under his breath. "Wow."

Before them stretched a wide clearing where the mountain had been sculpted into a natural terrace. At its center stood a magnificent log home—not a rustic cabin, but a grand lodge-type cabin built of massive timber and native stone. The two-story structure featured floor-to-ceiling windows that reflected the morning light and a wraparound porch adorned with hanging baskets overflowing with summer flowers. A wooden gate stood open at the entrance to the property, crowned with a wrought-iron eagle, wings outstretched as if in welcome.

Brad slowed the truck, gravel crunching under the tires as they approached. "This is... not what I expected."

"Impressive, isn't it?"

Brad parked beside a neatly maintained garden where native perennials attracted a cloud of butterflies and bees. As they stepped out of the truck, the vastness of the view struck Anna anew—rolling mountains stretched to the horizon, their blue-green ridges fading into distant mist, while the silver ribbon of the New River wound through the valley far below.

Brad stood motionless beside her, taking it all in. "This," he said finally, gesturing toward the log-and-stone architecture, the wide porch, and the perfect integration with the surrounding landscape, "this is the kind of home I imagine building one day."

The quiet longing in his voice caught her attention. Anna glanced at him, suddenly picturing what it might be like to build something permanent with someone—a home and a life.

"It's beautiful," she agreed.

The front door opened before they reached the steps, and Mayor Wilson emerged. He wore faded jeans and a chambray shirt with rolled sleeves, looking every inch the mountain man despite his silver-streaked hair and reading glasses perched atop his head.

"Welcome!" he called, descending the steps with an easy stride. "Glad you made it up okay."

"Anna's a good navigator; I would have never found your home on my own," Brad replied, extending his hand.

The mayor shook it firmly, then surprised Anna with a quick, avuncular hug. "Good to see you, honey. Your mom tells me the farm transition is going well?"

"It is," Anna nodded. "Katie's already revolutionizing our systems."

"You all are making a brilliant business move," the mayor approved. "Playing to strengths is always a good idea." He gestured toward the house. "Come on in. I've got brunch set up on the back deck."

They followed him through the home's interior, Anna's eyes widening at the soaring cathedral ceiling supported by massive timber beams. She had visited the mayor's home before, delivering potted plants and transforming his flower beds every spring and fall, but had never been inside his home. The great room featured a stone fireplace large enough to stand in, surrounded by comfortable leather furniture and rustic tables crafted from local wood. Natural light poured in through the windows, illuminating carefully curated collections of local art and historical photographs of Laurel Ridge through the decades.

"Your home is incredible," Brad said, pausing to admire a landscape painting of the New River Gorge.

"Thank you," the mayor replied, his pride evident. "My late wife designed it. She was an architect—specialized in structures that complemented their natural surroundings."

"She had a remarkable eye," Brad commented.

The mayor nodded, a brief shadow crossing his face. "That she did."

He led them through a set of French doors onto a spacious deck that seemed to hang suspended over the valley. A glass-topped table had been set with a simple brunch—a platter of assorted cheeses and meats, fresh fruit, muffins from Shirley's Bakery in town, and a pitcher of sweet tea beaded with condensation in the morning warmth.

"Please, help yourselves," Mayor Wilson said, gesturing to the chairs. "Nothing fancy, but the view makes up for it."

Anna settled into a chair that faced the panorama, momentarily speechless at the breathtaking vista. The deck provided an unobstructed view of the New River winding its way through the valley, flanked by rolling mountains that faded into blue haze at the horizon. Far below, patches of farmland created a patchwork quilt effect against the deeper green of forests.

"I can see why you built up here," she said finally. "It's like sitting on top of the world."

"My wife, God rest her soul, used to say that often. She loved living up here. We built a happy life together here."

Brad accepted a glass with thanks. "How long have you lived here?"

"Going on fifteen years now," Mayor Wilson replied, settling into his chair. "Built this home when Diane—my wife—retired from her firm. We had five good years here together before she passed." He gazed out at the view, a gentle smile softening his features. "She loved to sit right where you are, Anna, and watch the sunset every evening."

"I imagine that's spectacular to see from up here," she said.

The mayor nodded appreciatively, then straightened his shoulders, his expression brightening. "But you didn't come all the way up this mountain to hear an old man reminisce. So talk to me, Brad."

Brad reached for a muffin, breaking it apart with careful fingers. "Thanks for taking the time to meet with us, especially on a Saturday."

"Saturdays, Mondays—doesn't make much difference," the mayor said with a wave of his hand.

"I've been thinking a lot about how I can contribute to Laurel Ridge—how my skills might serve the community."

"And?" the mayor prompted, leaning forward slightly.

"And I believe there's an opportunity to enhance how visitors experience Laurel Ridge without changing the character here." Brad set down his glass and pulled an iPad from his messenger bag. "May I show you something?"

At the mayor's nod, Brad unlocked the device and slid it across the table. The screen displayed a clean, professional-looking interface featuring a stylized outline of mountains above the words "Discover Laurel Ridge."

Anna leaned closer, surprised by what she saw. This wasn't just a concept or a rough sketch—it was a fully designed prototype, detailed and polished.

"This is an app I've been working on," Brad explained, tapping the screen to demonstrate. "It serves as a digital guide to Laurel Ridge and the surrounding area, highlighting local experiences, businesses, etc."

The mayor adjusted his reading glasses, studying the interface with interest as Brad continued.

"It includes interactive trail maps with difficulty ratings and real-time updates," Brad swiped to demonstrate, "local business listings with rich profiles and seasonal offerings, a community calendar that could include direct ticket purchasing options for events, and storytelling features highlighting local history and lore."

Anna watched as Brad navigated through the app with ease, showing sections for Martha's Diner, Talbot's General Store, Adventure Tours, the church, and even Blooms Farm. Each listing featured beautiful photography, detailed descriptions, and practical information like hours, specialties, and historical significance.

"This is... remarkably thorough," the mayor said, clearly impressed. "How long have you been working on this?"

"A few days," Brad admitted.

Anna studied Brad's face as he spoke, noticing the quiet passion that animated his features. This wasn't just a casual project; he'd clearly poured significant time and expertise into it. She thought about the nights he must have spent in his Airstream refining this vision.

"The goal," Brad continued, "is to create something that benefits everyone—visitors who want real down-to-earth experiences, local businesses seeking new customers, and the town itself, which I imagine needs sustainable tourism growth."

The mayor nodded thoughtfully, continuing to explore the app. "And the business model? How would this be sustained?"

"Initially, I'd fund development and maintenance myself," Brad replied. "Long-term, it could be supported through a small commission on bookings made through the platform, plus premium placement options for businesses that want extra visibility during peak seasons."

Anna noticed something shift in Brad's demeanor—a subtle straightening of his shoulders, a clarity in his voice that suggested this was familiar territory for him. She was seeing the businessman beneath the casual exterior, the CEO who had built an entire company before arriving in Laurel Ridge.

"That's the digital side," Brad said, taking back the iPad and setting it aside. "But I'm also envisioning a physical component that would complement it—a Welcome Center for Laurel Ridge."

Anna felt her eyebrows rise. She watched as Brad pulled a sketchbook from his bag and opened it to reveal detailed drawings of a lodge-style building.

"Nothing elaborate," he explained, sliding the sketchbook toward the mayor. "But a place where visitors could orient themselves when they arrive in town. It would host brochures, maps, and information about local attractions. More importantly, it would be staffed by knowledgeable locals who could provide personalized recommendations based on visitors' interests."

The mayor leaned forward, studying the sketches. "Something like this would create several job opportunities for locals. Have you thought about where something like this could be located?"

"Ideally, just outside town near the junction of Main Street and River Road," Brad replied.

"The old Peterson lot," the mayor nodded. "The town's owned that land for years. Old man Peterson left it to the city in his will. Been trying to figure out what to do with it ever since."

Brad's sketches showed a charming timber-frame structure with a wide porch. The interior layouts included a large welcoming desk with room to display maps and brochures, a small retail area for local crafts, and a lounge where visitors could plan their stay.

Anna felt a strange mixture of emotions as she studied the drawings. Pride in Brad's vision and commitment. Admiration for his skills. But also a creeping sense of being caught off-guard—of realizing how much she still didn't know about this man who was becoming increasingly important to her.

"I see the need," the mayor said slowly, tapping his finger against the sketches. "And I agree, it could benefit the town significantly. But funding... that's the tricky part. The town budget is tight, and we've got the library roof repairs coming up soon."

Brad nodded understandingly. "Understandable," he replied. "But I may have some contacts who specialize in small-town development partnerships. I'm not saying I have answers yet, but I'm willing to explore options—and help pitch something at the next town council meeting."

There was something in his tone—a calm confidence, a casual assurance—that made Anna study him more closely. He spoke as though making things happen was second nature, as though resources and connections were simply tools at his disposal.

The mayor sat back, considering. "The app seems like a no-brainer—low risk, high potential benefit. I'd support moving forward with that immediately."

Brad nodded.

"As for the Welcome Center," the mayor continued, "I'd like to see a more formal proposal at the next council meeting. Budget estimates, timeline, staffing needs—the whole package. If you can address the funding question, even partially, it would go a long way toward gaining broader support."

"I understand," Brad nodded. "I'll put something together."

They spent the next hour discussing specifics—which businesses should be featured in the first version of the app, other potential locations for a Welcome Center, how to structure community involvement. Throughout the conversation, Anna noticed how effortlessly Brad navigated complex questions about project management, technology implementation, and business development. This wasn't just enthusiasm; it was expertise, honed through years of professional experience.

Who was this man, really? She'd known he'd founded a successful app company, but she was beginning to suspect there was much more to the story than he'd shared.

As they finished their tea and prepared to leave, the mayor walked them back through the house.

"I'm impressed, Brad," he said candidly. "Most newcomers need years to understand what makes Laurel Ridge tick. You've grasped it in months."

"I've had good teachers," Brad replied, his gaze finding Anna's for a brief, warm moment.

At the front door, the mayor shook Brad's hand firmly. "Looking forward to seeing that proposal. And Anna," he turned to her with a grandfatherly smile, "keep this one around. He's good for Laurel Ridge."

"I'll take it under advisement," she replied lightly.

Back in the truck, Brad was quiet as he navigated the winding road down the mountain. The air between them felt charged with unspoken thoughts, the gentle hum of the engine filling the silence.

"You okay?" he finally asked, glancing at her. "You're quiet."

"I'm fine," she said automatically, then reconsidered. "Just... processing, I guess."

"Processing what?"

Anna watched the passing trees, gathering her thoughts. "I didn't realize how serious you were about a welcome center. It was... unexpected."

Brad's hands flexed slightly on the steering wheel. "It evolved from our conversations about tourism. I should have shared it with you sooner—that's on me."

"It's not that," Anna said carefully. "It's just... those drawings were detailed. Professional. And the app prototype is practically finished. You've clearly been working on this for some time now."

"I have," he admitted. "It's given me focus, a purpose beyond just settling in."

Anna nodded, still processing. "The mayor was impressed. So am I. I just—" She paused, unsure how to articulate the jumble of questions forming in her mind.

"Just what?" Brad prompted gently.

"Sometimes you're a mystery," she said finally. "Like there are pieces of who you are that I haven't seen yet."

Brad was quiet for a moment, navigating another switchback before responding. "Is that a bad thing?"

"No," Anna said thoughtfully. "Not bad. Just... I guess I'm realizing how much more there is to learn about you."

The truck rounded a bend, revealing a sweeping view of the valley below. Brad slowed, then pulled into a small overlook carved into the mountainside. He cut the engine and turned to face her fully.

"What do you want to know?" he asked simply.

The directness of his question caught her off guard. "About?"

"About me. About my past. About what I did before coming here." His expression was open, unguarded. "I'm an open book, Anna..."

Anna felt a flutter in her chest at his earnestness. "It's not about specific questions. It's more... I keep glimpsing different sides of you.

The man who helps me transplant seedlings in the greenhouse. The man who bakes cookies for a church potluck. And then today, the businessman who presents polished proposals to the mayor like it's second nature."

Brad's expression softened. "All of those are me. I'm not hiding anything—I'm just... multifaceted, I guess. Like anyone."

"I know," Anna said. "And I like all those facets. I'm just still learning how they fit together. You're different from anyone I've ever met. I guess... it's a little jarring."

Brad reached across the console and took her hand, his thumb tracing gentle circles on her skin. "Then let's keep learning together."

The simple touch centered her, grounding her swirling thoughts. She looked at their joined hands—his larger one engulfing hers, warm and steady. Whatever questions lingered about his past, about his resources or his plans for Laurel Ridge, the connection between them felt real and present.

"I'd like that," she said.

Brad smiled, that genuine smile that never failed to warm her from the inside out. "For what it's worth," he said, "I'm still learning about you too. Every day I discover something new to admire."

Anna felt heat rise to her cheeks. "Like what?"

"Like how you listened at the meeting today—really listened. Like how you notice the details others miss when we're out and about—a monarch butterfly others might not notice, the subtle difference between shades of blue in your hydrangeas. Like how you have the mayor wrapped around your finger without even trying."

Anna laughed, the tension in her chest easing. "I do not."

"You absolutely do. Did you see how his whole demeanor changed when he talked to you? Pure grandfatherly affection."

"He's known me since I was born," she protested, still smiling.

"And clearly adores you," Brad said, squeezing her hand gently before releasing it to restart the truck. "As he should."

As they continued down the mountain, Anna found her thoughts settling. Yes, there was more to learn about Brad Knight—layers and complexities she was only beginning to understand. His vision for Laurel Ridge was bigger than she'd realized, his capabilities more extensive, his resources potentially far greater than he'd let on.

But at his core, he was still the man who'd held her hand under a canopy of lights, who'd kissed her with such tender care, and saw her in ways no one else ever had.

And maybe that was enough for now—to trust in what she knew while remaining open to what she had yet to discover. After all, wasn't that what any relationship required? The courage to move forward without complete certainty, faith that what was revealed would only deepen the connection rather than diminish it.

As the truck rounded the final curve and Laurel Ridge came into view in the valley below, Anna felt a sense of rightness settle over her. Whatever questions lingered, whatever the future held, this much she knew: Brad Knight was changing her world—and maybe that change was something she needed.

Chapter 27

The side-by-side utility vehicle bumped over the uneven terrain as Anna guided it toward Brad's Airstream. Daisy sat in the back, her golden coat gleaming in the August sunshine, nose tilted to catch the breeze that carried a thousand scents across the property.

Anna spotted Brad waiting outside his home-on-wheels. He wore faded jeans and a simple blue Henley pushed up at the sleeves, looking so at ease in the landscape that she couldn't imagine a time when he hadn't been part of her world. He waved as she approached, his smile brightening.

"There you are," he called as she cut the engine. "I was beginning to think you were standing me up."

"After you left, Mom wanted to chat with half the congregation at church. I should have ridden home with you," Anna explained.

Brad set the picnic basket in the back of the utility vehicle and scratched behind Daisy's ears. "No worries, I get it. The only reason I rushed off was to pack our lunch. It's nothing fancy—just some sandwiches, fruit, and water. Ready to go exploring?"

Anna patted the seat beside her. "Hop in."

Brad settled next to her, his shoulder brushing against hers in the narrow seat.

"Any particular destination in mind?" she asked, restarting the engine.

"Actually, I was hoping we could find that old apple orchard Mr. Taylor mentioned at Martha's the other day. The one he said was on the northern edge of my property."

Anna nodded, remembering the conversation. "We can try."

She steered the vehicle away from the Airstream, following a faint trail that wound through tall grass and scattered pines. Daisy sat behind them, ears flapping in the wind, occasionally releasing an excited bark when a rabbit darted across their path.

The heat of the day pressed down, but the movement of the vehicle created a cooling breeze. Anna navigated around a fallen tree, the tires bumping over exposed roots as they ventured deeper into the undeveloped portion of Brad's land.

"It's beautiful back here," Brad said, his voice filled with quiet appreciation. "So different from the cleared area around the Airstream."

"The land changes its character every few acres," Anna agreed. "That's what I love about this whole valley. You can walk ten minutes and feel like you're in an entirely different world."

They followed a grown-over winding path as it gradually climbed slightly upward, the trees growing more scattered as they reached higher ground. After maneuvering around several tight corners and a section where the path had nearly disappeared beneath encroaching vegetation, Anna slowed the vehicle.

"I think this might be it," she said, gesturing toward a clearing ahead.

As they emerged from the treeline, a small plateau stretched before them. Gnarled apple trees stood in crooked rows, their twisted branches reaching skyward like arthritic fingers. Though untended for decades, the orchard had persevered, wild and determined. The trees were spaced with the deliberate rhythm of human planning, evidence of the careful hands that had once tended this place.

Anna pulled the vehicle to a stop beneath the outstretched limbs of the largest apple tree. "June apples," she noted, surveying the different leaf patterns. "And Heritage apples, just like he said."

They climbed out, Daisy immediately darting forward to investigate new scents. Brad followed her, moving from tree to tree with childlike wonder, touching rough bark and examining clusters of tiny apples.

"The June apples are already done producing for the year. The others won't be ready until fall," Anna said, joining him. "I bet they'll taste incredible when they ripen. Old varieties often have flavors you can't find in commercial orchards."

"We'll have to come back and pick some."

Anna's attention caught on something beyond the orchard's edge. "Brad, look—there's a creek back there."

They made their way through the trees to discover a narrow stream cutting across the far edge of the orchard, its clear water bubbling over smooth stones. A natural clearing beside it created a perfect picnic spot, with flat rocks that seemed placed by design rather than chance.

"This just keeps getting better. It's like finding buried treasure," Brad said, returning to the vehicle for the picnic basket.

He then spread a checkered blanket over the flattest portion of ground, and Daisy explored the shallows of the creek. The sound of water tumbling over rocks provided a soothing backdrop as they settled onto the blanket.

Brad opened the basket, revealing neatly wrapped sandwiches, a container of fresh grapes, and bottles of water that had stayed cool in the insulated lining. "I hope turkey and Swiss is okay."

"Turkey and Swiss is one of my favorites."

The simple meal tasted extraordinary in the open air, with sunlight filtering through apple branches and the gentle music of the creek beside them. They ate while enjoying the simple pleasure of good food in a beautiful setting.

"Pastor Andrew's sermon was good today," Brad said eventually, reaching for a grape. "Recognizing blessings in unexpected places... gives me something to think about."

Anna nodded, remembering how the message had resonated with her. "I kept thinking about how much had changed in the last few weeks. The farm restructuring with Katie, Mom finally taking steps toward retirement, and you arriving next door."

"You have been my unexpected blessing. Coming to Laurel Ridge was a leap of faith, but finding such a welcome here—finding you—that's been the real gift."

The sincerity in his voice made her heart flutter.

"I've been thinking a lot about this land," Brad continued. "About what might be possible here."

"What kind of possibilities?"

He leaned back on his elbows, his expression contemplative as he gazed up. "I've had a few ideas floating around. Nothing concrete, but... I don't know, maybe some sort of retreat space? A few small glamping cabins tucked among the trees, or tiny houses for short-term rentals. Something for outdoor enthusiasts who are eager to explore the New River Gorge but still want to have a comfortable place to return to."

The ease with which he described such substantial projects caught Anna's attention. She took a sip of water, studying him over the bottle's edge. "That sounds... ambitious. And expensive."

Brad shrugged lightly. "Just ideas at this point. Trust me, I'm in no rush to do anything. I want to build a house first. And part of me worries about getting too caught up in another business and losing the peace I've found here." His gaze drifted to the creek. "But I do get restless every so often. My brain needs projects to chew on."

Anna nodded, turning his words over in her mind. It struck her how casually he spoke about developments that would cost hundreds of thousands of dollars, yet he lived in an Airstream and didn't seem to have any regular income. The disconnect nagged at her.

"How would you even manage something like that? That is, if you decide to put a few cabins somewhere out here for rent?" she asked, trying to keep her tone conversational. "It seems like a full-time job, and I thought you came here to step back from work."

Brad picked up a small twig, twirling it between his fingers. "If I did it, I'd start small. Maybe just three or four small cabins to test the concept. And I'd probably hire a company to manage it all." He glanced at her with a self-deprecating smile. "I'm learning a lot about maintenance and upkeep on something like that, and I know my limitations."

It wasn't really an answer to her question, Anna noticed. Not about how he'd fund such a project or support himself while developing it. But before she could press further, he changed direction.

"But honestly, I go back and forth on whether I want to do anything commercial with this land at all. Part of me just wants to let it be wild." His voice took on a wistful quality. "Some days that sounds like enough."

Daisy returned from her creek exploration, shaking water from her coat before flopping down beside them with a contented sigh. Anna absently stroked the dog's damp fur, considering Brad's words.

"What about you?" he asked, turning toward her. "Have you given more thought to your event venue idea?"

Anna's face brightened. "Actually, yes. I talked to Mom about it yesterday, and she loves the concept. She thinks it could be a good investment, another step up in expanding what we offer on the farm."

"That's fantastic," Brad said, his enthusiasm genuine.

"She even suggested we could start small—just clearing the area and adding a simple pavilion—then expand as bookings increase." Anna's voice quickened with excitement. "We could host spring and summer weddings when the gardens are at their peak, then shift to harvest celebrations and holiday gatherings in fall and winter."

Brad sat up straighter, energy radiating from him. "You could incorporate the natural features—that waterfall would make an incredible backdrop for photo ops." His eyes gleamed with possibility. "And imagine if we connected our properties with a footbridge over the creek. Your venue could offer packages that include hiking trails on my land, or sunset picnics at spots like this."

The image was captivating—their separate properties united in a seamless experience, each complementing the other. For a moment, Anna allowed herself to be swept away by the vision he painted.

"You could build a small chapel near the waterfall," he continued, gesturing as if mapping it out before them. "Nothing elaborate—just a simple structure with open sides and a few benches. The possibilities are endless."

Anna's practical side surfaced through her daydreaming. "That all sounds beautiful, but... the initial investment would be substantial."

Brad leaned back, his expression still animated. "There are options. Small business loans, grants for rural development. Maybe even private investors who believe in supporting local tourism." He waved a hand as though brushing away financial concerns. "The important thing is the vision. Money follows good ideas."

Again, his answer felt frustratingly vague, but his confidence was contagious. Anna found herself nodding, caught up in possibilities that had seemed like distant dreams.

They finished their meal as the conversation drifted to other topics—Katie's progress with the farm's new accounting system, the upcoming Founder's Day planning committee, a funny story about Brad's attempt to fix a leaky faucet in the Airstream. The afternoon sun shifted position, creating new patterns of light and shadow across the orchard.

As they packed up the remains of their picnic, Brad paused, his hand finding hers. "Whatever you decide with your event venue idea, it'll be beautiful," he said, his voice low and sincere. "You've got the heart and the land for it. That's more than most people start with."

The warmth of his palm against hers, the quiet conviction in his voice—it touched something deeply within Anna. She squeezed his hand, words momentarily beyond her.

On the ride back, with Brad at the wheel and Daisy dozing in the rear, Anna found her thoughts drifting not to event venues or apple orchards, but to Brad himself. For all the time they'd spent together, for all the connection that had grown between them, there remained puzzling gaps in what she knew about him.

He didn't seem to work, or maybe he did have a side business that he ran from the comfort of his Airstream. He spoke with ease and confidence about substantial projects. He lived simply but talked like someone with significant resources at his disposal. He'd mentioned selling his company but never spoke of anything beyond that.

These weren't necessarily contradictions, she reasoned. Just pieces of a puzzle she hadn't fully assembled. Brad hadn't been secretive about his past when directly asked. But she realized now that his answers, while forthcoming on the surface, left gaps. There was more to the man sitting beside her.

The side-by-side bounced over a fallen branch, jarring Anna from her thoughts. Ahead, the clearing where Brad's Airstream stood came into view, silvery in the late afternoon sun. As they approached, she noticed Earl's delivery truck parked nearby.

Brad slowed the vehicle as they entered the clearing. Earl waved from where he stood beside the Airstream, clipboard in hand.

"Afternoon, you two," he called. "Got the shipment of solar panels you ordered."

"Thanks," Brad replied. "I appreciate you bringing them out. I wasn't expecting you today."

"I had time. I stacked them all up on the side of your Airstream. You planning to power the whole county or what?" Earl's laugh was good-natured.

"Just preparing for winter," Brad explained. "Want to make sure the Airstream stays warm in case the snow flies early. There is no way I'll have a house built before the new year comes, and I have no desire to rent someplace to live in."

Earl nodded and climbed into his truck with a final wave. As he drove away, Anna turned to Brad with raised eyebrows.

"Solar panels?"

Brad shrugged, his expression neutral. "I plan on using solar power for the barn eventually. Seems practical."

It was a reasonable answer, and yet Anna felt the same nagging sense that there was more beneath the surface.

As they said their goodbyes, Brad's kiss was gentle against her cheek, his hand lingering at her waist. "I enjoyed today."

Anna smiled up at him, her heart pulling in two directions at once. "I enjoyed it too. Next Sunday after church, it's my turn to plan our adventure."

His eyes crinkled at the corners. "It's a date."

Driving the side-by-side back toward the farmhouse, Anna found herself thinking more and more about Brad and the questions tumbling around in her mind.

It wasn't that she distrusted Brad. Everything important between them felt genuine. The way he listened, his patience, and his respect for her and the community. Those things couldn't be faked.

And yet, a whisper of unease had settled in her heart alongside the growing warmth of deeper feelings. Who was Brad Knight, really? And why did it seem he was holding part of himself back from her?

Chapter 28

Anna squinted at the wholesaler's website on her laptop screen, trying to focus on the spring bulb pricing. The numbers kept swimming together as she scrolled through varieties of tulips and daffodils. Dutch Master. Golden Harvest. Tahiti. Mount Hood. The names blurred into a jumble as Katie's voice faded into the background noise.

"So I've completely reorganized our shipping system," Katie was saying. "We can save at least fifteen percent on packaging costs if we order in bulk for the whole season instead of—Anna? Are you even listening?"

Anna blinked, forcing herself back to the present moment. "I'm sorry. What were you saying about packaging?"

Katie leaned back in her chair, the ancient wood creaking beneath her weight. "Okay, spill it. You've been staring at the same page for twenty minutes, and you haven't written down a single thing in your planting notebook."

"I'm just tired," Anna said, rubbing her eyes. The office smelled of fresh paint and new filing cabinets—physical evidence of the changes taking place at Blooms Farm. Just last week, this had been a cluttered spare bedroom. Now it housed matching desks, Katie's ergonomic chair, and a wall of labeled bins containing everything from seed catalogs to customer contracts.

"Tired people don't look like they're trying to solve calculus problems while ordering tulip bulbs," Katie replied, reaching for her coffee mug. She took a sip and grimaced. "Cold. Want me to make a fresh pot?"

Anna nodded, grateful for the momentary reprieve. As Katie disappeared toward the kitchen, Anna closed her laptop and pressed her palms against her eyes. The questions that had been brewing for the past couple of days about Brad refused to be silenced.

Who was he really?

The Brad she knew for sure baked cookies for church potlucks, helped with seedlings in the greenhouse, and knew exactly how to calm Daisy during thunderstorms. But there was another Brad—one who casually discussed business investments, who designed professional apps and welcome centers, and who spoke of connecting with "associates" for funding as though it were as simple as making a phone call.

Two halves of the same person, but the edges didn't quite match up.

Katie returned with two steaming mugs, setting one beside Anna. The rich aroma of fresh coffee filled the small space.

"Okay," Katie said, settling back into her chair. "I know that look. This isn't about flower bulbs."

Anna wrapped her hands around the warm ceramic, drawing comfort from its solidity. "Can we take a break? I need some girl talk."

"Of course. What's going on?"

Anna hesitated, uncertain how to voice the confusion swirling inside her. "It's about Brad."

"Trouble in paradise already?" Katie asked, but her teasing tone faded when she saw Anna's expression. "Hey, what's wrong?"

"I like him. I really do." Anna traced the rim of her mug with one finger. "But lately... I keep wondering. Who is he really?"

Katie tilted her head. "What do you mean?"

"He talks about funding massive projects like its nothing. He designs professional apps. He builds business proposals with the confidence of someone who's done it a hundred times." Anna looked up, meeting Katie's gaze. "And whenever I ask about his past, he answers, but... it's like he's skimming the surface."

"Most guys aren't great at opening up," Katie offered.

"It's not that." Anna shook her head. "Brad is open about his feelings. But when it comes to his career, his resources... he's vague. The other day, he was talking about building rental cabins on his property like it was as simple as planting petunias."

"He did sell a successful app," Katie reminded her. "Maybe he has savings."

"Enough to live on without working? To fund potential cabin developments?" Anna set down her mug. "What do I really know about him? About his life before Laurel Ridge?"

Katie considered this, tapping her pen against her notepad. "Have you asked him directly?"

"Sort of. He answers, but somehow I still end up with more questions... and I don't want to be pushy or look like I'm being... nosy." Anna sighed. "I sound paranoid, don't I?"

"Not paranoid. Cautious. You've been hurt before. It makes sense you'd want to be certain."

"It's not that I don't trust him. I do. But there's something... missing."

Katie studied her for a moment, then swiveled toward her computer. "I'll Google him... probably won't find anything, but hey, it'll be fun. She wiggled her fingers above the keyboard.

"No! That's..." Anna started to protest, then stopped herself. Was it really so wrong to seek information? "That feels invasive."

"It's not like I'm hacking his email," Katie reasoned. "Just public information anyone could find."

Anna hesitated, torn between curiosity and principle. "I don't know... Googling him just feels creepy."

But Katie had already opened her browser. "What was his app called again? LocalLens?"

Anna nodded reluctantly.

Katie typed quickly: "LocalLens travel app Brad Knight."

For a moment, they both stared at the screen as the search engine processed the request. Then the results populated, and Anna felt the air leave her lungs.

The top headline glared back at them: "LocalLens Sold to Expedia for $150 Million—Meet Founder Brad Knight."

"One hundred and fifty million dollars?" Katie whispered, her voice rising to a squeak on the final word.

Anna couldn't speak. Her eyes fixed on the accompanying photograph—Brad standing on a stage, clean-shaven in an impeccably tailored suit, arms spread wide as he addressed a massive audience. He looked confident, polished, and utterly at home in that world of wealth and influence.

Katie clicked the article, and more images appeared.

Brad receiving an award for innovation.

Brad at a tech conference with Silicon Valley icons.

Brad's profile in Forbes "30 Under 30."

"Oh my goodness," Katie murmured, scrolling through the article. "Listen to this: Knight's remarkable journey from college dropout to tech mogul began in his University of Colorado dorm room, where he coded the first version of LocalLens after a disappointing spring break trip. Six years later, his company employs over two hundred people and serves millions of users worldwide."

Anna barely heard her. Her mind raced backward, replaying every conversation, every moment with Brad in this new context. His casual confidence with the mayor. His effortless design skills. The way he spoke of business strategies and funding sources.

It wasn't just that he'd had success. It was the scale of it. Brad wasn't just some app developer who'd done well. He was... enormous. A tech mogul. A millionaire.

And he'd never said a word.

"There's more," Katie continued, clicking through to another article. "Knight shocked the tech world by announcing his departure from LocalLens following its acquisition by Expedia. Sources close to the entrepreneur cite health concerns following a cardiac episode earlier this year, though Knight himself has declined to comment on his future plans."

Katie opened another tab, revealing a photo of Brad with a beautiful dark-haired woman at a charity gala. "Looks like he was dating someone in the tech world too—Michelle Reeves, VP at some social media company."

Anna stared at the woman—elegant, sophisticated, and perfectly at ease in Brad's world of success and wealth. Something cold and heavy settled in her stomach.

"Why wouldn't he tell me all this?" she whispered, more to herself than to Katie.

Katie closed the browser, turning to face Anna fully. "He said coming here was a fresh start."

"But this isn't some minor detail he forgot to mention," Anna said, her voice catching. "This is his entire life. His identity."

"Is it, though?" Katie challenged gently. "Or is it just his past?"

Anna pushed back from the desk, needing space to breathe as emotions crashed over her. Shock gave way to confusion, then to a sharp, unexpected pain. Not because Brad had money—that didn't matter to her. But he hadn't trusted her enough to share this fundamental truth about himself.

Or had he been right not to? A new, more painful question surfaced: what could a tech millionaire possibly see in a small-town flower farmer with no formal education beyond high school? Was she just a quaint diversion? A simple girl for a man tired of complexity?

"Anna, talk to me," Katie urged, concern etching her features.

"I feel so stupid," Anna said, her voice barely audible. "All this time, I've been worrying about my financial projections for the venue idea, talking about applying for a small business loan. And he's sitting there, probably thinking how adorably naïve I am."

"That's not fair," Katie protested. "He doesn't seem like that type of person."

"How do we know?" Anna countered, tears pricking her eyes. "The Brad we thought we knew doesn't exist. The real Brad Knight is... is..." She gestured helplessly at the computer screen.

"The real Brad Knight is the man who's been here the past several weeks," Katie said firmly. "The one who helps on the farm, who sits with you and your mom at church, and who looks at you like you're the most fascinating person he's ever met."

Anna shook her head, unable to reconcile the images in her mind. Brad helping transplant seedlings in her greenhouse. Brad on a technology conference stage, commanding the attention of thousands.

"I just don't understand why he'd hide something this significant," she said. "What could he see in someone like me?"

"That's your insecurity talking, not reality. Has Brad ever, even once, made you feel like you weren't good enough?"

"No," Anna admitted. "But maybe that's what makes it worse. He's been so... perfect. Like he was playing a role."

"Or maybe," Katie suggested, "he's just been himself. The version of himself he wants to be now."

Anna fell silent, considering this possibility. Could it be that simple? That Brad had left behind not just a stressful career but an entire identity that no longer fit?

She remembered their conversation by the waterfall, how he'd spoken of finding purpose beyond achievement. How he'd described his former life as "hollow success." At the time, she'd assumed he meant moderate success, not... this.

"I don't know what to think anymore," Anna said, wiping at a stray tear. "I thought I was getting to know him, but there's this whole other life he never shared."

"You need to talk to him," Katie suggested. "Ask him directly about all this."

"And say what? Hey, I Googled you and discovered you're secretly worth millions."

"Why not? Honesty goes both ways, Anna."

She paced the small office, arms wrapped protectively around herself. "I'm not ready for that conversation. I need time to think."

"Don't overthink this," Katie warned. "Money is just a thing... it comes and goes. It doesn't define who someone is."

"It's not about the money," Anna insisted, though part of her wondered if that was entirely true. "It's about trust. About whether anything between us has been real."

Katie sighed, recognizing the stubborn set of Anna's jaw. "Just promise me you won't make any decisions while you're upset. Sleep on it, at least."

Anna nodded, though her mind was already churning with more doubts and questions. Who was the real Brad Knight? The gentle, thoughtful man who'd kissed her beneath the string lights at the church potluck? Or the polished tech mogul who commanded millions with a signature?

And more troubling still: which version could possibly want someone like her?

What could she possibly offer a man who had already conquered the world?

Chapter 29

Brad looked up as Anna crossed the creek and approached his Airstream, his expression brightening in that now-familiar way that usually made her heart skip.

Now, it just made her chest ache.

She cut the engine, sitting motionless for a moment. From the passenger seat, Daisy whined softly, ears flattening against her head as she sensed the tension radiating from her owner.

"Stay, girl," Anna murmured, patting the dog's head before stepping out.

Brad was already rising from his chair, with that easy smile still playing on his lips. "Hey, you," he called. "This is a nice surprise. I was just—"

The words died on his lips as she approached. Whatever he saw in her face made him stop, his smile fading into concern.

"Anna? What's wrong?"

She stopped a few feet away, maintaining a distance that felt both physical and emotional. The late afternoon breeze ruffled her hair, carrying the scent of pine and freshly cut lumber from the half-built shed near his Airstream.

"Brad Knight," she said, her voice steadier than she felt. "Founder and CEO of LocalLens. The travel app that revolutionized tourism experiences across thirty countries. Sold to Expedia for one hundred and fifty million dollars."

She watched his expression shift—surprise, then recognition, then a quiet resignation. Not denial. Not even an attempt at it.

"Forbes 30 Under 30," she continued, each word another stone dropping between them. "Featured speaker at Silicon Valley tech conferences. Girlfriend Michelle Reeves, VP of some big social media company."

The last part slipped out before she could stop it. Brad's eyebrows drew together slightly.

"Ex-girlfriend," he corrected softly. "And that was many months ago."

"That's what you're focusing on?" Anna asked, wrapping her arms around herself despite the warmth of the evening. "Not the fact that you've been hiding your entire identity since the day we met?"

Brad ran a hand through his hair. "I wasn't hiding. I just... wasn't leading with it."

A humorless laugh escaped her. "Not leading with it? Brad, you're a millionaire. A tech celebrity. That's not minor details you forgot to mention—that's your entire life."

"My former life," he corrected, his voice gentle but firm. He took a step toward her, then stopped when she instinctively backed away. Hurt flashed across his features. "Anna, please. Can we sit down and talk about this?"

"Why?" she asked, hating the slight tremor that had entered her voice. "So you can explain why you thought it was okay to let me believe you were just... what? Some guy with a good app idea who did okay for himself? To let me ramble on about small business loans for the venue idea while you probably had enough in your savings account to fund the whole thing ten times over?"

Brad sighed, a deep sound that seemed to come from somewhere beyond simple frustration. "That's exactly why I didn't tell you. Because I wanted to be seen as a person, not a bank account. Not a success story or a potential investor."

"You didn't trust me enough to let me decide that for myself."

"It wasn't about trust, Anna."

"Then what was it about?" she demanded, her voice rising slightly. "Because from where I'm standing, it looks an awful lot like you were playing some kind of role. Country Living: The Brad Knight Edition. Slumming it in an Airstream, pretending to be just another guy starting over."

The accusation landed hard. She could see it in the tightening of his jaw, the slight flinch around his eyes.

"I've never pretended with you," he said quietly. "Not once."

"But you haven't been honest either."

"I told you I founded a successful app company. I told you I sold it and moved here for a fresh start after health concerns."

"You conveniently left out the scale of that success." Anna's throat felt tight. "You made it sound like you'd done reasonably well, not that you could buy half the county if you wanted to."

Brad took a deep breath, his shoulders rising and falling with the effort of maintaining his composure. "Sit with me, please? I want to explain, and I'd rather not do it standing in my yard like we're having some kind of showdown."

The reasonable request only fueled her frustration. Here he was, calm and collected, while she felt like she was coming apart at the seams. But she nodded stiffly and followed him to the wooden table and chairs near the Airstream's entrance. Daisy had jumped out of the utility vehicle and now sat at a distance, watching them with anxious eyes.

Brad sat across from her, his hands flat on the table between them. Up close, she could see the tension in his shoulders, the careful way he was controlling his breathing. This wasn't as easy for him as he made it appear.

"When I came to Laurel Ridge," he began, his voice low and measured, "I was running from more than just a stressful job. I was running from a life that had consumed me so completely I didn't recognize myself anymore."

Anna remained silent, watching him.

"The Brad Knight you read about—the tech mogul, the conference speaker, the CEO—that person was hollow inside. Everything revolved around the next milestone, the next acquisition, the next round of funding... and the next buck in the bank. I hadn't taken a real day off in years. I'd lost touch with my family and with any friends who weren't in the industry. Even Michelle—" He paused, his mouth twisting slightly. "She was with me because of what I represented, not who I was. When I got sick and then sold the company and bought the property here, she was gone the minute I told her I was beginning a new life."

Despite herself, Anna felt a twinge of sympathy.

"My cardiomyopathy was stress-induced; I already told you all of that," he continued. "The doctor told me if I kept living the way I was, I wouldn't see forty. So, I made a choice. I sold everything—the condo, the cars, and the vacation property in Aspen I hadn't used in four years. I put most of the money into long-term investments and charitable foundations. And I came here to figure out who Brad Knight really is, underneath all the success and status."

He looked up, meeting her eyes directly. "I didn't tell you about the money because it's the least important thing about me. And because the moment people know, everything changes. They see dollar signs instead of a person. They filter everything I say and do through the lens of wealth."

"That's not fair," Anna said, finding her voice. "You didn't give me the chance to prove I wouldn't do that."

"You're right," he acknowledged. "That's on me. But, Anna, can you honestly say nothing would have been different if you'd known from day one?"

The question hung between them. Anna wanted to insist that nothing would have changed, but she wasn't entirely sure. Would she have been as forthright about her farm struggles? Would she have offered herself so freely? Would she have felt as comfortable inviting him to church potlucks and town meetings?

"That's not the point," she said finally. "The point is, you made that decision for me. You got to know the real me while only showing me pieces of yourself."

Brad's expression softened with regret. "I showed you the parts that matter. The parts I'm trying to build a new life around."

"But I told you everything," Anna said, her voice breaking slightly. "I let you see all of me. And the whole time, I didn't even know who I was letting in."

"You know me better than anyone in Laurel Ridge," Brad insisted. "Better than anyone has in years."

Anna shook her head, tears threatening to spill over. "How can I believe that? How can I trust anything now?"

The question landed like a physical blow. Brad's face paled slightly, his hands drawing back from the table's center.

"I didn't hide anything to manipulate you," he said softly. "I just didn't talk about it because I wanted something real, without all the noise that comes with who I used to be."

"But that's still part of who you are," Anna pointed out. "You can't just erase your past, Brad. It shaped you. It gave you opportunities and perspectives I'll never have."

"Is that what this is really about?" he asked suddenly, his gaze sharpening. "The difference in our backgrounds?"

Anna looked away, uncomfortable with how close he'd come to a truth she hadn't fully acknowledged even to herself. "No. It's about honesty."

"Anna." The gentleness in his voice compelled her to meet his eyes again. "Talk to me. Please."

She swallowed hard, feeling exposed and vulnerable. "Why would someone like you be interested in someone like me?"

"What do you mean, 'someone like you'?" Brad asked, his brow furrowing.

"You know what I mean," Anna said, heat rising to her cheeks. "You've traveled the world. You've built something that changed how millions of people experience travel. You've given TED talks and been featured in magazines and dated sophisticated women who understand your world." She gestured helplessly. "And I'm just... me. A small-town flower farmer who's never lived anywhere else. Who's only been to three states in her entire life. Who wouldn't know the first thing about the world you come from."

Understanding dawned in Brad's eyes, followed quickly by something that looked like pain. "Anna, that's exactly why—"

"Don't," she interrupted, suddenly unable to bear whatever rationalization he might offer. "Please don't tell me some story about how my simplicity is refreshing or how you admire my authenticity or whatever else you might say to make this seem like less than what it is."

"And what exactly do you think this is?" Brad asked, his voice carefully controlled.

"I don't know anymore," Anna admitted. "Maybe a diversion. Maybe some kind of... experiment in normal living before you go back to your real world. Maybe you even believe you're serious about me, and building a new life here. But how can I possibly compete with everything you left behind?"

"It's not a competition," Brad said firmly. "And I'm not going back to Colorado or the old lifestyle I had. This is my life now."

"For how long?" Anna challenged. "Until you get bored? Until you realize there's only so much excitement to be found in a small town where the biggest event of the year is the Founder's Day parade?"

Brad's expression hardened slightly. "You're not giving me much credit here."

"And you didn't give me enough credit to handle the truth," she countered.

They sat in tense silence for a moment, the only sound the gentle rustle of leaves from the trees overhead as the evening breeze passed through.

"I was trying to live honestly," Brad said finally. "Not by reciting my résumé—but by being present. With you."

The sincerity in his voice made her heart twist painfully. Part of her wanted to believe him, to accept his explanation and move forward. But the larger part felt too shaken, too uncertain of everything that had passed between them.

"I need time," she said, standing abruptly. "I can't... I can't process all of this right now."

Brad rose as well, distress evident in his features. "Anna, please. Can we talk this through?"

"Not right now." She backed away, needing physical distance. "I need to think."

He didn't try to stop her as she turned and walked back to the utility vehicle. Daisy trotted after her, tail low, sensing her distress. As she started the engine and pulled away, she caught a glimpse of Brad in the rearview mirror, standing motionless, watching her leave.

The drive back to the farmhouse passed in a blur. Anna's vision swam with unshed tears as she navigated the familiar path across the property. By the time she pulled up beside the house, her hands were shaking on the steering wheel.

Inside, she found June and Katie at the kitchen table, papers spread between them as they worked on financials. They looked up in unison as she entered, their expressions shifting immediately to concern.

"Honey, what's wrong?" June asked, rising from her chair.

Anna stood in the doorway, suddenly unable to hold back the tears that had been threatening since she left Brad's. "I can't do this," she said, her voice breaking. "The venue idea. The app collaboration. All of it. I need to put everything on hold."

Katie and June exchanged a quick glance.

"What happened?" Katie asked.

"I just need some...," Anna said, wiping roughly at her cheeks. "I don't even know what I'm doing anymore."

June crossed the room and wrapped her arms around her daughter. "Whatever it is, it's all going to be okay," she murmured, stroking Anna's hair like she had when Anna was a child.

Anna allowed herself to be held, the familiar comfort of her mother's embrace providing a momentary harbor in the storm of her emotions. But even as she stood there, she couldn't escape the hollow feeling in her chest—the sense that something precious had been lost before she'd fully understood its value.

Chapter 30

Anna's hands trembled as she eased the delicate root ball of a celosia seedling into the waiting potting soil. Dirt clung to her fingers, lodged beneath her nails. The humidity of the greenhouse wrapped around her like a weighted blanket, both comforting and suffocating.

"...and Mrs. Finley said she'd need at least twenty arrangements for the church anniversary next month," June was saying, her voice floating through the greenhouse like distant music Anna couldn't quite focus on. "Anna? Did you hear what I said about the centerpieces?"

"Hmm? Oh, yes. Centerpieces. For Mrs. Finley." Anna nodded absently, reaching for another plant.

Katie and June exchanged glances across the potting table. Katie raised her eyebrows meaningfully, and June gave a small nod in response.

"You know," Katie said lightly, "I was thinking about those new dahlia varieties for fall. The catalog says they need to be ordered by next week if we want them for the September plantings."

"That's fine," Anna murmured. "Whatever you think is best."

Another look passed between Katie and June.

Anna didn't notice their silent communication. Her mind kept returning to Brad's face—the hurt in his eyes when she'd backed away from him yesterday, the careful control in his voice as he tried to explain. The moment replayed in her mind like an endless loop: "I wasn't hiding. I just... wasn't leading with it."

Was that really so wrong? The question had haunted her through a sleepless night. Had Brad actually lied to her? Or had he simply chosen which parts of his story to emphasize? Everyone did that, didn't they? No one offered his or her complete history all at once.

But $150 million wasn't just any detail.

She pressed the soil too firmly around the seedling, crushing its delicate stem. "Shoot," she muttered, lifting the damaged plant. Another casualty of her distraction.

"That's the third one you've mangled," June observed mildly. "Maybe you should take a break."

"I'm fine," Anna insisted, reaching for another seedling.

"Fine doesn't usually have you snapping the heads off perfectly good plants," June replied. She set down her trowel and wiped her hands on her apron. "Spill it. I haven't seen you like this since your ex took that job in California and gave you no warning. Don't pretend nothing's wrong. I've been quiet and have not pressed you about what's bothering you for long enough. Now talk."

The maternal directness hit like cold water. Anna looked up, startled by her mother's tone—gentle but brooking no argument. June Mitchell rarely pushed, but when she did, there was no deflecting.

"I..." Anna's voice caught. She set down the trowel, afraid she might break something else. "It's complicated."

"Life usually is," June agreed. "But keeping it bottled up never helps. What's going on with Brad?"

"How did you know it was about Brad?"

"Mother's intuition," June said. "And because you two have been practically inseparable for weeks, and suddenly you're in here destroying innocent plants."

Katie leaned forward, resting her forearms on the potting table. "Tell her, Anna."

Anna looked between them, feeling cornered but also a bit relieved. The heaviness of carrying her confusion alone suddenly seemed unbearable.

"I found out who Brad really is," she said finally, the words spilling out in a rush. "Or was, I guess. Before he came here."

June's eyebrows lifted slightly. "And who is that?"

"He founded a company called LocalLens. It was a travel app. A really successful one. But you knew all that." Anna paused, swallowing hard. "He sold it to Expedia for $150 million."

June's expression remained unchanged. "I see."

"No, Mom, you don't see," Anna continued, the words coming faster now. "He's not just some guy who did okay in tech. He was huge. Like giving TED talks huge. Speaking at major conferences. Being profiled in Forbes. Dating this beautiful social media executive. That kind of huge."

June glanced at Katie. "And you knew about this?"

Katie nodded. "We looked him up yesterday. After Anna had been worrying about... well, about the gaps in what she knew."

"We Googled him," Anna admitted, heat rising to her cheeks. "And found all these articles and photos. It was like discovering he was a different person. A person he never told me about."

"Oh, for heaven's sake! You both Googled him? Okay... that's beside the point. Did you talk to him about whatever it is that you discovered?" June inquired.

"Yes. I drove over there yesterday evening and confronted him."

"Confronted," June repeated, the word hanging in the humid air. "That sounds combative."

Anna flinched slightly. "I was upset."

"What did he say?"

Anna sank onto a nearby stool, suddenly exhausted. "He didn't deny anything. He said he wasn't hiding, just 'not leading with it.' That he wanted to be seen for who he is, not his bank account or his past success."

"And you don't believe him?"

"I don't know what to believe," Anna admitted. "He had a whole life he never talked about. A massive, successful life that he just... left behind. I mean... who does that? And he never thought that was important to mention?"

June was quiet for a moment. "When your father left," she began carefully, "I didn't tell anyone for almost two months."

The unexpected reference to her father caught Anna off guard. "What? Why not?"

"Because I was trying to figure out who I was without him," June said simply. "I knew the minute I told people, I'd become 'poor June Mitchell, abandoned wife.' Everyone would see me through that very narrow tunnel. Their pity, their assumptions, their well-meaning advice—it would all be colored by that one fact."

Anna stared at her mom, seeing something new in the familiar face. "I never knew that."

"Those two months were precious to me," June continued. "They gave me space to grieve privately, to find my footing, to decide who I wanted to be on the other side of that pain."

The parallel was unmistakable. Anna felt a shift in her understanding, like a kaleidoscope turning to reveal a new pattern from the same pieces.

"Are you saying Brad was right to keep his past from me?" she asked.

"I'm saying sometimes people don't tell you everything right away because they're still trying to figure out if you'll love the real them or the version everyone else wants to see," June replied. "The question isn't whether he should have told you sooner. The question is why it matters so much to you that he didn't."

The simple observation landed with a thud. Why did it matter so much? Anna had been so caught up in the feeling of betrayal that she hadn't stopped to examine its roots.

"I guess..." she began hesitantly, "I felt that if he didn't trust me with that part of himself, that maybe nothing between us was real. Maybe I was just... I don't know, some quaint diversion for a bored millionaire."

"Has Brad ever made you feel that way?" June asked gently. "In any of your interactions, has he ever treated you as less than his equal?"

"No," Anna admitted. "Never."

"He sees something in you, Anna," Katie added. "Something real. You told me once that no one's ever made you feel seen and heard the way he has. Don't let fear make you forget that."

Anna wrapped her arms around herself, suddenly cold despite the greenhouse heat. "But why would someone like him want someone like me? He could have anyone. Someone sophisticated, educated, worldly."

"And yet, he chose you," June pointed out. "Maybe that should tell you something about what he values."

The simple observation struck Anna speechless. She'd been so focused on what Brad hadn't shared that she'd overlooked everything he had shown her—his appreciation for her knowledge, his respect for her work, and his genuine interest in her thoughts and dreams.

"I think," Katie ventured carefully, "that you're afraid of not being enough. Just like when your dad left, and again when Ryan took that job without even considering you. You assume there must be something fundamentally lacking in you that makes people leave."

The observation was so accurate it stung. Anna felt tears prick her eyes.

"So when you discovered Brad had this whole other life," Katie continued, "it confirmed your worst fear—that you're just temporary. That once he remembers who he really is, he'll leave too."

A tear escaped, trailing down Anna's cheek. "Maybe."

June moved around the table and placed her hands on Anna's shoulders. "Sweetheart, Brad's past doesn't diminish who he is now. And it certainly doesn't diminish who you are together."

"But what if he gets bored?" Anna whispered, giving voice to her deepest fear. "What if this is just... a sabbatical from his real life?"

"What makes you think his life here isn't real?" June countered. "I've watched that young man these past few weeks. The way he engages with everyone, how he listens, and the care he takes with his plans or ideas or thoughts he has about adding to the value of our community. That's not someone playing tourist. That's someone putting down roots."

Anna wiped her cheek with the back of her hand, leaving a smudge of potting soil. "He says he's not going back. That this is his life now."

"Do you believe him?"

Did she? The question echoed in Anna's mind. Brad had been nothing but genuine in every interaction. He'd shown up consistently, with kindness and integrity. He'd integrated himself into the community, formed real relationships, and demonstrated commitment to Laurel Ridge's future.

The only thing he hadn't done was lead with his resume.

"I want to," she admitted finally. "I'm just scared."

"Love always involves risk," June said softly. "The question is whether he's worth the risk."

"You're not the only one who's afraid, you know," Katie added. "Think about it from Brad's perspective. He had a life where people valued him for his success, his money, and his status. Then, when he had his health scare and decided to change directions, his girlfriend left him. What lesson do you think that taught him?"

The realization struck Anna with surprising force. Brad had been abandoned too—not by a parent, but by someone who should have loved him, someone who'd chosen status and wealth over the actual person. No wonder he'd been cautious about sharing that part of himself.

"That people only want him for what he represents," she whispered, "not who he really is."

"Exactly," Katie nodded. "So maybe he wanted to make sure you were falling for Brad the man, not Brad the millionaire."

Anna stared at her dirt-covered hands, seeing them as a metaphor for her own messiness and her own imperfections. Brad had never seemed to mind those imperfections. In fact, he'd celebrated them.

"I think I messed up," she said finally. "I was so caught up in feeling deceived that I didn't stop to consider why he might have held back."

"It's not too late to fix it," June said, squeezing her shoulder gently.

"What if it is?" Anna looked up, vulnerability raw in her expression. "I said some pretty harsh things. I practically accused him of slumming it here, of playing some kind of role."

"Then you apologize," June said simply. "You tell him you were scared and reacted from that fear. And then you listen—really listen—to what he has to say."

Anna nodded slowly, something like hope flickering in her chest. It wasn't a complete resolution, not yet. There were still questions to answer, and fears to face. But the fog of confusion had begun to lift, allowing her to see the situation—and herself—more clearly.

"Not everyone leaves, Anna," June said softly. "Some people stay. Some people choose you, not because they have to, but because they want to. Brad might be one of those people—if you let him. Don't let the men who walked away—your father, Ryan—become the standard you measure everyone else by."

Chapter 31

"So when are you planning to go public with this Laurel Ridge project? The publicity could be huge. Just think—Brad Knight's triumphant return to the tech world after his mysterious disappearance. We could probably get you on the cover of—"

"Mark, stop." Brad pushed back from his laptop. Papers and file folders were scattered on the surrounding table—sketches of the Welcome Center, tourism data, and preliminary cost analyses. "That's not happening."

"I don't understand. You built an entire prototype app. You've drawn up plans for a physical welcome center. This is classic Knight innovation—solving problems people don't even know they have."

Brad pinched the bridge of his nose, gazing across his property toward the creek that separated his land from Blooms Farm. From where he sat, he could just make out the colorful patches of zinnias and cosmos. Anna would be there now, maybe cutting flowers for today's orders.

"That's not the point of this," Brad said finally, his voice quiet but firm. "I'm not doing this to be seen or to build another massive corporation. I'm doing it to serve and to put my skills to use. To build something meaningful for a community I care about."

"Brad, listen to yourself," Mark countered. "You're sitting on a fortune and designing tourism apps for some Appalachian backwater? You could be—"

"Living exactly the life I want," Brad interrupted. "Mark, I appreciate your friendship. I do. You're one of the few people from the old days who still calls just to check in. But I need you to understand that I'm not coming back. Not to that life."

A sigh crackled through the speaker. "Look, I get the health scare was serious. I get needing a break. But this... this feels like you're burying yourself."

The words stung more than Brad wanted to admit, especially after the confrontation with Anna. Her wounded expression flashed in his memory—the betrayal in her eyes when she'd listed off facts about his past life as though reading an indictment.

"I'm not buried," Brad replied, his tone softening. "I'm planted. There's a difference."

"Fine, fine," Mark relented. "But at least tell me you're not leaving all that money sitting in low-yield accounts. The market's been—"

"I have a financial team that handles all that." Brad absentmindedly shuffled the papers before him. "Most of it's in long-term trusts, anyway."

"Right. The Knight Foundation for Digital Access," Mark recited. "Another brilliant idea nobody knows came from you because you insisted on anonymity."

Brad glanced at his watch. "I've got to go, Mark. Send over those tourism trend analyses when you get a chance, will you? And... thanks. For understanding. Or trying to, anyway."

"Sure thing, buddy. Just... don't disappear on us completely, okay? Some of us actually miss your insufferable perfectionism."

Brad smiled despite himself. "Take care, Mark."

He ended the call and set his phone on the table. The sudden silence felt heavy.

Leaning back in his chair, Brad closed his eyes against the bright morning light. His chest tightened as Anna's words echoed through his memory: "Country Living: The Brad Knight Edition. Slumming it in an Airstream, pretending to be just another guy starting over."

The accusation had landed like a physical blow—not because it was true, but because it revealed how completely she had misunderstood his intentions.

He hadn't chosen silence out of shame. He'd chosen it out of a desperate need for freedom.

After years of being introduced by his net worth, reduced to headlines, and judged before he could even speak, Brad had just wanted to be seen as a man. A neighbor. A friend. Maybe, if life was generous, something more.

He opened his eyes and stared at the sketches for the Welcome Center. The design was simple, practical, but lovingly detailed—the kind of place that would serve Laurel Ridge for generations. He'd poured genuine care into every line, imagining visitors finding authentic experiences, locals finding employment, and the town finding sustainable growth without losing its character.

And he'd imagined sharing it all with Anna.

Brad gathered the papers into a neat stack, trying to impose order on at least one aspect of his suddenly chaotic life. The wind caught a loose sheet, sending it fluttering toward the edge of the table. He lunged to catch it, his fingers closing around the page just before it could escape.

It was the sketch of the waterfall and event venue idea for Anna's property—the one she dreamed about. He'd drawn it from memory after their visit there, capturing the natural clearing, the tumbling water, and the perfect view of the distant mountains. In the margin, he'd scribbled notes about solar-powered path lighting, a timber frame pavilion with retractable sides for all-weather use, and locally quarried stone for the foundation.

Dreams on paper. Dreams she'd shared with him.

Brad carefully set the sketch atop the others. The hollow feeling in his chest expanded, threatening to swallow him whole.

He hadn't hidden his past to deceive. He hadn't talked about it to protect something sacred: the chance to live as himself—not as someone's opportunity or someone's threat.

And now, maybe he'd lost Anna because of it.

But even as he grieved the distance between them, he stood by his choice. People didn't need to know everything to know him. His story was his. And he was more than what he had built.

Brad didn't plan to make a grand announcement or out himself to the town. He would continue showing up with humility, service, and kindness. He believed actions revealed a man's character far more than résumés.

Still, he missed her. And he wondered if she'd ever see why he had made the choice he did.

Closing his laptop with a soft click, he stood and stretched, his body stiff from sitting for so long. Restlessness propelled him toward the creek that formed the boundary between his property and Blooms Farm.

The path was becoming well-worn now, evidence of his frequent journeys to and from Anna's world. Wild blackberry bushes lined part of the creek bank, their fruit ripening in the July sun. He'd been teaching himself to identify the native plants—had even bought a field guide from Talbot's General Store. He knew the difference now between the high-bush blueberries and the potentially toxic pokeweed berries that casual observers might confuse.

Small knowledge, ordinary knowledge. The kind that anchored a person to a place.

As he approached the creek, Daisy's familiar bark sounded from the far bank. The golden retriever bounded along the opposite shore, tail wagging furiously at the sight of him. She splashed into the shallow water without hesitation, making her way toward him with determined paddling strokes.

"Hey, girl," Brad murmured, crouching to meet her as she scrambled up the bank, her coat heavy with creek water. "I've missed you too."

Daisy pressed against his legs, leaving damp patches on his jeans as she whined softly, looking back toward Blooms Farm as if expecting Anna to follow.

"She's not coming," Brad told the dog, scratching behind her ears. "Not today."

Daisy tilted her head, those soulful brown eyes somehow understanding more than an animal should. She leaned her weight against him in what felt like canine sympathy.

They walked together along the creek, past the spot where Anna had first come into his world, where Daisy had crossed the boundary between their properties and inadvertently introduced them. The memory ached with a particular sweetness now—Anna's initial wariness, the flash of surprise in her eyes, and the smile that had transformed her face.

Brad slowed where the wildflowers thinned, and the view opened to the distant ridge. The quiet was thick, holding everything he hadn't said.

The ache in his chest wasn't just regret. It was fear. Of losing her. Of being misunderstood. Of having something real—something good—slip through his fingers because he hadn't said the right thing at the right time.

He'd give anything to rewind. To have told her earlier. To help her understand that he wasn't hiding anything from her but trying to honor what they were building together.

Daisy nudged his hand with her wet nose, pulling him from his thoughts. She cocked her head toward a sound he couldn't hear, her ears perked forward.

"What is it, girl?" he asked.

The dog looked toward Blooms Farm again, then back at Brad, her tail wagging hesitantly.

"No, I can't go over there," he said, the words tasting bitter. "Not until she's ready."

Daisy whined softly but seemed to accept his decision, turning to sniff along the creek bank instead.

Brad ran a hand over the back of his neck and gazed toward the mountains. He missed her. He wanted her back in his world. But he also knew he couldn't force trust. It had to be given freely.

So, he'd wait. Patiently. He'd live with integrity, serve this town with everything he had, and hope that somehow, in time, Anna would see the man he was—not the name on a tech headline.

"Come on, Daisy," he called softly. "Time to head back."

The dog gave him a reproachful look but trotted along at his side as they turned toward the Airstream. Their pace was slower than before, as if they both felt the weight of what—who—was missing.

Back at his temporary home, Brad watched as Daisy shook herself vigorously, sending droplets of creek water in all directions before settling on the ground with a contented sigh. He smiled despite himself, grateful for the simple companionship.

Settling back at the table, he flipped open his laptop again. The work felt heavier now. For the first time, the Welcome Center wasn't just about community outreach or town improvement. It was about building something real, honest, and maybe—just maybe—earning Anna's trust again.

"God," he said. "I don't know if I did the right thing. I thought... I thought I was protecting something important. But now I've hurt someone I care about. Someone I—" He paused, swallowing hard against the emotion rising in his throat. "Someone I'm in love with."

The confession hung in the evening air, spoken aloud for the first time. Love. The word felt both terrifying and right.

"I don't want to lose her," he continued. "But I don't know how to fix this. How to make her understand that I never meant to deceive her. That I just wanted the chance to be known for who I am, not what I've done or what I have."

A gentle breeze stirred the leaves of the oak tree, sending dappled shadows dancing across the ground. Brad watched them move, finding a strange comfort in their patterns.

"If there's a way forward from this, show me. And if... if this isn't meant to be, help me accept that too." His voice dropped to a whisper. "But please don't let her think I was playing some kind of game."

Chapter 32

The clicking of Katie's keyboard filled the otherwise quiet office as Anna stared at the notebook before her, pen hovering indecisively over the half-finished planting schedule. Mid-morning sunlight streamed through the freshly washed windows, casting a warm light across the polished desktop and illuminating the colorful sticky notes that now organized their spring planning process.

"If we commit to these double early tulips, we'll need to order by next Friday at the latest," Katie said, scrolling through the wholesaler's website. "The 'Apricot Beauty' variety is always the first to sell out."

"Mmm," Anna murmured, adding another note to her page without really seeing what she wrote.

The scent of fresh coffee mingled with the lemony cleaner they'd used on the new filing cabinets. Everything in the room spoke of order and purpose—everything except Anna's scattered thoughts, which kept drifting.

Three days had passed since their confrontation.

Three days of replaying every moment, every conversation, every shared smile.

Three days of wondering if she'd destroyed something precious before fully understanding its value.

Brad had never once made her feel small. Not when he helped sort seedlings in the greenhouse, his hands gentle despite their size. Not when he fixed the farm's website code, explaining each step without a hint of condescension. Not when she'd shared her dreams for the event venue, his eyes lighting with genuine excitement rather than polite interest.

He'd shown up for her multiple times and stayed. He'd remembered how she took her coffee. He'd knelt in the dirt alongside her, asking questions and listening—really listening—to her answers.

Yet the moment she'd discovered his wealth, she'd made him a stranger. Cast him as the villain in a story about deception and manipulation that existed only in her mind.

"Anna?" Katie's voice cut through her thoughts. "Earth to Anna? Did you hear what I said about the lily bulbs?"

Anna blinked, focusing on Katie's concerned face. "Sorry, what?"

Katie studied her for a moment, then swiveled her chair away from the computer. "Okay, that's the fourth time you've zoned out in the last hour."

Anna set her pen down with a sigh. "I know. I'm sorry."

"Don't apologize. Just talk to me. You're thinking about Brad, aren't you?"

Anna pushed back from the desk, the wooden chair legs scraping against the floor. "Do you think I overreacted?"

"About Brad's money?"

"About all of it."

Katie leaned back, considering. "What's really bothering you about it? That he didn't tell you, or what it means about who he is?"

"I don't know." Anna stood, needing to move as the emotions swirled within her. She crossed to the window that overlooked the cosmos field, where purple and pink blooms nodded in the summer breeze.

"Well, that clears things right up," Katie teased gently.

Anna pressed her palm against the cool glass. "I keep replaying everything. Every conversation. Every moment we spent together. Looking for signs that he was... I don't know, laughing at me? Judging me? Finding my life quaint and simple?"

"And did you find any?"

"No, that's what makes this so confusing. He never once acted superior or impatient. If anything, he seemed to genuinely admire what we do here."

Katie nodded. "Because he does."

"But why wouldn't he tell me?" Anna turned back to face her friend. "Why keep something that significant hidden?"

"Remember what your mom said? She kept the fact that your dad had left to herself for two months. About wanting to be seen for who she was becoming, not who people thought she should be."

Anna nodded slowly, the parallel sitting uncomfortably in her chest.

Katie stood and moved to the coffeepot in the corner, refilling their mugs before wheeling her chair beside Anna's. "Let's talk this out, girl to girl. No judgment, just truth."

The familiar ritual of their friendship—coffee and conversation—created a space where honesty felt possible. Anna accepted the steaming mug, wrapping both hands around its comforting warmth.

"The truth is," Anna began hesitantly, "I feel guilty. The moment I found out about the money, I made Brad feel like a stranger. I accused him of playing some kind of role, of 'slumming it' here in Laurel Ridge. Who does that to someone they care about?"

"Someone who's scared," Katie replied simply. "And you were scared, weren't you?"

"Terrified."

"Of what, exactly?"

"Of being a charity case. A project. Some kind of small-town curiosity for a bored millionaire. Of not being enough."

Katie studied her over the rim of her coffee mug. "Has Brad ever treated you like a charity case?"

"No."

"Has he ever tried to throw money at you or buy your affection?"

Anna thought of their dates—picnics by the creek, stargazing on her porch, and dancing at the church potluck. Simple pleasures shared between equals. "No."

"Has he ever made you feel like your dreams weren't worth pursuing?"

"Just the opposite." Anna's voice caught. "He believed in my venue idea more than I did. He didn't try to take over or fix it—he just... added to it. Made it bigger and better while keeping it mine."

Katie reached out, touching Anna's arm gently. "So your fear wasn't based on Brad's actions. It was based on something else."

"My dad left. Ryan left. I guess I'm just waiting for everyone to realize I'm not worth staying for."

"And when you found out Brad had this whole other life—this glamorous, successful life he could go back to—it confirmed that fear."

"Yes." Anna wiped a stray tear with the back of her hand. "Which is so unfair to him. He's been nothing but good to me. And I threw it all back in his face because I was afraid."

"People do crazy things when they're scared. Especially when the thing they're scared of losing matters."

The simple observation struck Anna with unexpected force. Brad mattered. Not because of his money or his success or what he could do for her. He mattered because of who he was—thoughtful, kind, genuine, and funny. The man who remembered her coffee order and stood in the rain helping her cover the seedlings when an unexpected storm blew in. The man who saw her dreams and made them bigger without taking them away from her.

"I miss him. I miss talking to him and laughing with him and just... being with him."

"So what are you going to do about it?"

"I don't know. Apologize, I guess. Try to explain why I reacted the way I did." Anna set her mug on the desk. "But what if he doesn't want to hear it? What if I hurt him too badly?"

"Anna Mitchell, that man looks at you as if you're the center of his universe. Trust me, he'll listen." Katie leaned back in her chair. "But first, you need to decide what you're apologizing for, exactly. Because it matters."

Anna frowned slightly. "What do you mean?"

"Are you apologizing because you found out he's rich and now you want to get back in his good graces? Or are you apologizing because you judged him based on your fears instead of who he's shown himself to be?"

"The second one. Definitely the second one."

"Then tell him that. And while you're at it, maybe tell him how you feel about him. Because I'm pretty sure those feelings haven't changed, even if the circumstances have."

Anna's heart thudded painfully in her chest. Her feelings for Brad hadn't changed—if anything, they'd deepened, clarified by the absence of his daily presence in her life.

"What if he rejects me?"

"What if he doesn't? What if he's sitting over there right now, wondering the exact same thing?"

Anna was quiet for a long moment, thinking of Brad alone in his Airstream. Had he been replaying their fight too? Wondering if he'd lost her for good?

"I think I need to forgive him. Not because he's perfect or because I need to pretend this never happened. But because... he was real when it counted. He told me the truth when I asked. And because everyone deserves grace—especially the people who have only ever shown us kindness."

"That," Katie said with a gentle smile, "sounds like the Anna Mitchell I know. The one who sees the best in people and believes second chances matter."

Anna stood with a new determination, straightening her shoulders. "I'm taking the rest of the day off."

"Are you now?" Katie's eyebrows rose. "And what might you be doing with this sudden free time?"

"I think I need to go see a man about an apology."

"Your apology or his?"

"Both, maybe." Anna paused at the door. "Thanks, Katie. For listening. For pushing me to see what was right in front of me."

"That's what friends are for. Now go get your man."

The phrase made Anna laugh—a real laugh, the first in days. "I'll let you know how it goes."

Chapter 33

The hammer slipped from Brad's hand, clattering against the wooden frame of his half-built shed. He muttered under his breath. The August sun beat down mercilessly, turning the clearing around his Airstream into a shimmering oven of heat and humidity.

"That doesn't go there," he told himself, squinting at the YouTube video playing on his phone propped against a lumber pile. "The support beam needs to be... wait, did he say sixteen inches or sixty? Why can't people just speak clearly?"

He rewound the video, leaning closer to hear the instructions over the chorus of birds in the surrounding trees. The sound of an approaching engine made him pause.

Brad straightened, shading his eyes against the glare as a familiar utility vehicle bumped across his property. His heart stuttered as Anna drove toward him, her auburn hair catching fire in the midday sun. Daisy's golden head poked up beside her, ears flapping in the breeze.

For a moment, he couldn't move. Couldn't breathe.

Anna cut the engine and sat motionless, hands gripping the steering wheel as if it might anchor her to something solid. When she finally climbed out, there was a determined set to her shoulders that Brad recognized.

Daisy leapt from the vehicle and bounded toward him, tail wagging so vigorously her entire body shook with the effort. The dog circled Brad's legs, whining with joy, pressing her nose against his hands.

"Hey, girl," he murmured, crouching to scratch behind her ears, grateful for the moment to collect himself.

Anna approached more slowly. She wore a simple t-shirt tucked into worn jeans, her hair pulled back in a loose ponytail that left wisps framing her face. The simplicity of her beauty made his chest ache.

"Hi," she said, stopping a few feet away.

"Hi," he echoed, straightening to face her.

The silence between them crackled with unspoken words and lingering hurt.

"You're building the shed?" Anna asked finally, nodding toward the half-finished structure behind him.

"Trying to," Brad admitted with a small shrug. "Turns out watching YouTube tutorials isn't quite the same as having actual skills."

A hint of a smile touched her lips. "That support beam is crooked."

"Yeah, I know. I've reinstalled it three times, and it's still not right." He gestured toward his phone. "The guy in the video makes it look so easy."

"The video probably doesn't show all the mistakes he made before filming the perfect take."

The observation landed like a gentle truth between them—about more than just shed-building.

Brad cleared his throat. "You wanna sit? I've got water in the cooler."

Anna nodded, and he led the way to the table and chairs in front of the Airstream. Daisy flopped beneath the table, her tongue lolling as she settled in for whatever conversation was about to unfold.

He retrieved two bottles of water from the cooler, condensation immediately beading on the cold plastic. He handed one to Anna before taking the seat across from her.

Anna twisted the cap off her bottle, taking a small sip before setting it on the table.

"I've been thinking about what happened," she began, her voice steady despite the slight tremor in her hands. "About how I reacted when I found out about your past."

Brad watched her carefully, sensing she needed to speak without interruption.

"I was hurt," she continued. "Not because of your financial worth—though that was shocking. But because I thought we were getting to know each other, really know each other, and then I discovered this gigantic part of your life you'd never mentioned."

"Anna—"

She held up a hand. "Please let me finish. I need to say this."

Brad nodded, settling back in his chair.

"I felt betrayed. Like maybe everything between us was built on a partial truth. And that scared me, because..." Her voice faltered slightly. "Because I was already falling for you. I had already let you in—all the way in—to parts of my life and my heart that I don't share easily."

"But these past few days, I've been replaying everything. Every conversation, every moment we shared. And I realized something." Anna looked up, meeting his eyes directly for the first time. "You never once made me feel small or insignificant. You never talked down to me or treated me like I wasn't your equal. You were always just... Brad.

The Brad who helps transplant seedlings and bakes cookies for church potlucks and fixes my website when I break it."

Brad's throat tightened with emotion. "That's who I am."

"I know that now," Anna said softly. "And I owe you an apology. I accused you of playing a role, of slumming it here in Laurel Ridge. That wasn't fair. I judged you based on my fears, not on who you've shown yourself to be."

"What are you afraid of?"

Anna's gaze dropped to her hands. "That I wasn't enough. That sooner or later, you'd remember who you really were and leave for something bigger and better."

The vulnerability of her admission struck Brad to his core. He leaned forward, elbows on the table, desperate to bridge the gap between them.

"Anna, look at me," he said gently.

When she raised her eyes, the pain and uncertainty he saw there made him ache to pull her into his arms. Instead, he chose his words with careful precision.

"The Brad Knight who built LocalLens—the one who gave TED talks and closed million-dollar deals—that person was hollow inside. I was successful by every measure except the ones that actually matter. I had wealth but no peace. Recognition but no real connections."

He ran a hand through his hair, searching for the right words. "I didn't tell you about the money because it's the least important thing about me. Not because I was playing a role or slumming it, but because for the first time in years, I'm living authentically—being seen for who I am, not for what I've accomplished or acquired."

"I understand that better now. But Brad, you could have trusted me with the whole truth."

"You're right," he acknowledged. "I should have told you. That's on me, and I'm sorry. But, Anna, please believe me when I say it wasn't about trust. It was about... fear."

"Fear?"

Brad nodded, forcing himself to maintain eye contact. "When people know about the money, everything changes. Suddenly, I'm not just Brad—I'm Brad Knight, tech millionaire. A resource. An opportunity. A threat. People filter everything I say and do through that lens."

He took a deep breath. "After my heart episode, when I told Michelle—my ex—that I sold the company, bought land, and was moving... she left. Just like that. Because apparently, I was only worth loving when I came with a CEO title and the lifestyle she wanted."

"I came here looking for something real, and I found it—in this town, in this community. In you."

"The first day we met," Brad continued, "when Daisy ran across the creek and you came after her—you didn't know anything about me. You just saw a neighbor. A person. And the way you looked at me, talked to me... it felt like breathing after being underwater for years."

Anna's eyes glistened. "We just... clicked when we first met."

"That's what I was trying to protect. What we've been building, free from all the baggage of my past life. But in trying to push my past life aside, I ended up damaging your trust. And I hate that more than I can say."

A tear slipped down Anna's cheek. She wiped it away quickly. "I want to trust you again. I do. But I need to know that moving forward, there won't be any more significant omissions. That what I see is who you really are."

"You have my word," Brad said immediately. "No holding back. What you see is exactly who I am—a man trying to build something meaningful in a place that feels like home, with people who matter."

He hesitated, then added, "I came here to heal, to find a simpler life. But I found so much more than that. I found a purpose. Community. And most unexpectedly, I found you."

The intensity in his voice made Anna's breath catch.

"I've never felt this way before," Brad continued, his voice dropping to a near whisper. "About anyone. About any place. It scares me and excites me in equal measure."

Brad met her gaze, his heart hammering against his ribs. "I'm in love with you, Anna Mitchell. Completely, utterly in love with you. With your strength and your kindness. With the way you see beauty in ordinary things. With how fiercely you protect what matters to you."

"I know it's too soon," he added quickly. "And I know we have to trust to rebuild. I just... I need you to know that what I feel for you is real. The most real thing I've ever felt."

Anna sat very still, her eyes wide with wonder and lingering uncertainty. "I don't know what to say."

"You don't have to say anything," Brad assured her. "I just want a chance to show you—every day—that you can trust me. That I'm here, all in, for as long as you'll have me."

Anna reached across the table, her fingers tentatively brushing against his. The simple contact sent warmth cascading through him.

"I'm still hurt," she admitted. "And I'm still a little scared. But I'm willing to try. To move forward. Because the thought of not having you in my life hurts more than anything else right now."

Brad turned his hand palm up, letting her decide whether to take it. When she placed her hand on his, the relief was so intense it nearly undid him.

"That's all I'm asking for," he said. "A chance."

They sat in silence for a moment, the weight of honesty settling around them like a cleansing rain. Daisy sighed contentedly under the table, sensing the shift in the emotional atmosphere.

"So," Anna said finally, a hint of her usual warmth returning to her voice. "Tell me about this shed you're trying to build."

Brad laughed, the sound rusty but genuine. "It's a disaster. I've watched the same fifteen-minute tutorial about six times, and I still can't get that support beam right."

"Show me," she said as she stood.

He led her to the half-constructed frame. As they surveyed the wooden skeleton together, Brad felt something shift and settle within him—a quiet certainty that this moment marked a beginning rather than an end.

"See, the problem is," he explained, pointing to the crooked beam, "I can't get the angle right without someone holding it in place while I secure it."

Anna moved to the beam, wrapping her fingers around the rough wood. "Like this?"

"Exactly like that," Brad said, picking up his hammer. "Perfect."

As they worked together, adjusting and securing the frame, Brad knew with absolute certainty that whatever they built together—whether a simple shed or a complex future—it would be stronger for having weathered this first real storm.

And when Anna smiled at him, really smiled, the August sun warming her freckled skin and catching the auburn highlights in her hair, Brad knew he was home at last. Not in Laurel Ridge. Not in the Airstream. But in the space they created together, where trust, once broken, could be rebuilt into something even more beautiful than before.

Chapter 34

Brad straightened his tie for the third time, checking his reflection in the Airstream's small bathroom mirror. The navy blue fabric felt suddenly constricting against his throat, though he'd worn the same tie to church several Sundays before without issue. Today felt different. Today, everything mattered more.

He hadn't heard from Anna since yesterday afternoon when she'd left his side after helping him work on the storage shed for a couple of hours. Their goodbye had been warm but tentative—a brief hug that left him wondering where exactly they stood.

Smoothing his collar one last time, Brad stepped outside. The air already held the promise of another scorching day, heavy with moisture that clung to his skin the moment he left the air-conditioned sanctuary of his home. Birdsong filled the clearing—cardinals and thrushes calling back and forth across the property, their melodies floating through the hazy golden light that filtered through the trees.

Brad paused on the metal steps, looking across his land toward the creek that separated his property from Blooms Farm. From this vantage point, he could just make out the corner of the white farmhouse where Anna lived.

The thought of seeing Anna at church this morning sent a flutter of nervous energy through his chest. Would she acknowledge him? Sit beside him as she had in weeks past? Or would the careful distance between them remain?

"One step at a time," he murmured to himself, an echo of his mother's favorite saying.

Twenty minutes later, Brad pulled into the gravel parking lot beside Laurel Ridge Community Church. The familiar white clapboard building stood against the backdrop of green mountains, its steeple reaching toward the cloudless blue sky. Already, the lot was filling with vehicles—pickup trucks, sensible sedans, and the occasional SUV, all arranged in the unspoken assigned parking that seemed to develop in small towns.

He didn't see June's blue pickup yet. Relief and disappointment mingled in his chest—relief at having a few more minutes to compose himself, disappointment at the delay in seeing Anna.

Brad nodded greetings to several familiar faces as he climbed the wooden steps to the church entrance. Mrs. Henderson waved enthusiastically from where she was arranging fresh flowers in the foyer. Earl clapped him on the shoulder with a hearty "Morning, son!"

The sanctuary smelled of lemon polish and aging hymnals, with undertones of the wildflowers that adorned the altar. The familiar blend of scents had become synonymous with Sunday peace in Brad's mind.

He hesitated, scanning the half-filled sanctuary. His usual seat—beside Anna and June—suddenly felt presumptuous. Should he sit elsewhere? Make himself less conspicuous?

He walked down the center aisle toward the Mitchell women's usual spot. Something in him needed to be there, in the place that had come to feel right. If Anna chose to sit elsewhere, that would be her decision. But he would be where she could find him if she wanted to.

The polished wood felt cool beneath his fingers as he slid into the pew, leaving room for two more beside him. He placed his Bible in his lap, his thumb absently tracing the leather of its cover as he waited, trying not to watch the door too obviously.

The organist began the prelude, her fingers coaxing the ancient instrument to life with the first notes of "How Great Thou Art." The familiar melody filled the space, rising toward the rafters and settling over the congregation like a comforting hug.

Brad felt her rather than saw her. He glanced back, and his heart stuttered in his chest.

Anna stood in the doorway, her arm linked through Mom's. She wore a simple sundress in a soft shade of green that brought out the auburn highlights in her hair, which fell in loose waves around her shoulders. For a moment, their eyes met across the sanctuary, and Brad held his breath.

With barely a pause, Anna guided her mother down the aisle toward the pew where Brad sat. Her steps were purposeful, her gaze steady. Anna slid in beside him, close enough that the fabric of her dress brushed against his slacks.

"Morning," she said softly.

"Morning," he replied, his voice rough.

June leaned around her daughter to offer him a warm smile. "Beautiful day, isn't it?"

"Perfect," he replied, though he wasn't looking at the sunlight streaming through the windows.

As the congregation rose for the opening hymn, Anna reached for the hymnal in the rack before them. Brad did the same, and their hands brushed—a brief, electric moment of contact that sent warmth cascading through him. When he opened the book to the correct page, Anna moved slightly closer, turning so they could share the hymnal between them.

The congregation's voices rose in harmony, filling the sanctuary with sound. Brad sang the familiar words, acutely aware of Anna beside him—the subtle floral scent of her shampoo, the way her shoulder occasionally pressed against his arm, and the clear, sweet quality of her voice joining with his.

When the hymn ended, and they sat, Anna shifted slightly in her seat. Her hand found his on the pew between them, her fingers sliding between his with quiet certainty. The simple gesture felt like a declaration.

Brad squeezed her hand gently, a question in the pressure. She squeezed back, her answer clear: *Yes, I'm here.*

Throughout Pastor Andrew's sermon on healing and renewal, Brad found himself struggling to focus on the words. Anna's hand in his kept pulling his attention back to the miracle of her presence, her choice to sit beside him, and her choice to hold his hand where anyone could see. Each slight movement of her thumb across his knuckles felt like a promise written in invisible ink.

When the final hymn ended and the congregation began to stir, collecting purses and Bibles and children, Anna turned to him.

"Would you like to take a walk?" she asked, her voice low enough that only he could hear. "Instead of the usual coffee hour?"

"I'd like that," Brad replied, hope unfurling in his chest like the first green leaf of spring.

They made their way out of the sanctuary, navigating the clusters of people exchanging greetings and weekly updates. Brad felt the curious glances following them.

Outside, the heat of the day had intensified, but a gentle breeze stirred the leaves of the massive trees that shaded the church grounds. They walked away from the church, following a well-worn path that led toward a creek bordering the property.

Anna still held his hand, her grip relaxed but certain. They walked in silence until they reached the creek, where a wooden bench had been placed beneath a weeping willow. Its branches created a curtain of green that swayed in the breeze, offering a pocket of privacy.

"I wanted to talk away from everyone," Anna explained as they sat. "Martha's probably already texted Katie about us holding hands during the service and leaving without chatting with everyone."

Brad smiled. "Small towns."

"Small towns," she agreed, a matching smile tugging at her lips.

The creek bubbled over smooth stones, its gentle music providing a backdrop to the moment. A cardinal darted through the willow branches, a flash of brilliant red against the green.

"I've been thinking," Anna began, her eyes on the flowing water, "about what you said yesterday. About being in love with me."

Brad's heart thudded against his ribs. "I meant it."

"I know you did." She looked up at him then, her blue eyes clear and steady. "That scared me. The certainty in your voice. The depth of feeling."

"Scared you?" he asked, fighting the urge to pull his hand away, to protect himself from what might come next.

Anna's fingers tightened around his, as if sensing his uncertainty. "Not in a bad way," she clarified. "More like... when you stand at the edge of something vast and beautiful, and you know stepping into it will change everything."

"I understand that feeling."

"When I went home yesterday," Anna continued, "I couldn't stop thinking about everything. About us. About what I want my life to be." She turned toward him more fully, her free hand coming to rest on his forearm. "And I realized something important."

"What's that?" Brad asked, hardly daring to breathe.

"That I've been letting fear make my decisions for too long. Fear of not being enough. Fear of being left behind." Her voice strengthened with each word. "And I don't want to live that way anymore."

The willow branches swayed around them, dappling her face with shifting patterns of sunlight and shadow. In that patterned light, she looked both vulnerable and resolved, her eyes never leaving his.

"Brad, when you told me you loved me, I wasn't ready to say it back. Not because I didn't feel it, but because I needed to be certain I wasn't just saying the words out of relief or gratitude or the fear of losing you."

Hope bloomed in Brad's chest, tentative but growing.

Anna's smile was like a sunrise breaking through clouds. "I'm in love with you too, Brad Knight. Just because of who you are right now, sitting beside me on this bench."

"Anna," he breathed, her name a prayer on his lips.

She leaned forward, resting her forehead against his. "I know we still have things to figure out. Trust to rebuild. But I'm ready to move forward—together—if you are."

"Together," Brad repeated, savoring the word and all it promised. "That's all I want."

He reached up, gently tucking a strand of auburn hair behind her ear, his fingers lingering against the soft skin of her cheek. "I'm gonna kiss you... just fair warning."

Anna's answer was to close the distance between them, her lips finding his with sweet certainty. The kiss was gentle and unhurried. Brad cradled her face in his hands, pouring everything he couldn't yet say into the tender gesture.

When they finally drew apart, Anna's eyes remained closed for a moment, as if memorizing the sensation. When she opened them, they shone with a quiet joy that matched the fullness in Brad's own heart.

"I've wanted to do that again since the church potluck," she admitted, a touch of color rising to her cheeks.

"Even when you were mad at me?" Brad teased gently.

"Especially then," Anna laughed. "It's very difficult to stay properly angry with someone when you keep remembering how it felt to kiss them."

The honesty in her admission made Brad laugh too, the sound rising from somewhere deep and previously untapped. "Good to know for future reference."

The creek continued its steady flow, constant and clear. From the church parking lot came the distant sounds of car doors closing and engines starting—the congregation dispersing to Sunday dinners and afternoon naps. Yet here in their willow-shaded sanctuary, time seemed to move at its own pace.

"What happens now?" Anna asked, her head coming to rest against his shoulder.

Brad's arm encircled her, drawing her closer against his side. "Whatever we want," he said. "We take it one day at a time. Build something real. Something lasting."

"I'd like that," she murmured.

They sat in companionable silence for a few minutes, watching the play of light on water, listening to the symphony of birdsong and rustling leaves. Brad felt a profound sense of rightness settle over him, as if some essential piece had finally clicked into place.

"You know," Anna said eventually, "I was thinking about your Welcome Center idea."

"Oh?" Brad shifted slightly to see her face.

"I think the town needs it. And I think... I think you're undoubtedly the right person to make it happen."

The vote of confidence—especially after everything they'd been through—meant more than Brad could express. "That means a lot."

"I believe in you, Brad." She sat up straighter, turning to face him fully. "Not because of what you've accomplished before, but because I've seen your heart. How much you care about doing things right."

Her words washed over him like a blessing.

"And I was also thinking," Anna continued, a hint of mischief entering her expression, "that Blooms Farm's event venue and your Welcome Center might complement each other nicely. Visitors who come for weddings or anniversary parties... or just whatever, might want to explore the area. People who discover Laurel Ridge through your app might be looking for a beautiful venue for special occasions."

Brad immediately caught the thread of her thinking, expanding on it with natural enthusiasm. "We could create integrated experiences. Packages that highlight the best of the region while supporting local businesses. Your farm could be a cornerstone of authentic experiences."

Anna's eyes lit with matching excitement. "Exactly! See, this is another reason why we're good together. You take my ideas and make them bigger without taking them away from me."

The simple observation revealed how thoroughly she understood him—how clearly she saw what drove him. Not conquest or control, but collaboration and enhancement.

"We do make a good team," Brad agreed, squeezing her hand. "In more ways than one."

A gentle breeze stirred the willow branches, sending a shower of dappled light across her face. She looked so beautiful in that moment—hair lightly tousled, eyes bright with possibility, lips curved in a smile meant only for him—that Brad felt his heart expand almost painfully in his chest.

"Anna Mitchell," he said, his voice low and earnest, "I am so grateful that your dog decided to investigate my property that day."

She laughed, the sound bright and clear against the backdrop of flowing water. "Daisy has good instincts about people."

"Smart dog," Brad murmured, leaning in to press another gentle kiss to her lips.

When they finally rose to leave, walking hand in hand back toward the church parking lot, Brad felt a profound sense of homecoming. Not to a place, but to a person. To the knowledge that whatever came next—whatever challenges or joys awaited—they would face it together.

As Anna leaned into him, his arm circled her shoulders naturally, Brad pressed a kiss to the top of her head. The gesture contained no grand promises, no sweeping declarations. Not yet. But in its quiet certainty was something even more precious: the beginning of something real and lasting. Not a maybe anymore, but a yes.

EPILOGUE

Anna smoothed her flowing white dress as she stepped through the wide barn doors into a vision made real. Fairy lights twinkled overhead like captured stars, casting a warm, soft light across the exposed timber beams. The sweet fragrance of late summer blooms perfumed the air, their vibrant colors adorning every table. In the center of the dance floor, Brad spun her mom in a gentle circle, her laughter rising above the bluegrass band's melody.

Anna simply stood there, absorbing the scene with all her senses. The polished wood floor gleamed beneath dancing feet. Ice clinked in Mason jar glasses. Peach cobbler, their chosen dessert for the wedding reception, with its cinnamon-sweet aroma mingling with the floral notes in the air. Children darted between tables, their excited voices punctuating the hum of conversation and music.

This barn—this beautiful, rustic event space with its soaring ceilings and wall of windows framing the mountain sunset—had existed only in her dreams a year ago. Now she stood within its walls as both its creator and its first bride.

"There she is!" Martha called from a nearby table, raising her glass. "The most beautiful bride Laurel Ridge has ever seen!"

A chorus of agreement rippled through the nearest guests, and Anna felt warmth rise to her cheeks. She'd never been comfortable as the center of attention, but today—her wedding day—she couldn't escape it. Nor did she want to.

Daisy trotted up, a circlet of white daisies and baby's breath adorning her golden neck. The dog pressed against Anna's legs, leaving a faint dusting of shed fur on the simple silk of her dress.

"You were perfect," Anna said, crouching to scratch behind the dog's ears. "Best ring bearer ever."

Daisy had carried the rings down the aisle earlier that afternoon, the small velvet pouch secured to her collar with a blue ribbon that matched the wildflowers dotting the ceremony space outside. She'd performed her duty with unexpected dignity, walking straight to Brad without a single detour to greet guests.

"She's left a trail of cake crumbs all over the floor," Katie said, appearing beside Anna with two flutes of champagne. Her best friend looked radiant in her maid of honor dress, a shade of blue that matched the bachelor buttons growing wild along the farm's fence line. "But I think we can forgive her today."

Anna accepted the champagne with a smile. "I'd forgive her anything today."

Katie clinked her glass against Anna's. "To the Mitchell-Knight wedding. Or is it Knight-Mitchell? I can't remember what you decided."

"Just Knight," Anna replied.

"I like that," Katie nodded, her gaze drifting to where her boyfriend, Sam, chatted with Pastor Andrew by the gift table.

Anna followed Katie's gaze, noting the way Sam kept glancing back at her friend, as if he couldn't help checking that she was still there. The look was familiar—she'd seen it countless times on Brad's face over the past year.

"He's crazy about you... I sense an engagement in your future," Anna observed.

"Yeah, well. Let's not get ahead of ourselves. Today is about you and Brad."

The band transitioned into a slower number, and Anna watched as Brad kissed her mom's cheek before scanning the room. When he spotted Anna, his entire face transformed with a smile that still made her heart squeeze in her chest.

Her husband. The word felt new and ancient all at once.

Brad excused himself from June and crossed the room, moving with the easy confidence that had become more pronounced over the past year as he'd settled fully into Laurel Ridge life. His suit jacket had been discarded hours ago, his tie loosened, and his sleeves rolled up to reveal tanned forearms. He looked relaxed and joyful and entirely himself.

"There's my wife," he said as he reached her. "I wondered where you'd disappeared to."

"Just taking it all in," Anna replied, accepting his kiss with a contented sigh. "It's perfect, isn't it? Everything we imagined."

Brad's arm slipped around her waist, solid and secure. "Better. Way better. Did you see Mayor Wilson trying to teach Mrs. Henderson how to two-step?"

Anna laughed, picturing the town's dignified mayor with the church's most proper matron. "I missed that. Was it as disastrous as it sounds?"

"Let's just say there might be a bruise or two on his shins tomorrow." Brad's eyes crinkled at the corners, a sign of genuine amusement that Anna had come to treasure. "He was a good sport about it."

Katie excused herself to join Sam, leaving Anna and Brad in their small bubble of newlywed happiness. Around them, the celebration continued in full swing—Earl telling one of his famous fishing stories to an enraptured audience of out-of-town guests; Ben Turner from Adventure Tours demonstrating some complicated dance move to his wife, Grace; and the church ladies refilling platters of food that seemed endless.

"Cake's almost gone," Brad observed, nodding toward the cake creation that Shirley had insisted on making as her gift to them. "Did the top tier get saved? Isn't that traditional?"

"Mom already wrapped it up and put it in the freezer at the house," Anna replied. "She says we can have it on our first anniversary."

Brad's fingers found hers, intertwining with practiced ease. "Hard to imagine it getting any better than this."

The simple statement carried layers of meaning that made Anna's throat tighten with emotion. The past year had brought so much change, so much growth—not just for her business but for them as a couple.

The Blooms Farm Events Center had gone from dream to reality with breathtaking speed once Brad had introduced Anna to a grant program specifically designed for rural economic development. The grant had covered half the construction costs, with Anna's carefully saved profits from the farm's record year covering much of the rest.

"Remember when we sat by the waterfall and talked about this for the first time?" Anna asked, leaning into his solid warmth. "It felt so far away then. Almost impossible."

"Nothing's impossible with you," Brad replied, his voice low against her hair. "You make dreams grow like they're the easiest things in the world to cultivate."

The music shifted again, this time to a cover of "Tennessee Whiskey" that had couples gravitating toward the dance floor.

"Wanna get out of here for a little bit?" she asked, setting down her champagne glass. "Just for a few minutes?"

Brad's eyebrows rose in surprise. "It's our reception. We can't just disappear."

"Watch me," Anna challenged with a mischievous smile. "No one will even notice we're gone. Look—Katie's entertaining everyone with that story about the goat that somehow found its way into the greenhouse, and Mom's holding court with your parents by the dessert table."

Indeed, June had Brad's parents captivated with some tale that involved expansive hand gestures and periodic laughter. The two families had bonded instantly upon meeting, united in their joy over the upcoming marriage and their shared love of gardening. Brad's mother had even started volunteering at Blooms Farm during her increasingly frequent visits from Kentucky.

"Where to?"

"The footbridge. I want to show you something."

They slipped away unnoticed by their celebrating guests. The August evening embraced them with lingering warmth and the gentle symphony of cricket song. The sun hung low on the horizon, painting the sky in watercolor strokes of pink and gold that reflected in the surface of the creek ahead.

The path to the footbridge was well worn now, traveled daily as they moved between their properties and the event center. Blooms Farm had never been more prosperous; her flower business had increased in sales this past year. And on Brad's property, ground had been broken for their home just a few weeks before.

When they reached the wooden footbridge, Anna kicked off her satin shoes and stepped onto the weathered planks in her bare feet, feeling the grain of the wood against her skin—real and solid, just like everything else they'd built together.

Brad joined her, loosening his tie further and letting out a deep breath of contentment. Below them, the creek burbled over smooth stones, carrying petals from the ceremony site in its gentle current.

"I never imagined I could be this happy," he said quietly, gazing across to his property where the Airstream gleamed silver in the fading light. Nearby, the foundation of their future home was taking shape, the concrete footings marking the outline of their shared vision. "Sometimes I'm afraid I'll wake up back in that condo in Denver, all of this just a dream."

Anna squeezed his hand. "Not a dream."

"No, everything about my life now is a dream come true." Brad turned to face her fully, framing her face between his palms with infinite tenderness. "Because of you."

The truth of his words shone in his eyes, unguarded and complete. In the year since their reconciliation, they'd built a foundation of honesty that made their love unshakable. Brad had gradually shared more of his past life, introducing Anna to former colleagues and explaining the complex workings of his charitable foundation. Anna had worked through her own fears of inadequacy, finally understanding that Brad chose her not despite their differences, but because of the unique perspective she brought to his world and simply because he loved her.

"I've been thinking," Anna said, leaning against the bridge railing. "About our plans for the venue. I think we should add those glamping cabins you talked about before—maybe three or four to start, tucked back in the trees near the waterfall."

Brad's expression brightened with interest. "Really? I thought you wanted to keep it simple."

"I did. But after seeing how quickly we booked up for fall weddings, I think there's real demand for on-site lodging. Especially for wedding parties coming from out of town." She gestured toward his property. "We could connect them with hiking trails across your land, maybe even to that apple orchard we picnicked in."

"Our land... I love where you're going with this," Brad said, his mind already visibly working on the possibilities. "We could build them with those floor-to-ceiling windows facing the mountains. Minimal environmental impact but maximum views. And if we use local materials—maybe that reclaimed timber from the old mill..."

Anna smiled, watching his enthusiasm build. This was one of the things she loved—the way they expanded each other's thinking without diminishing individual dreams.

"What made you change your mind?" Brad asked, bringing his focus back to her.

"Something Mom said at our rehearsal dinner. About how the most beautiful gardens aren't the ones where everything is perfectly planned, but the ones where there's room for unexpected growth." Anna looked toward the barn in the distance, where light spilled from every window, silhouetting the dancing figures inside. "I think our life should be like that too."

Brad's expression softened with understanding. "Room to grow. Together."

"Together," Anna echoed, leaning into him. "That's the important part."

The last rays of sunlight gilded the creek below them, transforming ordinary water into something magical. In the distance, a whippoorwill called, its distinctive song carrying across the valley.

"Do you think we'll have a family someday?" Brad asked, his voice holding a hint of vulnerability she rarely heard. "Children running between our properties, learning to grow flowers and code websites?"

The question made Anna's heart swell with longing and possibility. "I'd like that. Not right away, maybe... We have the venue to establish, and your Welcome Center plans..."

"But someday," Brad finished, his arms encircling her waist.

"Someday," she agreed, resting her head against his chest where she could hear the steady beat of his heart. "We have time."

That was the gift they'd given each other—the certainty of time together, of dreams shared and nurtured to fruition. No more fear of abandonment. No more hiding behind partial truths. Just two people who had chosen each other completely.

From the barn came the sound of Katie calling their names, her voice carrying across the evening air. "Anna! Brad! Where are you? It's time for your sendoff!"

"We'd better get back before they send out a search party."

"One more minute," Anna requested, holding him in place. She wanted to fix this moment in her memory—the bridge between their properties, the sunset painting the sky, the sound of celebration in the distance, and Brad's solid presence beside her.

This was the foundation they'd built—not the concrete footings of their future home or the timber frame of the event barn, but something far more enduring. Trust. Understanding. A willingness to grow together while remaining true to themselves.

"I love you, Bradley James Knight," Anna whispered against his lips. "Every version of you—past, present, and future."

"And I love you, Anna June Knight," he replied, matching her tone. "My best friend, and my wife."

Their kiss was gentle, a promise renewed with the same reverence as their vows earlier that day. When they parted, Anna saw the future reflected in Brad's eyes—seasons changing, dreams evolving, and love deepening.

Hand in hand, they walked back toward the celebration waiting for them. Behind them stood the bridge connecting their properties. Ahead lay the barn filled with everyone who had witnessed their journey. And all around them sprawled the land they both loved—acres of possibility and a flourishing flower farm, no longer separated but united by the paths they'd worn between them.

Leave A Review

If you enjoyed this book, please consider leaving an honest review on Amazon

Visit Our Website:

www.tarabaisden.com

Visit Our Amazon Author Page HERE

Find Us On Social Media:

Facebook

Facebook Author Page

Instagram

www.ingramcontent.com/pod-product-compliance
Lightning Source LLC
Chambersburg PA
CBHW011848300726
48970CB00009B/2697